A Touch of Love

Adrianna Schuh

A Conquest Publishing Original

Conquest Publishing

https://conquest-publishing.com

Copyright © 2024 Adrianna Schuh

Cover Design: Ria Designs

Edited by: Brandi Shaffer and Nicole DeVincentis

All rights reserved. No part of this publication may be reproduced, distributed, or transmitted in any form or by any means, including photocopying, recording, or other electronic or mechanical methods, without the prior written permission of the publisher, except in the case of brief quotations embodied in critical reviews and certain other noncommercial uses permitted by copyright law.

Any references to historical events, real people, or real places are used fictitiously. Names, characters, and places are products of the author's imagination.

Chapter 1

NEW YORK CITY | MAY 1890

THIS HOUSE WAS MUCH too quiet. Elijah Jameson was used to constant noise. The incessant chatter of his little sister, the crackle of wood in the stove, the creak of the old floorboards under his feet, and the continuous hum of voices coming from the shop below.

But in this house, there was only him and the lawyer, a short, portly man with graying hair who droned on as Elijah nodded along, his body almost numb with shock.

He was now a very wealthy man, courtesy of the inheritance his very rich grandfather left him. A grandfather who, until a few moments ago, he knew very little about.

If money could buy happiness, he should be the happiest man in the world.

He simply nodded along from behind his grandfather's massive oak desk as the lawyer, Stuart Webber, read out the Last Will and Testament of his grandfather.

According to Mr. Webber, Elijah's grandfather was none other than Edward Jameson, owner and founder of Jameson Steel. The old man had recently passed and left everything to his next of kin—Elijah.

Elijah sat dumbfounded for a moment, his jaw hanging open in a most undignified manor. "I am sorry, could you repeat that? I must have misheard you."

Mr. Webber laughed, a slightly exasperated sound that grated on Elijah's nerves. "I said, you will receive an annual income of twenty-thousand per year. And a large amount already sits in your account at the bank. Profits from the business along with some earnings from investments your grandfather made over the years."

He was staring; Elijah knew he was staring, yet he could not stop. He just stared and stared at the man for far longer than was appropriate. And it was likely he would have kept on staring because his brain was not quite able to connect the dots to form logical thoughts. That kind of money just did not exist in his head.

"I assume you have questions," Mr. Webber finally said, his patience likely wearing very thin.

Elijah would apologize if he thought it would make any difference. Instead, he just nodded before speaking up. "Many. Many questions. I am not sure where to begin."

Mr. Webber's eyes softened. "Well, as I said, you will inherit that amount. And you will now gain sole custody of your grandfather's company and everything else he owned. This house, for example…" He gestured to the room around him.

The space felt cavernous to Elijah with its large stone fireplace and massive desk that seemed excessive for one man.

Mr. Webber continued, "It was to go to your mother, Abigail. But since she is no longer with us, it all goes to the next of kin. You."

"And I am to run the business?"

The solicitor nodded. "That was the elder Mr. Jameson's plan, yes."

Elijah looked around at his surroundings again, at the thick, plush carpet under his feet, and the gleaming chandelier over his head, this time trying to imagine it all belonged to him. This was to be his home, should he want it to be. And what a home it was. After a life spent on the verge of poverty, this clean and stately townhouse on the edge of Central Park might as well have been a castle.

And he should be grateful. He was grateful.

But he was also very overwhelmed. Suddenly he was a part of this great legacy, the great Jameson family, a name synonymous with influence and importance. And his mother had turned her back on all of it at just eighteen, running off with Elijah's father. There was so much he did not know. What was now expected of him? Was he supposed to run this company on his own? And run this big house on his own? He would be expected to navigate this new world, a world full of glitz and glamor and rules and judgment, all to be a gentleman, and that was probably the biggest joke of all.

Elijah was no dignified gentleman; he was not someone who was at all used to such an exorbitant amount of money and possessions. On the contrary, he was a young man from a poor home who was suddenly plucked from the dirt and placed amongst wealth and opulence.

He was completely out of his depth.

Growing up, all he had was his mother and then Vivian the year he turned five. And the friends he made working on the docks.

Their father had run off at some point and Elijah did not even remember him. He and Vivian, and their mother, were the three musketeers. And that had been enough. And when their mother passed, they soldiered on as they always had, his friends offering encouragement and support when they could.

For three years, they moved along as they until that letter turned up on their doorstep.

His mother would know what to do. She would know how to handle all of this, having grown up in this world. There was so much he wanted to say to her, so much he wanted to ask, so much he did not understand.

He walked to the office window, his office now, and looked out at the bustling street. Men with bowler hats and walking sticks marched down the road, back to their own offices from lunches where they discussed important affairs. Pairs of women strolled under parasols, chatting and shielding themselves from the hot summer sun. Young children were ushered on by their nannies on the way to the park to enjoy some fresh air.

He recognized no one. The feeling of loneliness buzzed under his skin and his palms slickened with sweat.

He did not belong here.

He ached for the smell of salt and sand.

And though he understood his new situation could lead to remarkable things, he wished he could go back to the small apartment above the rundown shop he and Vivian called home. Where they would sit in front of the fire, reading out loud from his favorite book of poems. The home where they spent nights lying awake, imagining the stars overhead and the pictures they could make. Back to the familiar busy streets on the other side of town where he spent each day working so hard he had little time to think of anything else. Back to the rank and order of a seafarer's life.

It may not have been much, but it was a life and work he took pride in. Earning every cent on his own.

Counting pennies and going to bed hungry he was used to, but this? This opulence, the quiet elegance, was uncharted territory. It was why he'd made arrangements for Vivian to stay with an acquaintance until he got everything sorted out with the lawyer.

He now had an annual income of twenty thousand dollars, investments in the railroad, and factories that produced cotton and steel. Things he knew absolutely nothing about apart from the cotton in the clothes he wore and the factories he sometimes made the odd delivery to for extra money.

He was an idiot. He had never dared to consider that the Jameson of Jameson Steele could be connected to him and his sister. Not that he had any reason to consider it.

Probably because his mother discouraged any discussion of the topic of her family, claiming it was just too painful, and out of respect for her, he stopped asking. But he always wondered. Sometimes he had found himself searching the faces of strangers, looking for long-lost relatives. After she died he went through her things searching for clues. Anything that would point him in the direction of her life before, but there was nothing. There was not much else he could do, no information to glean from anyone. Until he was standing in front of Mr. Webber in his secondhand clothes, with dirt under his nails and sweat on his brow, reading a letter from his mysterious grandfather.

It angered him to think that his mother chose to allow them to struggle when they could have been comfortable.

And that anger brought guilt with it. He could not remember the last time he felt truly at ease. The responsibility of taking care of his little sister was heavy on his shoulders. He was a young man of twenty-one with an eighteen-year-old sister he was now solely responsible for. And now this. Without his friends who now seemed a world away, he was truly alone.

But he supposed it did not matter now. His mother had been gone for several years. He was accustomed to hard work and making decisions on his own. So he pushed those feelings of anger and loneliness down. Feeling sorry for himself was a waste of time and energy.

He pulled his eyes away from the window and walked over to the desk, his grandfather's desk—his desk—and tried to focus on Mr. Webber's words.

"I have arranged a meeting with your grandfather's excuse me, with your—banker this afternoon. Just give them your name, and they will direct you to the appropriate individual. His name is Fisher."

Mr. Webber glanced up then, scanning him. He opened his mouth to speak and then promptly closed it, looking uncomfortable.

"What is it?" Elijah asked, fighting to keep the irritation from his voice.

The man had been generous with his time and explanations so far. But somehow Elijah knew that whatever Mr. Webber was about to say next, he would not like it.

"I was only going to say that you might want to clean up first. There should be some things here that fit you. Your grandfather's things." The man looked mildly uncomfortable before pushing on. "And then might I suggest you set up a tour of the factories and plan a visit to your upstate home to become familiar with everything. There is much for you to learn. In the meantime, I have taken the liberty of putting together an overview of what your estate entails. And what condition everything is in. If you'd like, we can go over it together."

He wanted to be offended, but he could not find it within himself to feel it. Instead, Elijah nodded his approval, extremely grateful for the offer, even if this man annoyed him greatly. None of this made much sense to him. But he had always been a quick study, and he was always eager to learn new things. An idea occurred to him.

He cleared his throat. "Before we discuss the business, would it be possible..." he trailed off, his throat dry from nerves."

"Yes?" Mr. Webber prompted.

"Could you tell me about my family?" He fought the urge to look away, embarrassment heating his cheeks.

Mr. Webber faltered for a moment. "Oh, yes. I, uh, of course. It is really quite simple. Your mother, Abigail, was your grandfather's only child. Because he had no male heir, your mother would inherit everything once she married. My understanding is that the man she chose was not suitable."

"My father, you mean?"

Mr. Webber paused, eyes darting around nervously. "Yes, your father. Your grandfather did not approve of the match."

"Why was no one else put in line to inherit? Surely there were other male relatives? Why me?"

"I cannot speak for your grandfather, but he had no other close family. My opinion is that he regretted driving your mother away, and this was his way of making up for it."

"I see," Elijah said quietly. He would have time to ponder all of this later. Right now he had work to do. "Thank you, Mr. Webber. Should we carry on with the business?"

The man looked relieved to be in safer territory once again. "Yes, let us begin."

Two hours later his head was stuffed full of facts and figures. And money. So much money. Amounts he could only dream of before. What he brought in, what he paid out, and how much his investments made him. And all kinds of lists with the names of people and places he was now either related to, associated with, doing business with, or responsible for. It was all overwhelming, and he was exhausted. And that exhaustion only doubled when the man unexpectedly brought up his Vivian.

"And then there is the matter of your sister. She will need to be presented upon society this season."

"I am sorry, what?"

"Your sister has just come of age, has she not?"

"Yes." He nodded slowly, still having trouble understanding what Mr. Webber was saying. Elijah had not even considered what this inheritance would mean for his sister, apart from the sense of security this money offered.

He had not considered what this would mean for her prospects, though he surely should have.

Truth be told, he was more concerned about her effect on the young men she set her sights on. His little sister was a true spitfire, and he loved her for it.

"Well, with your new position, she should have no trouble securing a husband. She will surely make a good match for any highborn gentleman hoping to find a wife in this uncommon season. It is most opportune timing."

Elijah resisted the urge to roll his eyes. But, of course, a man like Mr. Webber would assume all Elijah cared about was money. As if he would not first consider Vivian's feelings in all of this. It was, after all, her decision whom she was to marry and when. He cared far more about her happiness than increasing his fortunes.

He had tried to remain cordial. He really had, out of necessity, sure, but out of some respect as well. But this was a step too far for him.

"I hardly think my sister's marriage prospects are my biggest concern right now," he said, trying and failing to disguise his annoyance. His clipped tone was no doubt bordering on impolite. But he was finding it hard to stay calm with the way this man talked of marrying off his sister as if she were no more than an expensive prize to be sold to the highest bidder.

Of course, he knew she wanted to find a husband at some point; she mentioned it sometimes, mostly commenting on how she longed to marry for love, so different from what their parents had. But surely not yet and not like this, by being paraded around in front of dozens of rich little boys in the hopes that somebody would snatch her up. This was a private matter between him and his sister.

"Sir, it would be most prudent to settle the matter as soon as possible. I would be happy to assist you with any arrangements. Meetings with the fathers of eligible gentlemen and such. Whatever you might need."

Elijah stiffened, his jaw clenching with irritation. "I do not wish to discuss my sister's marriage prospects at this time."

He did not attempt to sound polite this time, and Mr. Webber finally seemed to catch on.

"I apologize if I have overstepped at all, sir. I only wish to help, as I am sure this must be very overwhelming. But do let me know if you change your mind."

He narrowed his eyes, then reminded himself of his earlier resolution to keep his temper in check and forced a smile onto his face.

"Thank you for your gracious offer, Mr. Webber. Should I decide to bring my sister into town for the season, I am sure we will take you up on it."

He had no intention of doing any such thing. No matter what Vivian did in the future, she would not be doing it under the tutelage of anyone associated with a slimy man such as this one.

A tense goodbye with Mr. Webber and a short while later, Elijah was freshly washed and dressed in uncomfortable clothes, standing on the steps of his townhouse, clutching the thick packet of papers Mr. Webber had given him. Everything there was to know about his estate.

The townhouse, the home upstate. All his holdings and real estate. Every bit of money he now had.

The very idea was still too much for him to grasp firmly.

Should he bother? Could he do this, make this life last? If he lost it all, he would be fine. But Vivian deserved this. He could not let her down.

He glanced down at himself and chuckled. A tailored waist coat with brass buttons, a pocket watch that surely cost far too much money, and shoes that pinched a little in the toes. He had never looked this put together in his whole life. Even his hair was artfully styled underneath his bowler hat.

Instead of hailing a carriage back to the dingy apartment he shared with Vivian, which he wanted to do more than anything, he walked until he left the quiet, glittering streets behind, hoping the fresh air would clear his head.

He walked until he was firmly ensconced among businesses and restaurants and the hustle and bustle of downtown, finding the bank easily enough.

The noise was comforting. There were all kinds of people on the streets here, not just the very wealthy. And for the first time in hours, he felt like he could breathe easy.

He stared at the entrance to the bank, watching the comings and goings for a few minutes. He thought of Vivian, waiting for him to return home with the news. She would be thrilled with this turn of events, he was sure.

There was so much to do. So many plans to create and decisions to make. So many people depended upon him now for their livelihood, not just his sister.

That, more than anything, made him determined to do everything right. To learn every piece of the business and to excel at it. To give no one any reason to look down on him.

He could do this. He would do this.

But first, he needed to disappear for a moment, to just be Elijah Jameson, brother, sailor, ordinary man for a little while longer. And he desperately needed a drink.

Chapter 2

Isabella Marin was the kind of person who would do something simply because someone said that she could not. For example, if her mother said she absolutely could not spend the entire day reading, that was precisely what she did.

But she was also the kind of person who would not do something simply because it was what was expected of her.

In a word, she was stubborn.

And that was why she flat out refused to participate in the upcoming social season that would begin in only a few short days. Because it was what her mother demanded of her, expected of her as a young woman of high rank who was as yet unwed.

Finding a husband for her only daughter was all Mrs. Marin seemed to want. There was little reprieve from it; it occupied every conversation they had, even if indirectly. Her mother had no interest or care for what her daughter needed.

And so, naturally, Isabella resisted as much as she could. She ignored her mother's glares from across the breakfast table. She spent hours roaming the gardens and put off as many social engagements as was possible.

But somehow, even that did not keep people at bay. The invitations kept coming.

Today's pile had looked particularly thick when she spotted it on the table in the entryway mere moments ago.

Her natural response was to hide away in her favorite room in their too-large townhouse, the library.

It was a warm and cozy room offering several navy-blue chairs with soft, plush velvet cushions so comfortable she sometimes fell asleep in one. Each wall was covered in floor-to-ceiling bookshelves of deep cherry red wood, and the large, high windows let in the sunshine. She often found herself sitting quietly for hours simply watching the dust motes in the air. This room was her happy place, books were her escape, they brought her comfort and companionship. And this room held so many of her favorite stories. It smelled of parchment and ink, with faint notes of charred wood. A chessboard sat on a small table in one corner where she and her father spent many happy nights together. Other times, they would sit in front of the fire, both lost in a book, simply enjoying each other's company.

Of course, that was mainly during the colder months. Currently, the temperature outside was warm, the air damp from a fresh rain. And though summer was officially on the way as the end of May approached, the day had not yet warmed enough to dry the puddles that littered the ground—all the more reason to stay indoors with a good book. Books were her escape. They gave her a sense of the freedom she so desperately craved.

But she so often retreated to this room that it was no hardship for her mother to track her down to deliver this morning's invitations.

"Today's letters," her mother said, dropping the pile into her lap. "That one on top is your obligation for today. I would appreciate it if you offered no arguments."

"What is it?" Isabella asked, not bothering to look up from the novel she was reading. Another small way to annoy her mother.

"An invitation to lunch at Mrs. Fisher's. You know Mrs. Fisher. The wife of your father's business partner and a dear family friend."

Isabella smiled inwardly. She had known Mrs. Fisher since she was a little girl and considered the woman a good friend. Truth be told, she enjoyed Mrs. Fisher's company and was more than happy to pay her a visit. But her mother did not need to know that, though she should have if she bothered to pay Isabella any real attention outside of her marriage prospects.

"Very well, Mother," she grumbled for effect. "You will hear no protest from me—this time."

Her mother stalked away, no doubt frustrated by her errant daughter's apparent lack of enthusiasm, but Isabella could not care less. Let her mother believe her uninterested; she was. It was all boring and repetitive. Her responsibilities were to pay calls, attend parties, and take daily strolls in the park with other upper-class young ladies, all hoping to catch the eye of an eligible, obviously wealthy young man.

But as one of the only Mexican American young women among a sea of white families, she had to work twice as hard. She constantly felt the need to prove that she belonged in this world, that she had every right to be here, even if she did not want to be.

Her parents had worked hard to give her this life. And so, she was at constant war with herself, torn between wanting to be a good daughter and her need for independence.

She picked up her book again, intending to finish the current chapter when a meow sounded from somewhere near her feet. She smiled and reached down to scoop up the fluffy black and white cat scowling up at her.

"Do not look at me like that. I can't help but be combative where Mother is concerned."

Jasper's scowl remained unchanged. He was judging her, as always. Her most loyal companion to a fault, he always knew when she was lying.

Call it a weird sixth sense. She had had Jasper since he was a kitten, finding him tangled in some brambles on the edge of their country estate. She had begged her parents to keep him and after lots of tears and a bath, they relented.

She rolled her eyes. "Fine. I will try to be kinder. But she could try too. It's like she doesn't care about my happiness. Only the illusion of it. She's trying so hard, but it's useless."

Isabella had no intention of taking a husband anytime soon, or at all if she could help it. She was not as eager as her mother to surrender her freedom to a man.

She sighed heavily while scratching behind Jasper's ear, her mind wandering far away.

If only her mother knew that it was all for naught, that her only daughter's prospects were ruined and had been since Isabella's third season this past year. But she could never tell her mother that;

she would never be able to look her in the eye again. So she took it all in stride for now and tried to keep her head down.

Meanwhile, her mother would be departing for their home upstate that very evening. She was allowed to hide away as she wished, while Isabella was not. Another wedge between them to further sour their already tense relationship.

And her father, not wanting to upset his wife, would remind her every single day of her responsibilities as the only daughter of such a prominent family.

Only that was the problem. She would much rather spend her days out in the gardens with a good book than don a beautiful gown and dance the night away.

But duty called, at least for now, until she could figure out a way to get what she really wanted.

And she did enjoy Mrs. Fisher's company.

She rose from her comfortable spot and carried Jasper up the stairs to her bedroom. Another one of her favorite places, her room was spacious but not so large that it felt unwelcoming. The walls were a pale green, a color that reminded her of quiet mornings at their country estate. The walls were dotted with frames filled with pressed flowers, some picked during walks in the park, some from their gardens. The hearth was adorned with small trinkets, keepsakes, and a few of her favorite books. The bed was plush and covered in pillows that she was always loath to part from each morning. She walked over to her wardrobe and threw the doors open, scanning the options for something appropriate. She wanted to be comfortable and cool, which was not easily achieved given the many layers of clothing a lady was required to wear. But a few dresses stood out in her mind that fit the bill.

She chose her favorite summer dress, a beautiful olive-green color, and her most comfortable pair of suede slippers, a lovely silver color, taking a moment to admire the look. The dress highlighted her deep, golden-brown skin and dark, almost black eyes. It was lightweight enough for the warm weather, a perfect material for her short frame because it did not overwhelm her. The hem stopped just above her ankles, and the straps hung lightly off her shoulders.

She found her favorite green parasol hanging in her wardrobe. Then, when she was satisfied with her appearance, she set off to walk the two blocks to the Fisher's townhouse. The trees lining the bustling streets were full and green. The sky above was a brilliant blue. People milled about, taking advantage of the perfect weather with a walk in the nearby park.

Only when she was alone, in the sunshine and fresh air, did she begin to wonder about the reason behind this lunch invitation. Perhaps Mrs. Fisher had been tasked by Isabella's mother to encourage her participation in as many events as possible this season. It was certainly possible. Or perhaps there would be other young ladies in attendance—an attempt to force socialization on her.

Or, worst of all, perhaps there would be young men there. She certainly would not put it past her mother to arrange something of that nature. As long as a chaperone was present, there would be nothing improper about it.

By the time she reached the Fisher's home, she had concocted several scenarios that might allow her to leave the lunch party early, including faking a stomachache, dramatic swooning, and a very pressing social engagement that she had conveniently forgotten about in her enthusiasm over Mrs. Fisher's invitation.

A little white lie would not hurt, right?

So, she was pleasantly surprised when the footman opened the doors to the drawing room, and she was met only by Mrs. Fisher and one other young lady seated on the couches within.

"Miss Isabella Marin, allow me to introduce to you Ms. Vivian Jameson, the younger sister of Mr. Elijah Jameson, the inheritor of Jameson Steele."

Oh, so this was one of the mysterious Jameson siblings? She had heard whispers of this situation from her father. He often did business with the late Mr. Jameson and was curious about what the young Mr. Jameson would be like. He seemed to have no such curiosity about the sister.

Typical man.

The name Elijah stirred a feeling in her stomach she dared not entertain. She knew that name. But this could not possibly be the same, Elijah. The coincidence would be too great. No. It was not him.

Vivian piped in then. "We had not even known Mr. Jameson was any relation to us. But after he passed last month, my brother received a letter from his solicitor. He inherited everything."

Isabella met the girl's eye, smiling before taking in her whole person. She was tall, almost a whole head taller than Isabella herself. She was thin, whereas Isabella was not, but looked very strong. Her eyes were bright and wide, a lovely hazel color above a small, almost button nose, and a mouth that was already moving a mile a minute.

Perhaps Mrs. Fisher intended for the two of them to be friends? Or maybe the young lady needed a lesson in etiquette.

It was truly an exercise in patience, fielding Mrs. Fisher's greetings and inquiries after her health. Then, of course, she had to be polite and inquire about her host, all while the mysterious young lady stole glances at her. This girl was a stranger, yet Isabella felt as if she was being judged and put to some silent test.

And she could not even fault her. Because if the roles were reversed, she would behave in the same way.

Mrs. Fisher interjected, "Mr. Fisher has always handled the banking for Jameson Steele and the personal fortune of the late Mr. Jameson, as I am sure you know from your father. He intends to keep the tradition going with the young gentleman, and offered any personal assistance should he require it. Young Vivian here preferred to stay in town while her brother attended to matters at their new home upstate. So, we have taken her in until he returns."

This would explain the invitation to lunch. Vivian was likely in need of some company outside of Mrs. Fisher.

Isabella smiled. "How very kind of you, Mrs. Fisher. And how fortunate for you, Miss Jameson. I am delighted to make your acquaintance."

"And I yours, Miss Marin," Vivian said with a nod of her head. "Given my circumstances before the inheritance, I fully expected to be completely overlooked."

Her heart went out to the girl. She was no stranger to being looked down upon. Her parents were prominent members of society, to be sure, but they had not always been so.

Still, she cared little for the expectations that came along with that, and she had a feeling Vivian would be the same way.

I have always had high expectations placed on me, with people waiting for me to fail. Something I have spoken to Mrs. Fisher about before."

That was true; she had often confided in the older woman. But she never told her the whole truth. No, that was a secret she was determined to take to her grave.

But at least she could help Vivian feel less alone by admitting her own feelings.

"Which is exactly why I wanted to introduce the two of you," Mrs. Fisher said with a wink.

"And how do you two know each other so well?" Vivian asked.

Isabella looked fondly at her friend. "My father owns the bank that Mr. Fisher works for, and they are very good friends. I have known him and Mrs. Fisher since I was quite a little girl, and we have always been close."

"And I am so very fond of you, dear Isabella," Mrs. Fisher said with a smile before continuing on. "Anyway, as I said, Mr. Fisher has offered his assistance to the young Mr. Jameson. He is largely unprepared for his new role, or to bring his sister out into society for that matter. But with our help, Vivian can have an absolutely lovely season. And even, perhaps, find herself a husband. If that is something she wishes to do."

Vivian laughed. "I do, yes. Much to my brother's horror."

Isabella tried not to cringe. Was that to be her mission, then? Helping Vivian to find a husband? The idea was almost laughable, considering she had absolutely no desire to find a husband of her own. Not that she could admit that to either of these women.

But that Mrs. Fisher had thought of Isabella to help Vivian navigate the battlefield that was high society in New York City was truly flattering. Some still looked down on her family, and some always would. Mrs. Fisher's easy acceptance and friendship still marveled her.

But would Vivian want her help? Vivian was white. And although Isabella was in a better social position, it was something that must be considered. She was not entirely sure she was the right person for the job.

Casting her eyes around the sitting room, she tried to find the words. She shifted in her seat and then breathed a sigh of relief when the footman arrived with tea. She picked up her cup and took a sip, giving herself a moment to collect her thoughts.

"I am truly flattered you would consider me for this, ma'am. But surely there are other, more qualified young women in your social circle who could help Vivian with these things."

She could name a few just off the top of her head; ladies who could, without fail, be found at one of the fashionable dress shops every time new fabrics came in. Ladies who spent most of their time at social events comparing their dresses to those of the other women in attendance while batting their eyes at every available young man who passed by. Women who never would have the same concerns Isabella had, even if she never wanted to marry. Lucky them.

Mrs. Fisher shook her head. "I do not believe that to be true, my dear. I know you don't like to hear it because you would happily be a recluse, but you are highly regarded in society. There is no one better for this task. This is not just about getting our dear Vivian a new wardrobe and teaching her the proper etiquette when sitting down to dinner. It is about ensuring her a grand debut and securing all the right connections so that she may have her pick of young men. She deserves the very best chance. And there is no other young lady who has your sharp wit and strong mind," Mrs. Fisher concluded with a twinkle in her eye.

She knew Isabella was never one to back down from a challenge. And while Isabella wanted nothing more than to hideaway for as long as possible, this would be a welcome distraction from her own hopeless situation. If she was busy fielding potential prospects for Vivian, there would be no time to focus on her own disastrous love life.

And maybe helping Vivian would work in her favor. She could attend social events, as her mother wished, but only in service of her new friend. Her mother would never know the difference. Killing two birds with one stone, as it were.

She glanced over at Vivian, who had been surprisingly quiet throughout the discussion. The girl looked positively giddy. "I take it you approve of this plan that has been made on your behalf, Vivian?"

The girl nodded enthusiastically, practically bouncing in her seat with a huge smile on her face.

"Well, then, let us get you ready to do battle."

The afternoon passed them by in a flurry of activity as the three ladies set about making appointments and filling their calendars with all of the upcoming social events.

There were to be dress fittings, lunches, dance lessons, and strolls through the park. All great ways to become acquainted with other members of New York's high society. There would also be outings to the museums and art galleries. More for the amusement of Vivian and Isabella than anything else, but good learning opportunities, nonetheless.

Her first official event would be the annual start of summer ball hosted by the prominent Whitney family. Everyone of importance would be in attendance.

Isabella and her family had been acquainted with the Whitney family since before she was born, and their son Eric was one of her very dearest friends. Getting an invitation for her new friend would be no problem. Perhaps she would even pay a call on Eric to introduce him to Vivian beforehand. She was certain the two would get on well.

And Vivian was completely over the moon about all of this. In fact, excitement seemed to be her permanent state of being, an attitude that would surely help her through this unprecedented situation.

"Now," Isabella said, "it will be next to impossible to instill eighteen years' worth of information onto you in only a few weeks' time. So, is there anything you already have experience in? Anything you are particularly eager to learn? Dancing? Or an instrument, perhaps?"

"Well," Vivian hesitated. "I am quite good at needlework. Before my mother died, she taught me very well. And because my brother and I had little money to our names, I have been sewing my own dresses for years, as well as my brother's clothes." She cast her eyes down then, seemingly ashamed of her admission.

Isabella walked over to the girl, clasping their hands together and looking her straight in the eyes. "That is an absolutely fine skill to have. And in that regard, you will be miles ahead of all the other young ladies, myself included."

"Really?" Vivian asked, that wonderful excitement beginning to creep back into her voice.

It made Isabella smile.

"Really."

"Isabella is absolutely right, my dear," Mrs. Fisher said from the sofa across from them. She had been so quiet Isabella had almost forgotten she was here.

"Now then," Isabella continued, "is there a particular skill you are most interested in learning?"

Vivian beamed up at her. "Dancing. I have never had many opportunities to learn or practice the very little I do know. I never had anyone available to accompany me to the public dances except once. And my brother would not allow me to dance with any of the young men. And he is not very fond of dancing, so—" Vivian trailed off.

Isabella chuckled. "Well, you are in luck because I love to dance. And I have been practicing with my father since I was very young. I would be happy to teach you."

The next hour or two was spent with Isabella leading Vivian around Mrs. Fisher's drawing room while the older woman watched on, making commentary here and there.

They started with a few of the easier round dances, twirling each other and trying not to giggle during every somewhat awkward hop and turn.

But Vivian was a natural.

Just then, the doors to the drawing room opened, and one of Mrs. Fisher's footmen announced a visitor.

Before Isabella even had the chance to catch the name of the newcomer as they entered the room, Vivian had thrown herself at them with an almost ear-splitting squeal of excitement.

"Elijah," she yelled as he lifted her up, twirling her gently around the room.

Elijah? Again, the name evoked a memory of shaved lemon ice, warm sand on her toes, and the ocean.

But this was Vivian's mysterious older brother, the young man who accidentally stumbled into an inheritance. He was not her old friend.

Already there was talk amongst Isabella's circle of friends about him. But she would be the first to see him in person. Whether or not she would contribute to the ongoing gossip remained to be seen.

She stood on her tiptoes to see over Vivian's head, silently cursing her short stature.

She could make out a dark red coat and cloak draped across broad shoulders and arms that held his sister so tightly Isabella was afraid he would crush the girl. Over the top of Vivian's head, she glimpsed a head of unruly dark curls, and a flash of warm brown eyes filled with love and excitement. It warmed Isabella's heart to see such true and open affection between the siblings, something she never got to experience as an only child.

The reunion went on quietly for a few more moments until Mrs. Fisher lightly cleared her throat, and the two broke apart.

"What a heartwarming welcome! Vivian, I know you must be very happy to be reunited with your brother, but please allow us to at least have a glimpse at him."

Laughing, Vivian let go of her brother only to grab his hand and lead him toward their hostess.

Isabella's heart stuttered in her chest, her breath catching in her throat. It was him; she felt it in her heart. The same Elijah from so many years ago. The same wild dark hair and kind eyes. The boy who used to chase her along the docks while her father and Mr. Fisher worked on the ships hauling the catch of the day.

She did not remember ever seeing or meeting Elijah's family.

"Mrs. Fisher, may I introduce my brother, Mr. Elijah Jameson, heir to the Jameson Steele fortune."

The gentleman in question straightened, his demeanor shifting. He bowed somewhat awkwardly to Mrs. Fisher as Vivian beamed up at him.

She glanced at him subtly so he would not notice. Would he remember her? Things were so different now; she was so different now. Did she want him to remember her?

Yes.

No.

He shifted, and she quickly looked away.

"Did I get it right?"

Her brother only gave an awkward laugh and lightly ruffled her hair, quite a feat as they were nearly the same height. Mrs. Fisher said, with fondness in her tone, "You got it perfectly right, my dear. Although you know we have already been introduced once. When you first arrived here."

Vivian blushed, ducking her head.

"But, it is no matter," Mrs. Fisher said, now addressing Mr. Jameson. "Welcome back to the city, Mr. Jameson. We are happy to have you here again."

Isabella waited for an introduction to the gentleman, but it never came as Vivian chattered on.

Should she say something? Or wait for Elijah to say something. Had he really not noticed her presence yet? That was rather rude behavior.

"It is so exciting to finally have you here—the city will be twice as much fun with you. I mean, now that our situation has improved so much," Vivian said, smiling at her brother.

Isabella doubted this man would add much in the way of fun. He was not what she remembered him to be. Young Elijah was always smiling and carefree, unapologetically himself. But this man seemed stiff and uncomfortable, reserved. Could she really blame him, though? Eleven years was a long time.

Still, she wanted to speak up, to make him look at her. Were his eyes as she remembered them? Always so full of kindness.

Perhaps Vivian and Mrs. Fisher had forgotten she was there?

"I am sure we will both find things to occupy our time," Elijah said as he settled onto the sofa across from Isabella with Vivian seated next to him. "In fact, I will be going to visit all the best shops to acquire a new wardrobe tomorrow. I have not had the opportunity to do so until now. Would you like to accompany me?"

"Oh, I would love to! But first, you must tell me all about what you have been up to as of late. I enjoyed your letters so much, but I am sure they did not do things justice. How did you find the home upstate? Was there much to be done?"

"Yes, there was much to do on the estate. The name is Jameson Hall; not very inventive, but it gets the job done, I suppose. I have been introduced to my new duties in depth and spent many nights learning the ins and outs of our new station. Apparently, having an estate requires all of one's time and attention."

At those words, Elijah's eyes locked on hers, and she was barely able to hold in her snort. Was he so naïve? If he wanted to make it in this world, he needed to wisen up and quickly. Did he not realize how many people's livelihoods relied on his ability to manage things well?

It was almost too much, which was why she could not help herself.

The words just slipped out. "It does if one intends to take good care of it and not let it go to ruin."

Chapter 3

"It does if one intends to take good care of it and not let it go to ruin."

The remark, and the near-hostile brittleness with which it was conveyed, finally drew his attention to the other occupant of the room, a dark-haired young lady whom he would guess to be only a couple of years Vivian's senior.

Anyone with eyes would agree that she was beautiful. She was the kind of woman he could happily spend hours admiring. It was the eyes. He got the impression that they hid many secrets, and if she would allow him, he would learn every single one.

But her impeccable posture, expensive dress, and polite, almost blank expression on her face told him that this was a woman who was far above his station. Someone who would not have spared him so much as a glance mere days ago, if she even bothered to acknowledge his presence at all, and he was immediately on edge. Who was this young woman? This stiff and uppity debutante who had such confidence as to criticize him so freely?

He was unsure what to do. Should he answer her or politely skirt over the question? Which one would be more inappropriate?

He looked to Mrs. Fisher for some guidance. But she only smiled at him, giving nothing away. The twinkle in her eye told him that she was not at all surprised by this turn of events, and that maybe she was enjoying this at his expense.

He shook his head to clear it before addressing the young lady.

"Are you very knowledgeable about managing an estate then, Miss…?"

"Miss Isabella Marin, daughter of Mr. Peter Marin, owner of Marin Investment Group."

Why would she supply her name and station?

To do so freely without waiting for a formal introduction from their hostess was odd. He was still learning the social graces of the upper class, but he knew that was not proper etiquette. A small smirk pulled at his face; the thought that his presence might have irked her enough to break decorum entirely too delightful to ignore. He had to find enjoyment somewhere, right?

"And I know enough to be aware of the weight of responsibility that comes with an estate and can only advise you not to take it too lightly. If you must know, my parents have always made it a point to teach me about the business of managing our estate whenever time allows. The tasks involved can indeed be daunting for some."

The implied meaning of her words were clear: "Someone like you has no idea what they are doing, which is why I am better than you in every way."

It was as good as a well-placed right hook, given that the only means proper young ladies like her had of cutting an opponent down was with their words. A small part of him was impressed.

Isabella Marin was likely not one to be trifled with, a quality his sister also possessed, which he prided himself on instilling in her from a young age.

Elijah was no stranger to a good fight. And he had no intention of letting Miss Marin off the hook. It seemed he had already crossed her without even trying. And his tongue could be rather swift and sharp when the occasion called for it.

"You might be surprised to learn that I know of your father, Miss Marin. He is the business partner of Mr. Webber if memory serves, and it is he who will be helping me to look after my new finances. I have not yet had the pleasure of meeting him in person, but I did have a very kind and courteous letter from him only a week ago. I see the apple has fallen quite far from the tree in that regard. But I shall endeavor not to hold that against your father when at last we do meet in person. And how very fortunate for you, Miss Marin, to have parents that possess such incredible foresight. They must surely see that you will need to know how to care for yourself. Given that, you will likely find no partner half as clever as you."

Vivian gasped, her mouth hanging open in shock for a moment before she spoke. "Elijah! I have only just begun with my etiquette lessons, but even I know that that was a terribly rude thing to say! And incorrect to boot—Isabella would never choose anyone but the most clever and sophisticated man for a partner."

He glanced at his sister, eyebrow raised in question. Apparently, she was already quite taken with their new acquaintance. Perfect.

He met Miss Marin's eyes again, waiting for some retort to come. But she only continued to watch him with that same blank expression, the fire in her eyes stoked for now. And he almost missed it, almost wished she would keep pushing him.

Vivian's outraged interjection kept the situation from turning even more unpleasant.

Still, he mumbled an apology, only meeting her eyes for a moment before pointedly looking anywhere else, but not before noticing the sadness in her smile, the way her facial muscles seemed to strain with the movement. There was a story behind that smile, and the young lady's prickly manner made him unexpectedly curious to learn it. Miss Isabella Marin may not be the most welcoming person, but he could not exactly judge someone he knew nothing about.

He took a steadying breath.

None of this really mattered in the end because she was of absolutely no importance to him.

He returned his attention to his sister, determined to cast all thoughts of this young lady from his mind. There was no need to concern himself with her sad eyes and the secrets they might hold.

Elijah was a good brother. If there was one thing he could state with confidence about himself, it would be that.

For the last two weeks, he had fumbled his way through learning the business, feeling incredibly inadequate the entire time. It was that feeling which made him so happy to be back in the city with his sister. They could finally start their new lives together.

"When will we be able to move home, Elijah?" Vivian asked as a footman entered with a tray of cucumber sandwiches and tea for the four occupants. Miss Marin rose from her seat to pour out the tea and they all busied themselves adding sugar and cream to their liking.

He took this momentary lapse in conversation to take in his surroundings. This was the first time he had spent an extended period of time in another high society member's home. Mrs. Fisher seemed to like pink. Pink velvet curtains, pink chairs with gold accents, pink lace adoring the tables. It was a sharp contrast to his grandfather's tastes of dark wood and burgundy red. This house felt inviting. It smelled of roses and citrus, brightness. He wanted that for Vivian and himself.

It was so strange to him that Vivian was already referring to the townhouse as home, but it also made him glad. He had always admired his sister's ability to just take life as it came at them.

"Everything is all ready for us. I sent a letter to the staff a few days before I departed from upstate. It felt very responsible of me," he said with a laugh.

Vivian and Mrs. Fisher laughed along with him while a certain young lady remained quiet. He tensed, waiting for her to cut him down over his bad joke when Mrs. Fisher spoke up.

"How very clever of you, Mr. Jameson. It seems you are learning our ways already."

It was things like this that reminded him of just how much he liked Mrs. Fisher. Not only for agreeing to take his little sister in but because she was a genuinely kind person. No one he had encountered so far in this new life had been as kind to him as she. She was warm and welcoming. Her interactions with him were genuine and not at all laced with curiosity, disdain, or superiority. And most importantly, she had shown incredible kindness and care toward his sister. To him, there was no greater evidence of good character than showing kindness and expecting nothing in return.

And from the looks of it, Vivian had indeed been treated well. His sister was positively glowing with happiness and wearing a new gown, well-made and tasteful but with a simple, natural air that filled him with relief.

When he had arranged for her to stay behind in the city and become equipped for the upcoming season, he had been afraid of returning to find her turned into a painted doll. Or find that her experience had been wholly unenjoyable. But the girl in front of him was still his little sister. The worry in his heart fully dissipated, and he felt more at ease than he had in days.

The suddenness of this status change was something that neither of them knew exactly how to handle. And it pained him that he was not equipped to guide her through this the way a true-born gentleman would have been.

He held on to that thought throughout his visit and all but ignored the young lady in the corner who threatened to bring his good mood down. Whatever she might think of his comments, he had worked hard and was committed to doing his very best. And it seemed incredibly unfair that Miss Marin would judge him so harshly upon their very first meeting. Did he not deserve the benefit of her doubt?

At times there seemed to be something she wanted to say to him. But Mrs. Fisher chatted on and on. And there was never any time for he and Miss Marin to exchange more than a few words until their hostess invited them to stay for dinner.

"Oh, Elijah. Can we please stay?" Vivian begged. "I am having such a lovely time. And it will give you more time to get to know Isabella. You have hardly said a few words to her all afternoon."

He cringed, his face undoubtedly turning red. Isabella turned to stare at him, eyebrow raised in challenge, and he bit back a groan. He hardly knew this woman, and yet she seemed determined to antagonize him. Had he never stood any chance with her at all? Did she consider herself so very far above him? Call him petty, but it only made him want to do the same in return.

And it was for that reason and that reason only that he turned to Mrs. Fisher and said, "We would love to."

***

Mrs. Fisher's dining room was truly something to behold. The long, large table could easily seat twelve people comfortably. Candles lined the entire length, placed in gold holders that glittered off the chandelier above their heads. The walls were covered in large paintings all framed in gilded gold. How much did each one cost? He did not want to know. But he made a mental note to familiarize himself with the artwork hanging in his townhouse.

The party of four was seated at one end of the large table, for which he was grateful. Did some people actually sit spread out when the table was not full? Did they have to shout at each other?

The wine was delicious, a White Zinfandel with notes of strawberry and watermelon, the food even more so. Roast beef, mashed potatoes, and glazed carrots. He should have been in heaven. Instead, his waistcoat felt uncomfortably tight, the room far too warm, and his palms would not stop sweating. All because one Isabella Marin would not stop asking him questions.

It started simply enough. Just chatter about the weather. Did he like being outdoors? Yes, he preferred it. Did he like living in the city, or would he be spending most of his time upstate? He and Vivian both declared their preference for busy city life. Isabella apparently preferred the country. Of course, they were opposites in this way. But then she started on the more difficult questions about his history and lack of experience.

He only wished he had the courage to ask what it was about him that seemed to vex her so. It was like she was trying to get him to confess something, but he had no idea what. And he was not about to ask her. If she wanted it to be this way, so be it.

"You had no idea of your family history?" she asked after her first sip of wine.

"That is correct. Not until the letter arrived at our door last month and I went spoke with the executor of our grandfather's estate."

The food was placed in front of them. And she watched him with shrewd attention as he placed a napkin on his lap and picked up the correct fork. If she was expecting him to be unsure, she did not show it. Not only had he spent the last two weeks learning the business, but he had schooled himself on proper etiquette as well. And he had instructed Mrs. Fisher to teach his sister the basics while he was away.

He was pleased to see that Vivian, too, seemed to know her way around the truly unnecessary amount of cutlery.

A few bites of food and Miss Marin continued on. "And you believe two weeks' time enough to know what it takes to run an estate?"

"I never said any such thing. I am still learning," he snapped before he could think better of it.

The other two ladies stopped speaking to each other, the tension in the air thick. Miss Marin regarded him coolly, assessing. His grip on his fork tightened.

"Perhaps not. But, in my opinion, you are far too cavalier about the whole endeavor."

He ground his teeth, trying to remain calm. "Funny, I do not recall asking for your opinion."

"Who would like some more wine?" Mrs. Fisher asked, her voice much too loud for the quiet room.

He sat back as the butler filled his glass and then reached forward to take a generous sip. He glanced at Miss Marin, relieved to see her focused on her food.

Vivian leaned forward to catch his eye. "Will we go to the shops tomorrow, Elijah? I have an entire list of things I must get in preparation for the season."

"Of course. We will see that you get everything you need."

Miss Marin cleared her throat, and he braced himself for another mark against his character. "Will you be taking Vivian on your own, then, Mr. Jameson?"

"I expect so, yes."

"Would it not be more prudent to have a woman accompany you? Someone to offer their opinions? Someone who knows the correct styles and what colors go together? That sort of thing? Surely that would not interest you."

"On the contrary, Miss Marin. I am more than happy to help Vivian in whatever way she needs." If she was fishing for an invitation, she would not be getting one. Only so she could criticize him more? He thought not. "I take my responsibility as a brother very seriously, and I will not have you suggesting otherwise," he bit out.

He was pleased to see that comment stopped her in her tracks. She lifted her wine glass to her mouth and took a hardy sip, and he breathed a sigh of relief, grateful for the momentary lapse in commentary on his life.

Vivian beamed at him. "You are the best big brother I could ever want."

And just that declaration was enough to soothe his nerves, because in the end that was all that mattered to him.

He met Miss Marin's eyes again, eyebrow raised, waiting for her to contradict him this time. Instead, he noted a hint of color on her cheeks. Embarrassment? And something that looked suspiciously like shame in her eyes. Or was that just a trick of the light? He could not be sure, but he hoped that he made it clear to her that he took every bit of this situation seriously. And that perhaps she would cut him some slack in the future. Not that he had any great desire to see her again anytime soon.

Finally. Mrs. Fisher declared they move back to the drawing room for dessert and coffee. He was ready to decline, but again, Vivian asked to stay, the promise of strawberry shortcake too good to pass up.

He pointedly ignored the curious sense of loss that bloomed in his chest as Miss Marin took her leave of the party, declining dessert and thanking their host. She pulled Vivian into a hug, but when it was his turn to express his goodbyes, she only extended her fingers for him to barely grasp. The feeling that touch left behind was surely a trick of his mind.

It was only after Mrs. Fisher's driver had safely driven Miss Marin home and returned, as he and Vivian finished up their dessert and donned their coats, that Mrs. Fisher told him just how much he would be seeing of their new acquaintance over the next few weeks.

Apparently, Miss Isabella Marin, due to her impeccable manners, impressive accomplishments, and vital connections, was to be his sister's companion for the upcoming season.

Dread settled in his chest as he recalled every word they had volleyed back and forth this evening and the impertinent way he spoke to her. Had he ruined his sister's chances before she had even begun?

Chapter 4

By the time Isabella returned home, she was exhausted. The day of planning, scheming, and endless conversation left her feeling tired all the way to her bones, and a headache was forming behind her eyes.

The housemaid collected her wrap, and she paused in the foyer to remove her gloves, the chill to the night air made her grateful she had thought to bring them along. She could not wait for warm summer nights, the scent of jasmine floating on the breeze, crickets singing her their song each night.

The house was quiet as she slipped up the carpeted stairs to the second floor where light was spilling from under the drawing room doors, her parents likely reading or playing cards together. She softly slipped by, heading to her bedroom at the very end of the hall. Her parents had chosen the room for her because it had the best view of the back gardens. And every morning, no matter the weather, she always took a moment to admire that view. It was like a special present from her parents to her every day.

As she readied for bed, her mind wandered, seeing Elijah again should have been a joyous moment, yet she felt unworthy. She did not want to think too hard about why.

Meeting Elijah was one of her happiest days. Here was a boy, a white boy, wanting to be her friend. She was cautious at first, but eventually they had formed a friendship. He earned her trust when another boy tried to bully her for her pocket change. Elijah shoved the boy into the sand, grabbed her hand, and they ran. They shared a lemon shaved ice that day and sought each other's company for the rest of the summer.

In the privacy of her bedroom she could admit that she may have gone a bit overboard with her criticism of him today. She suspected that the person she was really angry with was her mother's incessant nuptial pursuit. To have a hand in her family's business was a dream of hers, and while her father was encouraging, it was tempered by the fact that she would eventually need to marry.

She would endeavor to be kinder to him in the future. But she would not apologize for pointing out the ways in which he was incredibly fortunate. She was far too stubborn for that.

Her feelings were a jumbled mess: anger that he did not remember her, shame that he might discover her secret, and jealousy because he was just handed what she craved most—freedom.

And then there was his annoyingly handsome face and deep, smooth voice.

He was incredibly cavalier and glib.

She breathed a sigh of relief as she pulled the pins from her tightly wound hair. It flowed freely down her back as she walked over to her chest of drawers to pull out a nightgown.

But what had really made her blood boil was the nonchalance with which he dismissed the duties and responsibilities of his new position. And regardless of her complicated feelings toward him, she felt it her responsibility to school him on what he did not understand.

Once she was dressed for the night she crawled into bed and settled in.

And perhaps that was part of her anger. She had never felt their differences as children. Neither of them had fancy clothes, spending money was rare and always treasured, and you could not have paid either of them to know the difference between a salad fork and a dinner fork. But now, there was a big difference between the two of them.

Freedom.

And his throwaway remark about choosing a good husband had only served to enrage her further. Because it had laid bare a truth that she always tried so hard to push to the back of her mind. The man she eventually married would be the only thing she had any influence over, and even that was no guarantee. Her choice of husband would be the deciding factor in how she lived her life. Was she to be something only there for aesthetic purposes? Or would her husband value her opinion and treat her as an equal?

But of course, well-bred young ladies did not shut themselves up in their rooms to rage against the man—they put on a nice dress and a demure smile and got on with their lives.

Which was exactly what she was planning to do where Elijah was concerned.

Unfortunately, that resolution was tested the very next morning.

***

She came down from her room to join her father for breakfast just as she did every other morning, only this time someone else was already present.

The toe of her boot caught on the edge of the thick carpet, and she stumbled into the dining room. Everything else was just as it was every other morning. A fire burned low in the hearth to her right, and the sidebar was filled with the usual delectables: toast and oatmeal, eggs benedict and sausage, and plenty of coffee for her father and juice for her. The table had two place settings, one at the head for her father, and one directly to his right. Everything mimicked an ordinary day.

Except for Mr. Jameson.

Both men were so engaged in lively conversation it took them a moment to register her presence. A moment she took to admire Elijah's annoyingly handsome face, not that she'd admit it.

When he caught her eye, she quickly looked away, choosing instead to focus on her father.

And it took another moment for Mr. Jameson to remember what little manners he had, get to his feet, and bow in her direction. Then he just stood there, watching her, his eyes entirely too intense for her comfort.

Was it warm in here?

Her father broke the tension by beckoning her over and pulling her chair out for her.

"Good morning, my darling. As you can see, we have a visitor. Of course, you are already acquainted as Mr. Jameson has been telling me. We have been getting to know each other as well."

"And what have you been discussing?" she asked.

Our mutual passion for sailing, and about all the recent progress in building ever bigger and faster vessels. He has some experience working on them. It is truly fascinating. I have read about them of course, but it is quite another thing to hear from someone who has sailed aboard one."

She smiled fondly at her father's enthusiasm. He loved to learn, something he instilled in her from a young age. She could recall many an evening hidden away in the library with him reading her passages from his favorite books. So content was she to see her father's smiling face, she almost forgot about their guest.

Almost.

She also noted that Mr. Jameson did not mention already knowing her father. Her hopes were truly dashed then, he must not remember her or her family after all.

It did not exactly change her feelings, except to lessen the guilt she felt over her rudeness yesterday. Though she still felt compelled to teach the man a lesson; that would not change.

She glanced over at Mr. Jameson to see him looking almost shy at her father's praise. And while she found the blush on his face to be endearing, the sight did not help to make this situation any less strange. What was he doing here? In her dining-room, this early in the morning?

"That sounds fascinating, Father. But surely a report on the advances in shipbuilding is not the only reason for Mr. Jameson's visit?"

"It is not, my darling girl," he said with a smile. Whatever the reason, it seemed to bring her father joy. "Mr. Jameson has come by to ask if you will accompany him and his sister on a walk through the park this afternoon."

He wanted to spend time with her? Even after their tense exchange yesterday? She held back a groan. Perhaps she would have to try harder to make sure they had less interaction.

She glanced over at the gentleman again, waiting for him to confirm her father's words. But he said nothing. He only looked at her silently, deep, chocolate eyes laser-focused, then suddenly his eyes widened, as if it finally occurred to him that she might like to hear the invitation directly from him.

He cleared his throat, his cheeks reddening slightly. Was he nervous? The very idea filled her with giddy excitement.

"Yes, of course. My sister has asked that you accompany us on a walk this afternoon. If you are not otherwise engaged."

She flinched ever so slightly. He did not say that he wished for her company. Only that his sister had. If nothing else, she could certainly appreciate the gentleman's honesty. Even if it stung.

And while her pride might insist she decline the invitation, she was eager to see Vivian again. She never made friends easily, and to have Vivian in her life was something that already brought her great joy. Not to mention that her day was surprisingly empty, her mother forcing no social engagements on her today.

Glancing out the window, she noted the day looked to be a mild one. The sun was shining bright and clear, so a walk might be just the thing to occupy her mind today.

She focused again on Mr. Jameson. "I would be delighted to accompany your sister. And you, of course. I do so enjoy her company," she said with a twinkle in her eye.

There. Let him make of that comment what he would.

He looked slightly surprised but managed to keep his composure long enough to fumble through a goodbye before hastily making his exit. It was an effort to hold in her laughter.

Her father eyed her curiously but said nothing for several long moments.

She was able to pour herself some juice and tuck into her breakfast before he finally spoke up. She was so lost in thought about spending the afternoon with Mr. Jameson, she almost forgot her father's presence.

"What an intriguing young man Mr. Jameson is," he said as he sipped his coffee, a wistful look in his eyes.

She did not like that look, because she knew what it meant. Her father liked Mr. Jameson. Her father who, more often than not, preferred the company of books to people, who had only a handful of close friends, had taken a liking to that smug, arrangement man. It would be funny if it was not so frustrating.

And then he added insult to injury by continuing on. "And handsome, too."

Now she openly gaped at him, though he hardly seemed to notice. Intriguing? Handsome? Had her father met the same Mr. Jameson she had? Because while she might reluctantly agree with the second assessment – she had already admitted it to herself, after all—she could most assuredly say that their "new" acquaintance was not intriguing, nor pleasant, nor any other praising word, nor was he likely to become so anytime soon.

And she could not hold her tongue on the subject.

"He is rude, judgmental, arrogant, and abrasive. I find it difficult to show any respect for him beyond that which his title and his sister's affection demand."

His brow furrowed and he shook his head. "Really? I found him to be nothing but polite, if a little insecure about the finer details of etiquette—an understandable deficit in his case, which I do believe we must forgive."

By now her father's voice had taken on a slight tone of reproach, and she bristled at the suspicion that she was being lectured.

"I am certainly willing to forgive a few gaps in his education – it would be more than cruel of me to expect him to excel at the duties of a station he was not born to fill..."

"How very gracious of you, Miss Marin."

The voice that filled the dining room was easily recognizable—and her stomach filled with dread as she slowly turned to look behind her. She rose even more slowly from her chair, the urge to run far and fast away singing in her blood.

Mr. Jameson stood in the doorway, looking at her with an angry glint in his eye, chin raised defiantly. He held her gaze for a moment before turning to her father.

"I regret having to interrupt your breakfast for a second time, but there is something I forgot to say before. May I speak freely for a moment?"

Her father glanced between the two of them, set down his coffee, and prepared to give the gentleman his full attention. But not before glancing at her, eyebrows raised in silent question.

She gave a subtle nod and then invited Mr. Jameson to take a seat again. The whole thing was mortifying. In this moment, she wished she could just disappear. He declined a seat and instead walked slowly toward her, coming to stand mere inches away.

She was so close now that she could make out the light dusting of freckles above his nose. The same as when they were young, only there were more of them now. And there were crinkles near his eyes that suggested he loved to laugh. She remembered that, too, how she used to delight in making him laugh. No doubt he found life to be endlessly funny, if his attitude the previous day was any indication. And yet, she could not find fault with that. For she loved to laugh. What would it be like to make Mr. Jameson laugh again?

She shook that thought away quickly and caught his eyes, waiting for him to speak. Yet he did not. Tension seeped slow and thick into the air around them.

She could feel her father's gaze upon them as they both waited for Mr. Jameson to speak, but he seemed almost stunned. She cleared her throat rather unsubtly, hoping he might take the cue. He shook his head and finally began speaking.

"You see... the thing is..." He paused as one of his hands reached up to scratch at his chin. A nervous gesture, perhaps? Again, she was giddy at the thought that she might make him nervous. Some things never changed, it seemed. "I have come here to apologize for the way I treated you during our meeting yesterday. I am by nature mistrustful where my sister's well-being is concerned, and I was wary of your motive in befriending her so quickly. But, Mrs. Fisher has told me that she specifically asked you to be a companion to Vivian. To help her find her way in society, and I... I wanted to ask you for myself if you would take that burden upon you, even after I have been unforgivably rude."

She was stunned. Of all the possible reasons for his sudden return, she had not expected this. Perhaps he deserved more credit; it was never easy to admit one's faults. She met her father's eyes that were now wide with surprise. She had not told him of the way Mr. Jameson had spoken to her, only that she had scolded him. That he would come here to apologize would only endear him further to her father.

Fantastic.

But there was nothing to be done about it.

So, she would give him this, if only for Vivian's sake. "I would not think that Vivian should suffer simply because of silly conversation between two people." Let him see how little she cared about him. "I shall be very happy to continue in my friendship to your sister and help her whenever she should need me."

He inclined his head in acknowledgement of the offer. "Thank you. My sister will be thrilled to hear it." He looked relieved, the tension now gone from his shoulders.

After the way she spoke about him to her father, she expected anger. Or down right refusal to speak to or see her ever again.

He must love his sister a great deal to still be here. She could appreciate that. And yet, she could not resist needling him a bit. Just how eager was he for her help?

"You should also know that as eager as I am to help Vivian have a grand season, I cannot accomplish the task alone. You will need to play your part, too."

He looked surprised, but to his credit, did not protest. He only looked at her with open curiosity before asking, "What would you have me do?"

"You must be out in society. Get to know people. Make acquaintances, attend events, perhaps join a social club. You have been given a very prominent position in society. Not everyone is so lucky. Use that to the advantage of your sister. So that when she is presented to society, everyone will already know her name as yours."

"How do I do that? I have no connections," he stated, his shoulders slumping in defeat. "All the money in the world could not give me that. No one knows me."

Her heart tightened at his words. *I know you, Elijah, but you do not know me. Not anymore.*

"You have me now. And my father."

You had me once before as well. For some of the happiest times of my life.

"True, my boy," her father said with a smile. "You would be most welcome at my club."

Isabella began speaking again. "There, you will make the rounds, tell people of your new station, and of course, you will let it slip, none too discreetly, that you have a beautiful sister with a sizeable inheritance."

At this, his posture went rigid, his eyes turning cold. "You mean to say I should dangle my sister like bait on a hook?"

"I mean to say you should make sure she has her pick of young men when the time comes."

He still looked angry and a little ill at the thought.

Her body moved of its own accord, closer still to him. The tips of her boots now touching his.

Somewhere in the back of her mind, she knew that this would be considered inappropriate. And not just because her father was present. But because two unmarried people with no attachment to one another should not be this close.

She did not care. She could not care. Because of that vulnerable look in his eyes.

"I know it sounds distasteful, and it is," she said in a quiet voice. She understood how he felt. "The marriage mart is not as cheerful a place as its name suggests. But this is important, especially for your sister. Believe me, I understand this better than any man ever could." Her words, so honest and intimate and accidental, prompted a surprising change in his demeanor. The angry steel in his eyes softened like melting chocolate.

This was not who she knew him to be from their first meeting only the day before. The kindness in his eyes threatened to soften her heart. Kindness was dangerous. His anger was easier, and she wished for it back.

Before he could speak, she rushed on, "If you make sure your sister's marriage prospects and your reputation attract suitors, I will make sure she will not fall prey to rakes and fortune hunters. I will make sure that she is not taken advantage of." *The way I once was*, she thought. She continued, "Vivian deserves the very best, and I want her to have it."

She wished she could tell him why. But she could not do that. She could not say that she would do anything to help Vivian because she did not want the girl to be like her, to repeat her mistakes. With very little choice as to the trajectory of her life, holding onto whatever small scrap of independence she could get.

His eyes stayed locked on hers for several long moments before he finally looked away. A quiet "Thank you" just a whisper on his lips.

He retreated then, and she pretended not to feel the loss of him. He caught her eyes again, a bemused smile on his face, as if he knew how his closeness affected her. Arrogant man. She met his stare head on, eyes hardening.

It took her father's gentle cough to break through the moment. She looked down at her feet, her cheeks hot.

"Wonderful. That is settled, then. Mr. Jameson, I will escort you to my club tomorrow for lunch. We will put you up for membership as soon as possible. Should be no problem at all, lad. And the two of you can work out the other details between yourselves. Perhaps with Mrs. Fisher's assistance?"

She nodded along. Including Mrs. Fisher was the appropriate thing to do, of course. "Yes, of course, Father."

Her father beamed at them. "There you go, Mr. Jameson. You are in my daughter's very capable hands."

He spared her father a quick glance and the hint of a smile before his eyes fell on hers again, warm now, yet intense as always. "Capable indeed," he said, his eyes now sparkling with mischief.

Was he flirting with her?

For a moment she was flattered. And then he smirked. That same arrogant look on his face from yesterday.

The nerve of him. She only just suppressed the urge to roll her eyes.

He turned to her father again. "I cannot thank you enough for your generous hospitality, Mr. Marin." He turned to her now, his face once again serious and hard. "And you, Miss Marin, for your gracious offer to help me and my sister."

The words she spoke about him earlier came back to her. She had hoped foolishly he had forgiven and forgotten. Perhaps she was wrong. Now that he got what he wanted, he could be as angry as he liked.

She cleared her throat. "You have no need to thank us. Vivian is a lovely young lady, and I am honored to help her."

An idea occurred to her. Just how serious was he in helping his sister?

"You might consider joining us for etiquette lessons. Calling upon an acquaintance so early in the day, particularly one you have only just met is quite irregular. It suggests a high level of intimacy, one that has yet to be established between our two families if ever. And while neither my father nor I will hold it against you, others certainly will. Clearly you have much to learn."

She waited, watching his face for a reaction. He would not like being scolded by her again, she was sure of it.

"I will keep that in mind," he said, tone clipped and stiff. But he did not rebuke her. He only seemed resigned to the idea. He said a quick goodbye and then he was gone.

"Go easy on him, my dear," her father said with a laugh and a kiss to the top of her head.

She smiled to herself as she dug into her breakfast. Perhaps Mr. Jameson would surprise her. She thought of his rough manners and cavalier attitude. But then again, perhaps not.

She sipped her coffee, buttered her toast, and tried not to think of that tender look in his eyes when she let herself be vulnerable. Nothing good would come of it.

Chapter 5

IF EVER ELIJAH FELT that he did not fit into this world of the wealthy, it was now, as he briskly strode away from the Marin residence

Not that he had not already felt that way every single moment of every single day for the past few weeks, but this was somehow so much worse.

Her father earned their place here, she earned hers. They were not the same, and it was so obvious to him.

Miss Marin's harsh words floated around in his head. She thought so little of him and had no trouble voicing those opinions. And still, he asked for her forgiveness.

Embarrassment clung to him like the smell of smoke. Lingering, irritating, and nearly impossible to be rid of.

He felt a little like a dog, begging for scraps at the feet of its master, only to be smacked on the nose and sent away.

He took a deep breath, savoring the warm summer breeze. The scent of flowers and dust from the road filled his nose. He still missed the smell of the salt from the ocean, but there was something about the buzz of city life.

Why he still cared so much about what she thought of him, he could not face. But care he did. He wanted to prove her assumptions about him wrong. He wanted to impress her.

And even though he was embarrassed, he had to admit her advice made sense. It was not only his sister that needed assistance navigating this world. He was unprepared. And if Miss Marin could notice just how much after only one evening, he had no doubt it would be just as obvious to anyone else willing to pay him any attention. And they would be paying him close attention, of that he was sure.

It was lucky, then, that he was introduced to Miss Marin and her father; he could admit that. The invitation to join Mr. Marin at his club was more than generous. And he had no doubt that it would prove fruitful. At least Elijah had managed to catch the favor of one Marin. And he had every intention of working to gain the favor of the other.

It seemed that this young lady, who looked down on him with such disdain, would not only be a permanent fixture in his life for the foreseeable future, but might be a valuable addition.

The realization that he was looking forward to their afternoon together hit him like a ton of bricks.

What was happening to him?

***

The Isabella Marin that first appeared in the park that afternoon was nothing like the harsh, sharp, and determined young woman Elijah had encountered only that morning.

Instead, she was all giggles and fluttering lashes, and demure looks aimed at any young gentleman who passed her by. The picture-perfect daughter of a captain of industry. She was dressed smartly in a bright yellow dress, the color of which flattered her skin tone. Not that he would admit such a thought. And the sensible boots on her feet told him she was prepared to battle on his sister's behalf. Her dark hair was pinned neatly atop her head, a few loose strands framing her face.

A light breeze picked up, and he caught the faint scent of amber mixed in with the roses that lined the pathways. Her perfume?

The full picture of who Miss Marin was now was beginning to take shape in his head. She knew the rules of this game they were playing. And she could follow them if she wished, would follow them if absolutely necessary. But she also had no problem bending them when it suited her.

Hence the practical boots in lieu of more fashionable footwear.

She acknowledged him only with a quick curtsey before rushing forward to meet his sister. The two of them immediately linked arms and began strolling, already looking like the best of friends. He noted with fond amusement the way Vivian was already trying to emulate Miss Marin. From the way she walked and held her head to the way she smiled, her lashes fluttering and all. Vivian always was a quick study.

He just never thought that skill would be applied to a situation like this. But he was grateful for it when all was said and done.

He contented himself with admiring the nature around him. The trees full and green against the bright blue summer sky looked almost like a painting. Birds flitted from branch to branch as groups of people moved all around them. And the breeze brought with it the sweet smell of honey and dew from the nearby pond.

If he closed his eyes, he could almost imagine he was walking along familiar streets on the other side of town. Friends calling out hellos in the distance, ocean waves crashing in the distance, the smell of salt in the air. The life of a deckhand was not so bad by his estimation. It was not glitz and glamor, but it was a good and honest life. He missed it. He missed the salt and sea of the ocean.

But he was also afforded the opportunity to study Miss Isabella Marin uninterrupted for the very first time.

She was a sight to behold, a true beauty. So confident and sure. Her steps measured, head held high. The picture of innocence and decorum.

But he knew better. And he felt a secret thrill at knowing her true nature. Even if that nature was never on his side.

His eyes caught on two dark moles on the back of her neck, and he found himself wondering what it would feel like to touch them, to connect them with an invisible line only he would know was there. Her smooth, dark-honey skin so warm and soft under his fingertips, her sweet perfume filling his nose.

A peal of laughter from Vivian snapped him out of his fantasy, and he quietly chastised himself as he sped up to keep better pace with them. If either of the ladies guessed his train of thought, he would never know it.

Miss Marin was still all smiles, laughter, and warm conversation. And he began to wonder if the unforgiving, sharp-tongued girl from this morning had been nothing but a figment of his imagination. He found himself almost missing that hard edge in her voice, that voice that seemed so fond of telling him off. If only because it was more familiar to him.

But he needn't have worried, because Miss Marin soon shed that innocent skin as they truly made their way into the park and off the main path. The idea that she felt comfortable enough to be more herself around him suggested one of two things—that she trusted him or that she thought so little of him that it made no difference to her.

He refused to spend time thinking about which was more likely.

"What is the plan for today?" he heard Vivian ask as he caught up to the pair of them, not bothering to hide her eagerness and excitement. It did help to ease his mind that she was excited about all of this instead of dreading it like he was.

"Today," Miss Marin pulled Vivian even tighter to her side with a Cheshire cat-smile, "we are going to stroll through the park, where perhaps we might run into some eligible young men. You will have your dance card full before you even set foot into a ballroom."

He stifled a groan. The thought of eager young men clamoring for his sister's attention made his skin itch no matter how much he tried to stop it.

As if she could sense his disapproval and discomfort even a few paces ahead of him, Miss Marin turned to glare at him with a roll of her eyes before continuing on in her explanation. This time speaking directly to him. "Several of my acquaintances like to take walks in the park at this hour. It is the perfect way to socialize outside of a ballroom. You do not necessarily need a formal invitation to be introduced to someone if you happen upon them in a setting like this. And among these park patrons should be Mr. Eric Whitney, an old family friend and heir to Whitney Oil. The Whitney family ball is next month, and once I introduce Eric to Vivian, I have no doubt that she will receive an invitation before the end of the week." With a final glare she turned her attention back to his sister.

It was at this moment that he again had to admit, however reluctantly, that Vivian really might be in good hands with the companion Mrs. Fisher had chosen for her. He let Vivian's excited chatter excuse him from replying to the carefully laid-out plan, magnanimously deciding not to let Miss Marin's triumphant look goad him into an apology or positive acknowledgment. However petty it made him seem.

And her prediction, of course, turned out to be true: Not only was Eric Whitney in the park just as she said he would be, but they encountered him within an hour of their arrival. Eric appeared thrilled to see his friend and even more thrilled to be introduced to both Elijah and Vivian.

"Miss Marin," Mr. Whitney greeted her warmly, pressing a kiss to his friend's outstretched hand. His smile was bright and friendly. Elijah studied the man, his blues eyes had a kindness to them. He was tall with broad shoulders and sandy blonde hair that was expertly styled. And the way he carried himself, with an air of quiet confidence. That was certainly something he wished he could emulate.

The four of them chatted about the warm weather, the ducks in the pond, and eventually, upcoming social events.

They were extended an invitation to the ball and to a small gathering at the Whitney home later in the week. And while Elijah was grateful, Eric's eagerness made him wary, even if the young man seemed genuinely nice. Would he be one of the young men vying for his sister's attention?

It certainly seemed so to him. But the whole thing brought such happiness to his sister, her smile was radiant, her eyes alight with excitement, and he could never deny her that. So he followed Miss Marin's lead, accepting the invitation and thanking Mr. Whitney with all the grace he could possibly muster.

Just like that, Vivian had gained her first suitor and her first invitation to a social event. And he had further reason to feel equal parts humbled by Miss Marin's social proficiency and irked by being forced into a debt of gratitude to her—a predicament he was sure would soon become all too familiar to him.

***

Elijah had received quite a few shocks recently. And maybe he should have been accustomed to the feeling by now.

But nothing could have prepared him for the gentlemen's club. Assembled here were the city's elite. The wealthy men who, until very recently, had such power over Elijah.

They made the rules. And he and so many like him were dependent on these men and the money they spread around. Captains of industry. The very best of the best.

Yet, here they were lounging about in plush armchairs, sipping expensive scotch, exchanging rowdy banter, and placing high bets on everything from the ridiculous to the outrageous. The room reeked of cigar smoke, coin purses jingled, and decks of cards were shuffled. A few women filed in through another door and joined some of the men around the tables.

He found the whole thing to be incredibly uncomfortable. Like finding out someone you greatly admired was nothing more than a schemer.

These were the kind of men he desperately wanted nothing to do with. And if it had not been for his sister's happiness, he may have run from the place screaming.

As Mr. Marin led him through the elegantly decorated club, making introductions left and right, his frustration grew and grew. All these powerful men, idling about. All this money and free time, and what did they have to show for it? Overworked, underpaid employees who killed themselves every day.

Not so long ago he worked in those factories, cleaned those ship decks, and walked those crowded streets. He thought of his friends who were still living that way. He promised to keep in touch, but looking around these rooms made him realize just how far removed he was from that life now. It was terrifying, the idea that he might become this someday. He would do everything in his power to avoid that.

But for now, he held his tongue, planted his feet firmly on the ground, and politely greeted each man that Mr. Marin introduced him to. Funnily enough it was Miss Marin's words that rang out in his mind. Her voice in his head saying that all of this was in service of his sister. He could do this for her, he would do this for her.

After years of scraping together what he could of his wages and hoping it would get them through the next few months, he finally had the chance to grant her a secure future. He would not squander this chance out of anger or pride.

As if sensing his internal debate, Mr. Marin steered him away from the crowded gambling tables and raucous noise and into a quieter room for the luncheon. Smaller groups of men were seated at the tables around them, engaged in conversation as they ate. This was a more comfortable setting for him. As much as he felt awkward and out of step in this new world, he was, at heart, a people person. He found himself relaxing at the thought of spending the afternoon having a simple conversation with a friend.

Lunch was cream cheese and cucumber sandwiches, and an assortment of fruit and beer to wash it all down. That was something he would never turn up his nose at: an ice-cold beer. Add that to the list of things he missed enjoying with his friends.

"It is not all gambling and drinking here. Business deals take place, politics are being discussed, and connections are made that can shape the fate of families for decades."

He only hummed noncommittally; the idea that fates were decided in small rooms over lunch by a handful of men was worrisome to him. But now that he was on the other side of things, perhaps he could enact some real change. Though it certainly would not happen in an afternoon. So, he focused on the food and his companion. He made a mental note to look into his finances and set aside some of his money to donate to a few charities.

"You will find great company here, young Mr. Jameson. Scientists, professors, bankers, and other oil tycoons the likes of your late grandfather. Anything you find of interest, you will find someone here who knows something of it."

He smiled. "I am glad to hear it, sir. I am a great lover of learning, and I have not had much opportunity to continue my education, with leaving school early to provide for my sister."

Mr. Marin, ever the gracious companion, only nodded his head in understanding. He never made Elijah feel lesser for the circumstances from which he came. And for that, Elijah was always grateful. The man could easily turn up his nose; he owed Elijah nothing. Especially considering the difference in their circumstances.

But he had to wonder, if such men frequented these types of establishments, why had he not been introduced to them? All the acquaintances he made were young men who inherited their father's money. Some were of the college age, but they did not seem particularly interested in the pursuit of higher education.

Vivian always told him that his face was like an open book. He could never hide anything from her. And it seemed that it was something he would need to work on in the company this new life afforded him. Because Mr. Marin leaned forward with an amused smile on his face.

"And now you are wondering why I did not introduce you to these types of men, instead of the ones you met—the raucous young men, the gamblers, and the rakes. I have done so for two reasons: The first is that the men who can be found most often at the card tables are often deeply in debt and will welcome any new member to the club as long as they are rich, which you are, lad. They will back your nomination for membership and try to win you as a partner at the gambling tables. They will want you on their side, and that can only work in your favor." He shot Elijah a questioning look. "Have you ever gambled before, Mr. Jameson?

The skill will come in handy at some point. Even if only to make an acquaintance."

"Not like the gentlemen here." That was the truth—of course there was gambling among his friends, often during breaks at work when they needed a bit of escapism. And they never bet much money, instead preferring to wager for silly favors and stupid things like candy. There had been no elaborately set-up card tables to play hazard, baccarat, or other fashionable card games. And there had certainly not been entire fortunes gambled away in the span of a few hours. They could only ever dream of such things.

Mr. Marin chuckled and nodded understandingly. "And I can only advise you not to emulate these men that I have introduced you to in any way. And certainly not when it comes to their gambling habits."

"Then why...?"

"Why make introductions if it would be in your best interest not to befriend these men?"

He nodded.

"Because you now have a list of all the men you should keep away from your sister." He held Elijah's gaze for a few moments, perhaps wanting to make sure that the younger man understood the gravity of his words. And for the very first time he could see where Miss Isabella Marin got her tenacity from.

"Brilliant, sir," he said with a laugh. He glanced back toward the room with the gambling tables. He could just make out laughter and yelling. The handful of men Mr. Marin introduced him to were around Vivian's age. They were the kind of young men who would only see dollar signs when they looked at her. In this moment he could see how lucky he had been to be introduced to Mr. Marin and be able to call him a friend.

"What men should I make a point of getting to know," he asked Mr. Marin.

His companion leaned forward, a sparkle in his eye, "You are smart and capable, use your intuition, my boy. But should you need counsel, I am always available to you."

Elijah blushed, not able to hold back the feeling of pride that swelled in him from being complimented by a man he respected. Mr. Marin had faith in him.

And now he could simply relax and enjoy Mr. Marin's company as well as the excellent food and wine, only the first few sips of which were still infused with guilt. As shocked and repulsed as he had been by the luxuriating lifestyle on display at this establishment, he was beginning to understand the attraction of such a place. The wine was leagues better than the watered-down swill that was available to him in the lower parts of the city. And the rooms, while lavish, were pleasant and comfortable, with their decor of dark woods and rich red fabrics. Bookcases lined almost every room and the allure of all that knowledge called to him greatly.

And then there was the club's selection of newspapers and magazines which Mr. Marin showed him after the luncheon and which made his heart leap with excitement. The club's subscriptions encompassed all the latest and most influential daily papers as well as political, philosophical, and scientific periodicals. It was a treasure trove of knowledge and reason, and he could barely tear himself away even after perusing a variety of titles for almost an hour, to his companion's great amusement.

But Mr. Marin had business to attend to, and Elijah was reluctant to be away from his sister for such a prolonged period of time, and so they left the club and parted ways.

Of course, Vivian was not actually alone. The townhouse had servants that, though they took some getting used to, he actually enjoyed having around. They were all wonderful people who seemed to appreciate the change in leadership at the house. And early this morning as he was leaving the house to run errands, Mrs. Fisher and Miss Marin had arrived and the three of them shut themselves into the drawing-room, no doubt to strategize now that Vivian had secured her very first invitations.

But when he arrived back home and went inside, ready to just relax, it was to find the house turned upside-down in his absence. The drawing room, where he had expected to find Vivian and her new friends, was deserted but looked like a cannonball had smashed right through it and left it in shambles: There were bits of cloth, ribbon, and other frippery strewn about, interspersed with books, music sheets and, oddly, an empty tea set. His first irrational thought was that, somehow, someone had abducted the ladies and trashed the room rather than robbing it, but just as panic threatened to settle in, he heard voices drifting over from the next room.

Following the sound to the dining room, he found the missing ladies—as well as even more cause for bewilderment: The chairs had been pushed aside, leaving the long dining table sitting in the middle of the room like a lonely, rectangular island. Circling it in slow, measured steps was Vivian, with a book balanced on her head and a long tablecloth pinned to her shoulders to swish after her like a train, while Mrs. Fisher and Isabella were watching from the side of the room, both wearing critical expressions.

"What on Earth are you doing?"

Vivian whirled around to face her brother, causing the book to fall off her head and the tablecloth to get tangled under her feet.

Chapter 6

It was all Isabella could do not to laugh as Vivian righted herself, giggling, and smoothing out her hair.

Glancing at Mr. Jameson, Isabella noted with delight that he, too, seemed to find the situation amusing. His eyes sparkled with held in mirth and one corner of his mouth was turned up just so.

Isabella could hardly blame him.

Especially given the contrast of the room they were in. It depressed her. The furnishings were dark on dark on dark. Very much the home of an older, single man. It desperately needed a few pops of color and some decoration to warm it up.

Would it be overstepping to suggest re-decorating to Elijah? Perhaps Vivian would be better. She resolved to mention it at some point.

"I am practicing my balance and posture. It's important for when we attend the Whitney Ball. And next week, I am to participate in a class to learn etiquette, table manners, and things like the proper way to curtsy."

Unsurprisingly, Vivian's enthusiasm failed to infect her brother. In fact, he looked dumbfounded.

"You need to attend a class for those things? You already know how to curtsy. And how to eat. Surely a class would be a waste of your time."

"Yes, but it must be perfect as she will have many more eyes on her. If Vivian were to trip or stumble…" Mrs. Fisher trailed off, suggesting that Vivian's fate in such an event did not bear mentioning.

All three ladies sank into respectful silence for a moment, Isabella remembering all too well the anxiety that had plagued her before attending her very first big event. Years later and the memory had not faded. Even if she was surrounded by people she had known since childhood, the stakes were suddenly very high. And for Vivian, perhaps much higher.

"Elijah," Vivian said, her voice turning into a whine. "You simply do not understand these things. Never before have I been expected to curtsy and act proper in front of people of such high society. It matters now more than ever that I do not make mistakes."

"Of course, you should do whatever you think will be most helpful for you," he conceded, though he still seemed utterly unimpressed by the mention of Vivian's daunting trial.

He would never understand these particular circumstances. Men were not expected to perform at these events. All Elijah was expected to do was admire the women who put in so much effort to be seen. His performance came when he entered business meetings and negotiated contracts.

"So, what else will you ladies be getting up to for the rest of the day? Besides pilfering the library for your funny practices," he said as he stooped to pick up Vivian's discarded book, holding it carefully.

That was something they at least had in common, a healthy respect for books.

"We are visiting the dressmakers and a handful of other shops," Vivian answered with a bright smile.

"Again? Did you not shop just yesterday? Did you not get everything you needed?"

Mrs. Fisher looked almost affronted by the question. "Certainly not! We have not even had a fitting for any ball gowns."

The look that graced Elijah's face was one of pure boredom mixed with a little irritation, he eyes were glazed while his mouth was pinched into a frown and Isabella had to stifle a laugh before addressing him, taking care to infuse a little mischief into her tone of voice.

She walked across the room to stand near him. "This is simply the way things are done Mr. Jameson—shops must be visited; money must be spent. A young lady needs a varied wardrobe."

"It does look like it," Mr. Jameson sighed. "But may I assume my presence will not be needed again so soon?"

Isabella's mirth dissipated at the dismissive words. Could he not at least feign interest in the things that were so central to Vivian's success? She was well aware that dress-shopping and curtsy-practicing were not quite as life-and-death as the running of a business, but they were Vivian's battles right now, and surely it would not hurt him to show some support.

Luckily, Vivian seemed unfazed by her brother's lack of interest, as she promptly snatched the book from his hands and went back to gliding across the room, her natural grace helping her look as if she had done this all her life.

A sense of pride bloomed in Isabella's chest. Her new friend was a true wonder, and seeing the young lady blossom under her tutelage brought her great joy. If only she had had someone to guide her at the beginning of it all. If her mother had tried to connect with her over etiquette lessons, had laughed with her when she made a misstep, maybe she would not have made the same choices. Being the only young lady of color in the room meant that she was overlooked by some of the young men. And despite her status in society, it could feel very lonely. Maybe his attention would not have felt so important if she had not always felt the odd one out.

Most days she still felt that way. Alone with her secrets and her shame.

But Vivian would not feel that. She will shine at any event she attends; of that Isabella was certain.

"Well," Mr. Jameson said, clearing his throat. "If you will please excuse me, I have a million things to do today. I will be in my office if you need me."

Vivian waved him off, focused only on the task at hand. He offered a bow first to Mrs. Fisher and then to her. Isabella watched him go happily, fully expecting not to see him again for the rest of the day.

After a long afternoon of shopping, during which they spent an obscene amount of Mr. Jameson's money, Vivian invited Isabella to dine with them.

"Your brother will not mind an unexpected guest?" she asked, hoping for a reason not to have to interact with the man. Even if her racing heart suggested she may truly feel otherwise.

Vivian shook her head. "He will not be there. He left a note with our man before we left for the shops earlier in the day. He is having dinner with some important business contact. I have no idea; it is all dreadfully boring to me."

Isabella laughed. How very opposite she and Vivian were in this regard. Isabella loved hearing about everything to do with her father's business.

No one could know that she helped him with the books and helped him strategize ideas. No man wants to take business advice from a woman, no matter how good the advice is.

"Well then, I accept."

Vivian only laughed, not at all bothered by her friend's dislike for her brother.

A brother who was indeed absent for their dinner until they had nearly finished. When he strode into the dining room with a sense of purpose she had not witnessed before, walked over to Vivian, and handed her a box.

He hardly spared Isabella a glance before watching Vivian intently, nervously running his hand through his hair before settling it on his thigh, fingers tapping a rhythm.

Obviously curious, Vivian tore the box open, tissue paper flying over her head, and peered inside. She squealed with delight before pulling out the gift and holding them up for Isabella to see.

Gloves. Beautiful, expensive white satin gloves. The kind a young lady wore to an event.

Elijah laughed nervously. "I did some enquiring and was told that a young lady could never have too many pairs of gloves. And I wanted to contribute something to this whole affair. I know how important it all is to you. And I apologize if I made it seem like I did not understand that. I still have much to learn."

Not even Mr. Jameson's gruff tone could mask the sweetness of the gesture, and Vivian was accordingly pleased.

But as she pressed a grateful kiss to her brother's cheek, his eyes sought Isabella's, a strange blend of insecurity and defiance in them. Was he seeking her approval? If he was, she was not above giving it in this moment. The smile she directed at him came easily and openly for once. And she melted just a little at the softness in his eyes.

***

After weeks of purposeful seclusion at her parents' home upstate, being suddenly thrust back into society was quite the change of pace for Isabella.

Add to that her two new acquaintances, and she suddenly found her days very full. But to her great surprise, she found that she liked it. There was a certain gratification to be found in introducing someone to the perks of her lifestyle who had not seen its downsides yet. Someone who could still be impressed with anything from a beautiful piece of jewelry to a newly published novel.

Surrounded by lengths of fabric, fashion plates, music sheets, and gossip magazines, Isabella sometimes felt like she was eighteen again, and looking forward to the excitement of her first season with flushed cheeks.

With her boundless energy and quick wit, Vivian was always ready for any adventure, and Isabella went on more outings in her first week as Vivian's companion than the last few months combined. Sometimes they were accompanied by Mrs. Fisher, and even her father once. But never by a certain young gentleman. Personally, she could not say that she minded the elder Jameson's rare appearances. But she did still wish he would show more of an interest in Vivian's affairs, glove purchase notwithstanding.

But as Isabella soon found out, Vivian's enthusiasm was not bestowed equally on all aspects of her new life. While she was ready to wholly apply herself to subjects that interested her and was always willing to follow instructions when they pertained to dancing, singing, or choosing dresses, she was unwilling to use her faculties when it came to things she considered boring or unnecessary.

And she was incredibly stubborn.

A quality that Isabella herself possessed but was loath to have to deal with in anyone else.

For example, when Mrs. Fisher had attempted to teach Vivian the finer points of serving tea, the fine China had almost ended up smashed to pieces on the floor, and Isabella congratulated herself on suggesting they practice with cold water instead. This way at least they would not ruin the carpet in the Fisher's home.

The problem, it soon became apparent, was that the very things that had endeared her to Vivian so quickly – her open laugh, quick mind, strong will, and a certain unpredictability of her actions—could very well work against her in different company. As strongly and openly as she showed it when she enjoyed something, Vivian was just as quick to demonstrate when she disapproved of the contents of her lessons, and she disapproved of many of the rules of ladylike behavior Isabella and Mrs. Fisher tried to instill in her.

It came as no surprise to Isabella that a brash and candid girl like Vivian would find it hard to hide her emotions, keep her opinions to herself, and submit herself to other people's judgment.

But that did not make the issue any easier to navigate.

And it all came to a head one afternoon when they were practicing tea serving etiquette for what seemed like the millionth time while seated in the Jameson's drawing room. It was a drab room in desperate need of some color. The were seated on couches that looked a bit worse for wear. And though they looked plush, they absolutely were not. The elder Mr. Jameson was most certainly a fan of burgundy. Every curtain she saw in their home was velvet and burgundy. All the wood was a very deep cherry red, and all the other furniture matched. The home smelled of bergamot, not a bad scent, but it reminded her of her own grandfather. She was curious to see what Vivian's bedroom looked like. Perhaps they needed to switch from fashion to furniture on their next shopping trip.

"Why must you always lecture me, Isa? I thought we were friends. But lately I have felt more like a student to you. I cannot be perfect at everything. And I am trying very hard, I swear it," Vivian huffed, her face red and her eyes blazing with anger. She looked so much like her brother at this moment.

Isabella was struck dumb by the eruption—and by the truth in it. She should have expected this eventual blow-up. Perhaps she had treated Vivian more like a student than like a friend lately. She was forgetting that this was supposed to be a fun time for the young lady. So, instead of chastising the younger girl for her impolite tone, Isabella sat down next to her on the sofa and took her hand.

"I'm sorry you feel this way. I do not mean to lecture you, but I have been tasked with helping you have a successful debut, and if you refuse to follow my advice, I'm afraid I shall fail in my task."

Vivian tensed for a moment, before letting out a sigh as she slumped onto the couch. "But why does making a successful debut require me to change so much about myself? Am I not good enough as I am?"

The girl sounded genuinely distraught now, and Isabella felt for her. Had she not suffered the sting of that very same question herself? She longed to tell her something reassuring, but she was afraid if she wanted to protect Vivian from rejection and ridicule, she would have to tell her the brutal truth.

"For many people, you are not." Vivian's eyes flashed with anger, so she quickly pressed on. "To them, the very traits that have endeared you to your friends, to me – your candid opinions and lively manner—will be taken as a blemish upon your reputation. I am an example of that, though not in the exact same way."

"What do you mean, Isa?"

"My family moved to New York City from New Mexico when I was only a baby. We had nothing, seen as less than citizens. My father scrubbed floors and my mother mended clothes to get by. Until my father made a smart investment and with the help of Mr. Fisher built his investment company up from the ground. Everything we have is rightfully ours. But some people will never try to recognize that the color of my skin does not make me less than them, nor does where I come from. They will always treat me as someone who does not belong. I will not lie, you do not face the same barriers that I do. But make no mistake, Vivian, the moment you set foot in a ballroom, you will be judged. You will be judged harshly."

Seeing Vivian's stricken expression, Isabella steeled herself against any sympathetic softening of her heart that might lead her to take back the words. She found no pleasure in trying to cast a lively young woman into a duller, less sparkling mold, but her task was to do precisely that, and she should not let her personal feelings interfere.

Nonetheless, she well remembered struggling through that very same process herself, and had lately begun to wonder if, in the battle between her own nature and society's expectations, society had won. It was an uncomfortable thought, one she pushed aside eagerly. This conversation was about Vivian and having it would be in her best interest.

But Vivian's spirit was not so easily crushed. Nostrils flaring and cheeks flushing with anger, she asked, with venom in her voice, "Am I to transform myself completely, then? To stifle every one of my natural impulses and believe every opinion I have?"

"Not completely, no. There is something my mother once told me that might help: That we all have our parts to play in the theatre of public opinion, and sometimes that means hiding our true character. It does not necessarily mean altering ourselves, simply taking better care as to how and when we let out glimpses of ourselves as we truly are."

Vivian nodded slowly, her skepticism giving way to understanding. "All the world's a stage, and all the men and women merely players. Elijah used to read to me, before I learned myself. We only possessed a handful of books, so our tastes were hardly discerning, but my favorites were Shakespeare's comedies. Of course, Elijah always left out the inappropriate jokes. I only learned about those when I found an issue of the comedies in our library here in the townhouse."

She could not help but laugh, amused by Vivian's delight at finding an uncensored version of the bard's comedies and secretly moved by the mental image of Mr. Jameson as a boy, reading plays to his little sister that were altogether inappropriate for a child.

"Well, Shakespeare had the right idea, at least in part. Sometimes we have to hide our true nature from those who seek to judge us, especially as women."

Vivian nodded in agreement before her brow furrowed in confusion.

"But if I am never allowed to be my true self in mixed company, how am I to find a husband who will appreciate me for who I am?"

Isabella smiled wistfully. "Quite a puzzle, is it not?"

Vivian seemed understandably unsatisfied with this answer. But as much as Isabella wanted to help, she had nothing more to contribute on this particular subject—her own memories pertaining to it were particularly painful to relive.

"Well, I suggest we cross that bridge when we come to it since you have yet to meet any young men apart from Eric Whitney. But we shall make sure that you will have your pick of them once you do. Perhaps you will find that your true match is the man you find safe enough to be your true self with," she said. That was the dream of any young woman in this day and age, apart from complete and total independence.

And thus, Vivian was appeased, and they spent the rest of the afternoon in companionable ease, practicing a few more songs and choosing a dress for Vivian to wear to the Whitney Ball in a few weeks. They also picked out another simpler gown for the casual gathering at the Whitney's. It was only a few nights away now, and she was looking forward to it almost as much as Vivian was. A chance to spend a carefree night with a few of her dearest friends. A night she desperately needed.

Chapter 7

Their intimate evening spent at the Whitney's home was an unmitigated success. It was such a success that Isabella almost felt jealous.

The gathering turned out to be a quaint and intimate affair that served as the perfect first taste of mixed company for Vivian, who soon lost her initial shyness and proceeded to charm everyone in the room thoroughly. Though still a far cry from the demure and delicate ideal of a proper young lady, she was on her best behavior, and Isabella could congratulate herself on having chosen the right approach in being candid with her charge.

By the end of the night, she had made a handful of new friends, had a dozen calls to pay in the next few days, and had secured several requests for the first dance at the Whitney Ball.

But the event also made it clear that there were still many pressing matters where Vivian's upper society education was concerned. First and foremost was the question of how to properly and quickly teach Vivian all the dances she would need to be proficient at when she made her full debut at the Whitney Ball.

This close to the start of the season, it was impossible to find a good dance teacher, as all the good ones had been employed by other families in upper society whose daughters also stood to make their debut this year. Isabella had started teaching Vivian some steps, quickly progressing from basic positions to some more elaborate patterns, but the girl would have to start practicing with a real partner soon. Particularly someone who was used to leading.

Luckily, coincidence intervened on her behalf when, on a trip to the shops with Vivian, Isabella ran into an old friend.

Mr. Wes Dugray was one of the most polite and well-spoken men in Isabella's circle of acquaintants, and she was always happy to see him. But because his father was a solicitor for the lower classes, not everyone treated him with the respect he deserved. Often dismissing the kind and friendly man as not worth their time. She knew exactly what it felt like to be looked down on because of her situation. Some of the young ladies in high society loved to remind Isabella of where her family started and that she still was not welcome. She was a grown woman, confident and sure of herself. But the words and looks and snubs still hurt.

So, she always tried to make sure he felt her joy to see him whenever they encountered one another.

And she happened to know from past experience that the gentleman was an excellent dancer. Perhaps he would be willing to take Vivian on as a student.

So, she seized the opportunity to ask him, in between browsing for books, if he would do her the great favor of helping to teach her protégé how to dance.

"And this," she said as she led Mr. Dugray over to Vivian, "is Miss Vivian Jameson. The young lady you would be teaching." Isabella stepped back, allowing the two to size each other up. Only they stood there silently for a moment, eyes wide before Mr. Dugray accepted the proposal with a quickness that would have alarmed her had she not trusted him to be a man of honor. All the while, Vivian was mysteriously shy.

During a quick visit with Mrs. Fisher, it was decided that bringing in a friend to teach Vivian how to dance was perfectly acceptable as long as their matronly friend would be present to chaperone. And with Mrs. Fisher offering her large ballroom and beautifully tuned piano for the lessons, all Isabella had to do was watch and offer notes when the time came.

Much to her annoyance, Mr. Jameson insisted on accompanying Vivian to Mrs. Fisher's house for the first lesson. Did he not trust her judgment? Did he not trust that she would always look out for Vivian?

It seemed that he did not. According to Vivian it was because Elijah trusted no young man to be around her without her older brother's supervision. And so, Isabella was on edge as she introduced the two gentlemen the next afternoon.

"Mr. Elijah Jameson, may I introduce you to Mr. Wes Dugray," she said, and then stepped back purely out of self-preservation.

As she expected, Mr. Jameson looked the man up and down, assessing him and said nothing, remaining cold almost to the point of being impolite. All while Mr. Dugray flashed a genuine smile and offered his hand.

"A pleasure," Mr. Jameson said quietly while shaking the man's hand.

Isabella fought against the urge to groan. Is this how he would behave at the upcoming ball? He would scare off any potential suitor before they even had a chance.

It was not her responsibility to ensure that Mr. Jameson behaved properly, but did the man have to be so damn infuriating at every single turn?

But Mr. Dugray let the hostile welcome pass without comment and seemingly chose to ignore Mr. Jameson's bad attitude.

Instead he turned his attention to Vivian and only Vivian, asking her to show which of the basic steps she had already practiced with Isabella.

This was why she was loath to have Mr. Jameson join them. Apart from the inevitable way he reacted to Mr. Dugray, ultimately, it left the two of them with nothing to do but stand together awkwardly at the edge of the room. Mrs. Fisher was standing closer to the dancing couple and offering suggestions every few minutes.

But between herself and the gentleman, things felt stilted and awkward. There was no polite chatting about the weather or anything of that sort. Not only because she had no great desire to speak to him, but because she honestly had no idea what to talk to him about.

She could bring up business; they had that in common. But that would almost certainly end in an argument. It was a pity. She so wished to have someone in her age group to confide in about her desire to work.

But would he really understand a woman's desire to work? Doubtful.

And he looked as if he would rather be anywhere but here.

She distracted herself for a while by counting the black and white checkered tiles on the floor. And then she counted the number of sconces lining both sides of the room. This room was beautiful but devoid of people to watch, and with Mrs. Fisher instructing Vivian, it could only hold her attention for so long.

The longer they stood there, the more bored she became. And when Isabella was bored, her mind wandered. And it was this particular habit that led her to decide to poke a little fun at Mr. Jameson. The same way she would when they were young when he got too lost inside his head.

He looked as bored as she felt, and perhaps she could work with that.

She sighed loudly but kept watching the dancing couple. Out of the corner of her eye, she saw him glance over at her. "You look positively enthralled by this particular activity. Not at all bored," she said, biting back a smile.

He stiffened. "I am fine."

She held in a giggle. "Is that so? There is nothing at all that you would rather be doing than watching your sister learn how to dance?"

"It is important that I be here for my sister."

"Right," she scoffed. "You standing there staring daggers at her and at Mr. Dugray will surely improve her dancing skills immensely."

He opened his mouth, no doubt ready with some witty retort, when Vivian suddenly halted and blurted, "What about Elijah?"

Isabella looked up at him, sure that the same confusion over Vivian's outburst was reflected on her own face.

"Yes, what about him?" Isabella asked.

Was Vivian perhaps thinking what she had been thinking? The idea was too hilarious.

"He should participate in the lessons too," Vivian said, looking at her brother with the most serious and commanding expression that Isabella had ever seen on the young girl's face. There was no smile to be seen, and her eyes were hyper-focused on her brother. "You will be attending the ball as well, and you have had less opportunity to learn than I have."

She wanted to jump for joy. She truly could not ever love Vivian more than she did at this very moment. She had intended to tease the gentleman a bit about his dancing skills, or his suspected lack thereof.

"But I am not the one who is going to be dancing."

Isabella rolled her eyes. Of course, he would say that. How in the world did he expect to get to know eligible young ladies if he was not planning to dance with them? Or did he feel as she did? That he had no desire to marry anyone? If only she could ask.

Vivian raised a brow at him as if to say, "Are you kidding?" And then she spoke, "Of course, you will be dancing too. It is a ball, Elijah. Do not be ridiculous."

Mrs. Fisher rushed over, practically shrieking, "My dear, Mr. Jameson, what are you saying? Of course you will be dancing! A gentleman does not sit out a dance when there are ladies in need of a partner—and there are always ladies in need of a partner."

Dread pooled in Isabella's stomach at the sight of Mr. Jameson's suddenly blank expression. Was he angry? Was he offended? Had they finally pushed him too far? Concern overwhelmed her, old feelings rushing back.

"Do you know how to dance?" Mrs. Fisher asked, not bothering to conceal her horror. The older woman certainly had a flair for the dramatic.

Mr. Jameson seemed determined not to meet anyone's eyes as he quietly mumbled, "I know a reel or two, but that is all. Nothing suitable for a ball, I am sure."

At his words, Mrs. Fisher went so still Isabella wondered if she was somehow frozen from shock. "Oh, for heaven's sake," she said, exasperation coloring her tone. "That simply will not do at all. Mr. Dugray, surely you can teach Mr. Jameson alongside his sister? We have not much time, but the young man seems a quick study to me. He'll pick it up in no time at all."

Mr. Dugray smiled, though he looked apprehensive. "Certainly, I can instruct him as well. But he'll need a partner since Miss Vivian is still learning the steps herself. Someone who already knows these dances well."

Isabella froze at his words. She could already see where this was going, and there would be absolutely no getting around it.

Mr. Dugray looked at her, a teasing smirk now planted on his face. The man knew exactly what he was doing. She would get him back for this someday.

Though if she was being honest, she would have to admit that this was the best solution to the problem. And she would simply ignore the fact that she was also going to suggest that Mr. Jameson join in the lessons, just to poke fun at him, and would have absolutely ended up in the same position.

"I suggest Miss Isabella join us as Mr. Jameson's partner. You are a practiced and elegant dancer, my friend. You can take the lead and help him learn the steps."

Mrs. Fisher beamed at the smirking Mr. Dugray. "What a splendid idea. Isabella, would you be so good as to step in? It really does seem like Mr. Jameson will need some help."

She forced herself to nod and smile politely as she moved out onto the floor where Mr. Jameson was now standing. He was scowling at her, which seemed to be his natural reaction to her. But there was also a fierce determination in his eyes. Another quality she recognized from their past friendship. He was always up for a dare. Like the time she dared him to stow away on one of the ships with her. And she was beginning to understand just how honorable of a man he was. Always willing to do what needed to be for the sake of his sister.

Damn him, but it was very endearing. Something else she would store in the secret part of her mind that thought about the gentleman far more than she cared to acknowledge.

That did not mean she wanted to dance with him, or have to be so close to him. But there was no way around it. They made their way to the middle of the room, only a few feet away from the other couple. They turned at the same time to face each other, and she stepped into his space and waited for him to take his position.

She had to tilt her head back to look at him fully.

When her partner made no attempts to take her hand, she did it herself. Ignoring how warm and strong it felt, she placed her hand in his and pulled him into the first position, Vivian and Mr. Dugray taking their places beside them to complete their interesting quartet. Due to there being only two couples, their options for which dances to practice were a bit limited. But there was still much to learn.

Upon the first step, Mr. Jameson's hand tightened around hers, causing Isabella to flinch despite all attempts to keep her composure. Of course, Mrs. Fisher's sharp eyes had not missed the awkward moment.

"Mr. Jameson, ease your grip. You are holding something delicate and precious. It demands a soft touch."

Properly chastised and blushing, the gentleman loosened his grip. From that moment on, so careful were his movements that she felt warmth blooming in her stomach and on her face.

Lord, but she was sure she was blushing.

She was thankful when the dance required her to twirl out of his immediate space, allowing her a momentary reprieve from the wonderful heat coming from his body.

But soon enough, they were facing each other again, and though only their fingertips were touching, she imagined she could feel his warmth and strength all throughout her. It was positively vexing, and her own body did nothing to hide the way she was feeling inside. Her face constantly flushed with heat, her hands becoming slick with sweat.

She was nervous and it was all too confusing. He did not like her, and she certainly did not like him, not anymore, and yet he continued to hold her in his arms as if she were the most precious thing in the world.

He followed her every move with his eyes as if he would be content to watch nothing but her for the rest of his life. Of course, she knew that was a common effect of this kind of dance, where eye contact was frequent, couples were pulled apart and brought back together just by that little point of connection created by their joined hands, and where each participant must always be aware of where their partner was as they moved about the room.

Surely it was the dance and not her that pulled him in so. He had forgotten her after all. Or he did not think their past connection was important enough to recall or remark upon.

She distracted herself from this internal struggle by continually checking in on the progress of Vivian and Mr. Dugray. She noted with satisfaction that Vivian's footwork was impeccable, her posture straight and elegant, and that she let herself be led by her instructor as if she had never done anything else in her life. Her friend was doing well, and there was very little reason to keep watching her instead of her partner.

She reluctantly turned her eyes back upon Mr. Jameson, only to find him already looking at her with a suspicious look on his face, an almost angry look. But what could she possibly have done to anger him? The intensity in his eyes sent a shiver down her spine. And not because she was afraid.

So intent was she on studying his expression, her steps faltered, and she stumbled.

When she righted herself, ignoring the way his grip tightened in hers to assist her, she looked to him again. This time he was looking over her head.

She let out a sigh of relief.

It occurred to her, then, that perhaps she should try to engage him in conversation. At a ball, a gentleman would be expected to carry on a conversation with his partner.

"I hear you have made quite the impression at my father's club," she said.

In his surprise at the sound of her voice, he almost missed a step, only catching himself at the last moment. "How so?"

"My father told me that several of his acquaintances spoke very highly of you to him."

His eyebrows drew together; either in confusion or due to the difficulty of conversing and dancing at the same time she could not tell. "I thought the purpose of a gentlemen's club was to provide a space for men to be free from the prying eyes and ears of ladies?"

"Oh, please. Gentlemen have plenty such rooms. In any case, my father told me nothing that could threaten my opinion of you. He merely mentioned that everyone was captivated by your tales of the life you led before. You are quite fascinating to them."

She had intended her words as a compliment, but Mr. Jameson's eyes iced over with anger and a sneer appeared on his face. At least now he was focused entirely on the conversation, his feet working automatically as he held her curious gaze with his harsh one.

"Fascinating, am I? The poor boy who stumbled into such great fortune? I had no intention of inspiring any such notions."

Just then the dance pulled them apart, their eyes remaining in contact, but their conversation interrupted while they both executed a few turns with a different partner before coming close enough to talk once more, and he continued. "There is nothing fascinating about poverty. It is either working yourself to the bone or sitting around, feeling helpless, because there is no work to be found. It is hard and harsh and dirty."

"You think I don't know that?" she snapped back.

"No, I kn—" he stopped, suddenly refusing to meet her eyes.

Was he going to say he knew she understood? Did he remember her?

Ugh. She wanted to scream, to blurt it all out. But again her shame stopped her.

The bleak picture he painted was a shocking contrast to their elegant surroundings, but she refused to let it deter her. After all, he spent his entire life living this way, the least she could do was listen to him talk about it. She owed him that much.

She said quietly, hoping he could hear her sincerity, "I guess it must be strange, hearing your own life talked about like some fairytale when you have lived the grim reality of it."

The look he gave her was one of surprise, mouth gaping open, followed by a softening of his eyes. The warmth she saw there almost stole her breath.

"Yes, I think that may be what it comes down to."

I understand you, she wanted to say, but her shame kept winning.

Silence settled once more, not hostile, but not quite comfortable either. She scrambled for something to say when he said, with obviously forced lightness, "But at least I did manage to impress them. After all, that is my allotted task in the grand scheme of Vivian's debut, is it not?"

"You have been paying attention, Mr. Jameson. I am truly impressed," she said, giving him a teasing smile. "But I do believe your grand inheritance should go a long way toward that end by itself."

His eyes widened comically. "How do you know that it is a grand inheritance?"

"I am a young, unmarried woman of high society. We know who the most eligible, and by that I mean richest, bachelors are. As do our mothers, so be careful how you conduct yourself around any and all mothers you meet. If they have daughters of marriageable age, you will be naught but prey in their eyes."

"Prey? Am I to be hunted, then?"

"Absolutely. You are the ultimate prize, sir. As soon as you make an appearance, I am sure you will be positively pounced upon by the most lovely, ferocious kittens and their mothers."

He suddenly looked nauseous, and she felt laughter bubbling up within her at the sight. She squeezed his hand in what she hoped was comfort and tried to keep the laughter in.

"But do not fret, sir. I will protect you if need be. You only have to ask."

Before her partner had a chance to reply, the tune reached its final notes and they parted on a bow and a curtsy, respectively.

And then Mr. Dugray and Mrs. Fisher immediately launched into a very thorough critique of poor Mr. Jameson's first real attempt at dancing that soon chased all remnants of their conversation away.

Chapter 8

WITH THE WHITNEY'S BALL, and Vivian's formal debut into society fast approaching, Isabella had little time for anything else outside of helping her friend to prepare, and for that she was immensely grateful.

There was less time to worry about her marriage prospects or listen to her mother worry about them, and even less time to think about the actions of a certain gentleman during their last interaction. In fact she proudly had managed to push him out of her mind altogether on most days.

But her biggest triumph during the days following the Jameson's first dancing lesson was not expelling Elijah from her thoughts but persuading a highly sought-after seamstress to take an order for Vivian's ball gown on such short notice. If she had ever put this much effort into her own preparations for her first season, she would no doubt have a husband already. At least that is what her mother liked to remind her of almost every night at dinner since she had taken on this endeavor.

Vivian's other lessons were moving along well, and the young lady was becoming more and more perfected by the day. She would be the envy of every other young lady in high society, a thought that filled Isabella with an overwhelming sense of pride.

But it was also a stark reminder of her own failures, when she allowed herself the time to dwell on them. Was this how her mother wished to feel about her? Proud. When Isabella knew she most certainly did not, and the idea made her heart ache.

She and her mother had never had an easy relationship. No matter how hard she tried, Isabella never felt like she was enough for her mother. She tried not to dwell on it often. But it was always there, looming over her like a specter in the night. It weighed on her, all wrapped up in the secrets she was keeping from the rest of the world.

Sometimes she just wanted to blurt it out during dinner, when the only sounds coming from the table's occupants were forks scraping against plates and sips of wine. She wanted to scream at the top of her lungs how sorry she was; how embarrassed she was of her own naiveté; how she thought the man loved her; and that she was a fool.

But then she would remember the night everything came crashing down. How she cried on her mother's shoulder, and how her mother had only dressed her down, scolded her, lectured her, and offered her no comfort.

They decided to keep it from her father. She could not bear the way he would look at her.

***

Vivian continued to provide an excellent distraction.

"I must admit, I am rather nervous about this whole marriage business," the young lady admittedly quietly while the two of them were practicing their embroidering in the drawing room of Isabella's home. She could not remember the last time she had a friend in her home as she always preferred to be elsewhere. But today, it was pouring rain, and thus, it was the perfect day to curl up in front of the fire.

What young lady is not, Isabella thought before she nodded. "That is understandable."

"So you feel the same way?"

"Of course I do. Finding someone to share the rest of your life with is a very daunting task indeed. And one that should not be taken lightly."

"Oh, that is not what scares me. I trust that my heart will not lead me astray. I will know the right man when I have found him."

She blinked in surprise at Vivian's sincere words. If only it could be just that simple. If only Isabella's own heart had not led her so far astray.

Vivian continued, "It is the thought of what my husband will expect of me once I have found him that unnerves me. I know he will expect me to be supportive and attentive, to keep his house in order and do the family name proud by being a gracious hostess and a pleasant guest to our friends." Vivian's droning tone suggested she had learned the words by heart rather than internalizing their message. "But I want so desperately to be more than just a maid and a cook. I want him to see me as his equal and to be his very best friend. And that is to say nothing of my worries over what he will expect of me when we are alone? Surely the reason some things are supposed to be kept between a husband and wife is that they are especially precious and important?"

Her breath caught in her throat, a nervous blush rising to her cheeks. Was Vivian inquiring after... marital relations? Of her? An unmarried, barely older friend? Why would she do such a thing?

Her blood ran cold in her veins, and her chest felt tight. Did Vivian know her secret? How could she?

But as she studied her friend's open and curious face, she realized that such a thing was not possible. Only two others knew of the situation.

Vivian only seemed to want someone to talk to. And what were friends for if not that? The young lady apparently just had an unfiltered sense of curiosity.

She forced her heart rate to slow and her face to remain neutral.

"Yes, Vivian, some things are indeed to be kept between a woman and her husband, or between two committed lovers of any kind. Because some things are just that intimate. And as long as both parties have agreed, there is nothing wrong about it."

The whispers in her mind picked up as they did when she was alone. Liar. You are a liar, and someday everyone will know. You cannot hide what you did. What person will ever want you?

But Vivian was far from done with her questions. "But are you not the least bit curious? After all, we are in the same situation. You are to marry as well, and soon, I would think. Would you not prefer to know... something? And after all, it cannot be that much of a secret, seeing as how the men at the club have no qualms about asking my brother when he'll set about producing an heir."

She stared at Vivian in shock as her needle slipped out of her hand and onto the carpet. "How do you know what the men at the club have been asking your brother? That is hardly proper conversation for a young lady's ears."

Vivian rolled her eyes. "Oh, please, Isa. I was raised by my brother. He did his best to shield me, but I have perfected my eavesdropping skills over the years," she said with a smirk. "I know that intimate relationships are not always between a man and his wife, or even just a man and woman. And even I know heirs are not produced by polite conversation alone. Surely, if providing heirs is to be among my duties, I should know something about it."

Isabella could no longer listen to this. It was not something she ever anticipated having to discuss with Vivian, and she knew Mr. Jameson would hate the very idea. And he would blame her. "Please, Vivian. Enough. This is not something we should be discussing."

Vivian looked indignant. "It is only us two here and no one else. Surely such things are allowed to be discussed among friends in the privacy of their own home? And if I cannot ask you, who else is there? I could hardly take these questions to my brother. To him I am still but a little girl. There is only you."

And that was the thing about her young friend: she may be excitable and easily distracted, but she was also shrewd and observant, and almost brutally honest when she wanted to be. Qualities that made situations like this incredibly difficult.

On the one hand, that kind of bravery, to seek out knowledge, was something that should be rewarded and encouraged. On the other hand, she really did not want to give Mr. Jameson any more reasons to dislike her.

She was both proud and horrified that Vivian would even deign to ask such questions. But she certainly could not fault her friend for it. Not without being a hypocrite. And Isabella was anything but that.

She had asked similar questions only years earlier before her own first season. But instead of some deep and heartfelt talk, or even a little reassurance, her mother had seemed scandalized, and then handed her a pamphlet by way of explanation. The kind that gets made in secret for just such occasions as this, because heaven forbid mothers and daughters ever have open and honest conversations with each other.

All the advancements happening in the world: electricity, new railroads, men earning their money instead of inheriting it, but women were still expected to remain the same. It was infuriating. And that said nothing of the struggles of the women who were not white. Her mother was such a forward thinker, but in this she remained unchanged. Women had to keep their passions and desires in check in every respect.

It was precisely her memory of that awkward and embarrassing exchange that made up her mind. She would talk to Vivian in the way her mother had not. Because she wanted her friend to know that they could talk about anything. Impropriety and Mr. Jameson's feelings on the subject be damned.

She excused herself for a moment to go and find the aforementioned pamphlet given to her by her mother. It was still in a box at the bottom of her wardrobe where it had lived for two years, hidden underneath old trinkets. Even though it represented negative feelings between Isabella and her mother, it was very informative. And at least this way Vivian would have something to look at while she was on her own.

When she returned, she retook her place on the sofa and grabbed Vivian's hands in her own. "I will tell you what I know. But you must promise me that you will not speak of it to anyone else, especially your brother. I am sure it has not escaped your notice that he does not care for me, and I do not want this to cause any trouble for either of us, for I very much enjoy your company, and I want to keep it."

Vivian nodded solemnly as she took the paper into her hands. There was information on the intimacies between a man and a woman and accompanying pictures. Isabella took a steadying breath and began speaking.

Heaven help her.

***

She should have known that her conversation with Vivian would not remain between the two of them. Of course, it could not be that easy. No, two young ladies could never have a conversation like that, even in private, without it coming to light somehow.

For not two days later, Mr. Jameson paid Isabella a visit, and it was not a friendly one in the least.

In fact, she was certain courtesy and decorum were not to be found anywhere near the Marin residence from the moment Mr. Jameson stormed into the drawing room where she was sat reading the paper.

She had been having such a lovely morning too. Both her parents were out of the house, her mother on her way upstate to check on their holdings and their estate, and her father at his office, and she intended to take full advantage.

Starting with a delicious array of pastries for breakfast, Isabella was particularly fond of cheese danishes and several cups of coffee, then a stroll to the park. followed by an evening of reading, Isabella had nothing but her own thoughts to keep her company.

And it was going very well, until Mr. Jameson, completely ignoring the outraged footman's protests, strode up to her, his face red with anger, waving the cursed pamphlet at her. She barely had time to register what his anger was about before he was all but shouting at her.

"What is the meaning of giving Vivian something like this? This is what you consider to be appropriate?"

She forced herself to remain calm. She set her book on the small table next to her chair and stood to face him. "It is if she intends to get married."

"You are overstepping your bounds, Miss Marin. If I had wanted someone to teach my sister about inappropriate things, I would not have put up with you for weeks on end!"

"That sentiment is mutual—if it were not for your sister, I would have been glad to see the last of you long ago as well, sir."

That was not exactly true, but she never could resist a good argument.

"Surely, if you cared so much about my sister, you would make more of an effort to keep such filth away from her," he snapped, his nostrils flaring and the color rising in his cheeks.

"It is not filth!" she snapped, stepping closer to him, her anger pushing her forward. The double standard of society was outrageous. Women should be allowed to be curious. It was not his fault, but he was the only one present, so she unleashed her fury on him.

She looked up at him, jaw hard and eyes fierce. "It is something every young lady should know before getting married if she does not want to be terrified and woefully unprepared on her wedding night. She asked me questions she did not feel comfortable asking anyone else. And while I was hesitant to answer them at first, it was important to do so. And I am honored that she felt safe enough with me to ask. I gave your sister that pamphlet to ensure her marriage would begin and continue with the utmost happiness."

"Happiness? What does this..." he raised the pamphlet into the small space between them. His hand coming dangerously close to brushing against her chest, "have to do with her happiness?"

"Rather a lot, I think. When it comes to a woman's happiness, I dare say a little education goes a long way. Although clearly it is not education you have been privy to, or you would understand what I'm talking about."

He gasped.

Her eyes shut in horror as silence descended on the room. How could she have said something like that? As if outright yelling at him had not been bad enough, now she was resorting to vulgar innuendo? She had not even meant to say it. But he had a remarkable knack for getting under her skin. This man was not good for her common sense.

When she opened her eyes again Mr. Jameson had not moved even an inch. And now, instead of having that small pamphlet between them for a buffer, there was just him. His face so close she could see the flecks of amber in his eyes, feel his breath ghosting her face. He glowered down at her. And she thought, in this moment, he looked quite intimidating. And very appealing. The boyish face she used to know replaced with the strong, angular face of a man.

Damn him.

But he would not intimidate her. He would not bully her. She stood firm behind her decision.

But when he spoke, oh, his voice was like liquid silk, dark and a little bit dangerous. And when she shivered, not able to control herself, it was not from fear. Oh no, she felt a quiver of desire.

"Oh, I know enough," he whispered harshly into her face. His breathing rough and labored.

Did she have the same effect on him that he had on her? Did he know the way his words played havoc with her emotions?

And then he licked his lip, quick, like a nervous tick.

Her mind went altogether blank then, struck dumb by the combination of his tongue against his lip and his close proximity and the thoughts of what exactly it was that he knew of the intimate matters between two people.

Tense silence fell between them: dark and heavy but altogether alive with the possibility of words that might be said, space between them that might be erased, skin that might be explored...

He sucked in a breath before speaking again. "The experience of the wedding night need not be nearly so disappointing as you seem to imagine."

Her eyes widened at the words, so forbidden, yet said so boldly but spoken so softly. It was not right, the familiarity with which they were speaking to each other. Regardless of their past. This type of speech was meant for a lover. Yet she did not want it to stop. His words were reassuring and promising, too good to be true.

She heard similar words before. From a man who ruined her. The thought, and the memory that came with it, brought her back to her senses with a thud. She could not do this, not with him, not with anyone.

Not again. Words meant nothing.

She shoved at him, desperate for some air to clear her head and slow her pounding heart. She succeeded in moving his sturdy frame only because he did not expect it. Only when she had put a safe distance between them did she dare to meet his eyes once more—and immediately wished she had not. They were still as wide and dark as they had been just a moment ago, his cheeks still as flushed. Lord, but he was so handsome it almost hurt to look at him.

It only made her hate him a little more. Hate him and still yearn to be so close to him again.

What was wrong with her? They could never be. Because then she would have to reveal their past. And her embarrassment at not being memorable to him. And her awful secret. It was too much. Too much risk. Too much potential for more heartbreak.

When he spoke again, it was with a softness she had not expected. "If you must tell my sister about these things, tell her this: It need not be terrible, and she need not be afraid."

The sincerity in his eyes nearly did her in. He was trying his best, even if he could not understand women did not have the luxury of certainty in these situations.

He was trying to help. That counted for something.

And just like that, her opinion of him was changed again. Just who was this man that continued to surprise her so?

She moved to take a step closer to him, not sure of her own intentions when the door to the room opened, her maid storming in followed by the angry footman, surprised expressions on both of their faces.

Heaven help her if anyone noticed their flushed complexions and heaving breaths.

Mr. Jameson gave her one last fleeting look before he excused himself and rushed from the room. And she was left to sort out all the confusion his visit had brought, the pamphlet gripped tightly in her hand.

Chapter 9

ONE DAY. SHE ONLY had one day of reprieve before she had to face Mr. Jameson again. But at least she would not be alone with him.

Today would be spent with Vivian and Mrs. Fisher trying on the young lady's new wardrobe. Vivian wanted their opinions on everything. And since she had no idea what had transpired between Isabella and her brother, Isabella could hardly turn her down.

The morning air was cool as she stepped out onto the sidewalk of her parents' home. But she could tell the day would be incredibly hot for mid-May. She did love the colder months for the excuse to stay in and read all day long. But she also loved the warm days of summer when she could walk any and everywhere with little trouble.

When she arrived at the Jameson's home she was relieved to be greeted at the door only by the footman. And when she entered the drawing room, her shoulders sagged in relief when Mr. Jameson was nowhere to be found.

"Isa, you made it," Vivian cried from across the room before flinging herself into her friend's arms.

She heard Mrs. Fisher chuckle from her place in a chair near the fire. "It seems everyone Vivian cares for receives a greeting like that."

The girl pulled out of the hug, an embarrassed smile on her face. "Only for my dearest friends. And only in the privacy of my own home."

"Well then, I suppose it is more than acceptable. And I am honored to be greeted with such enthusiasm. So, have the many dresses arrived yet?"

Vivian shook her head, taking a seat on the sofa by the window beckoning for Isabella to join her. "The seamstress sent a note letting me know that they will be here in a few hours. Apparently she is very busy today."

"Oh. So, should I come back later, then?"

"No, no. I was thinking we could practice some more etiquette lessons."

"You were thinking?" Isabella asked, not bothering to hide the surprise in her voice.

Mrs. Fisher laughed. "My sentiment was much the same when she told me her idea."

"Yes, it is shocking that I, Vivian, might want to learn a little bit more instead of just whiling the day away."

And that was how the three women found themselves when Mr. Jameson eventually entered the room.

Isabella's hands were mid stitch into a particularly difficult pattern of her needlework. But she froze the very minute he announced his presence.

She did not move a muscle as he walked over to greet them, taking Vivian's and then Mrs. Fisher's hand to his lips for a kiss. Surely he would not do the same to her? But if he did not, how would that look?

Suddenly her hand was in his. He did not meet her eyes as he placed a feather light kiss on her hand. If not for the gloves she would have been able to feel his lips on her skin. And oh, how she wanted that.

When exactly had her feelings for him taken this sharp turn? Was she always going to end up here? Wanting after the childhood friend who forgot her completely and now seemed to love to anger her?

If she was being honest, it was his willingness to argue with her that endeared him to her. It was all she had ever wanted, someone in her life who was not afraid to show their true self.

An almost non-existent occurrence among the city's elite.

She blinked, the kiss only lasting a moment, and then he was gone, moving across the room, book in hand.

Over the next hour she found her attention straying across the room to where Mr. Jameson had taken a seat. And more often than not, her gaze was met with his own. It happened so often she eventually resigned to focus on other aspects of his person. This strategy only made things worse for her as her mind provided images that made her flush hot.

When a nervous swallow caused his Adam's apple to bob, it drew her attention to the column of his neck and made her fingers suddenly itch to touch the warm skin there, all the way from his jaw to the hollow of his clavicle. When she lowered her eyes to his shoulders, she succeeded only in noticing how snugly his black overcoat was stretched across them. And worst of all, when her gaze quite accidentally fixed on his mouth, she could hear the words that had come out of it the day before; half promise, half defense: I know enough.

After a long afternoon of pretending Mr. Jameson was not driving her wild, and etiquette lessons, embroidery, and singing, the dresses finally arrived. Mrs. Fisher only lingered for a few moments longer before she gracefully bowed out. Not surprising since she had been trying to hide her yawning for the last twenty minutes.

And Vivian began trying on and proudly showing off the dresses in order to decide which one to wear to any and all of the upcoming events, among which was the fabulous gown she would be wearing to the Whitney Ball. It was a light lilac color with capped sleeves and beaded embroidery along the bodice. It was perfect.

The newly-minted debutante was in high spirits, twirling around to watch her skirts billow out and flouncing about the room to strike exaggerated poses.

Isabella for her part was glad for the entertainment. Because while Vivian's debut promised to be a shining success, it reminded her that her own future was looking less than bright.

A family matter was settled only this morning that Isabella had been dreading. Since her first season three years earlier, her father promised her that she would not have to marry if that was not her dearest wish. And that if she did marry, it could be for love the way she always wanted. That he would stipulate in his will that the family estate be passed onto her upon the deaths of her parents and not to the closest male relative as was the standard at the time the will was declared. Never mind that these days, it was perfectly acceptable for a female to inherit money.

But, her father informed her over breakfast this morning that the will of his father, her grandfather could not be contested. And it stipulated that should his son, the current Mr. Marin, have no sons, his money and estate would pass to the closest male relative, not to his one and only granddaughter.

Wretched old man that he was, Isabella had not one fond memory of him. She was grateful for the happy relationship with her own father, and she appreciated all the effort he had put forth on her behalf. That did not mean that she was not incredibly sad.

She had been counting on her father to make this happen, which was why she had been so free with her affections during her debut season. It was why she had let that man into her heart and into her bed. She did not need to worry.

Her mother warned her not to put all her eggs in one basket. She did not listen, and she was paying the price now.

Thus far, she had not allowed herself to dwell on the matter at length, but interpreting the implications of the court's decision for any designs she may have had for her future required very little mental effort. She would have to focus all her capacities on finding a husband and abandon all interests detrimental to that cause or suffer the consequences not just for herself but for her mother as well, who had been even more grievously neglected by her father-in-law.

It was this tense, dejected mood of hers that Mr. Jameson interrupted when he interjected just as Vivian finished a series of twirls with a perfect curtsy in one of her many dresses. And judging by the look on his face, Vivian's antics failed to have the same uplifting effect on him which they had on Isabella. It was not entertaining to him, just confusing, and probably a little annoying.

"You are still practicing curtsies?"

"Of course," Isabella interjected. "Where a lady's accomplishments are concerned, there is always room for improvement."

Her tone was light and humorous despite the harsh truth to her words, but her attempt at a joke seemed to be lost on Mr. Jameson, whose expression was as unamused as ever.

"And do those accomplishments include any sort of reading or other training of the mental faculties?"

Vivian laughed. "Don't be silly, Elijah, my mental faculties will not help me much at the Whitney's ball."

"Learning is always helpful. And anyone who does not see the value in it is not someone you should be determined to spend time with or try to impress."

Vivian was beginning to look put out, so Isabella took it upon herself to intervene.

"Mr. Jameson, I am sure Vivian's mind will suffer no serious neglect if she fails to read whatever instructional tomes you have in mind for a few hours."

Never mind that between learning etiquette, pianoforte, a little bit of French, and sewing, Vivian's mental faculties were in no danger of being stifled. Not that Mr. Jameson had deigned to recall any of those things. For all his insistence on the powers of the mind, his had ventured no further than the superficial image of pretty dresses and a girl daring to have fun.

Mr. Jameson turned abruptly to look at her, fire in his eyes. "As far as I am aware, my sister's reading is not one of the areas you were tasked to supervise. I must ask you therefore to stay impartial in this matter."

The look on his face spelled danger, but as always when it came to the elder Jameson, she ignored every warning sign and plunged headfirst into the storm known as his temper and her pride.

"And I must contest that assessment. I have been tasked with instructing your sister on all that is most necessary to her at this moment. If my efforts are to bear fruit, I need to have some say over how she allots her time..."

Elijah cut her off with a tone of voice that surpassed even the unpleasantness of their last unchaperoned meeting.

"Not when your efforts seem to be aimed entirely at turning my sister into a vain, useless doll."

She reeled back, the sharp words landing a physical blow against her. The implication of his words was clear, and she knew now exactly what this meant.

Whatever had occurred between them in the past was gone. Whether he remembered her or not, the way he viewed her now was crystal clear.

"Like me, you mean?"

Vivian let out a shocked gasp, the only sound in the silence that had fallen suddenly over the room.

She felt tears welling up in her eyes and cursed herself. This was what it came down to, then. She had always had a suspicion as to his intense dislike of her. Though to have it all but confirmed was quite another thing entirely. He thought her vain and frivolous. Useless. And in saying so, had managed to pour salt on what was already an open wound for her. She tried so hard to be more than just another daughter of high society. As a Mexican American woman in a world of white, she wanted to be worthy of her heritage, of the work her parents put into this life.

But with the distressing news this morning and now this, it was hard not to think that Mr. Jameson was right. She was nothing more than a useless thing that only served to further the plans of others.

Suddenly, she found it hard to breathe. She could not stay in this room a second longer, with Mr. Jameson's eyes still staring down at her, cruel and merciless. She got to her feet, ignoring the shakiness in her knees.

"I should go."

She should not. But she just could not resist chancing a glance at the angry gentleman one more time, the pull entirely too strong.

Mr. Jameson's expression suggested that perhaps he regretted his words, his mouth now pulled into a frown, a deep crease between his brows. But at this point, she did not have it in her to care what he thought. It seemed just as likely that he was simply afraid of losing her and her father's patronage.

Well, her father could associate with whomever he pleased. And she would certainly not abandon Vivian to navigate high society on her own. But she was through with the stubborn and judgmental Mr. Jameson.

Done.

Out of the corner of her eye, she saw Vivian glare at her brother and move as if to accompany her, but Isabella gave a quick shake of the head, and her friend remained where she was. She may be too distraught to defend herself in this moment, but she could still manage to make it out of this room, down the hall, down the stairs, and out the door on her own.

She moved quickly and with purpose, anxious to be out in the open air. She made it down the hall and was about to turn the corner when the sound of heavy footfalls behind her signaled that someone was following. She was sure it was not Vivian. She quickened her steps, but to no avail. On the first landing of the staircase, a hand closed around her arm and pulled her to a stop.

"Wait," and when she whirled around to tell him to unhand her immediately, "Please."

Despite her anger and pain, something in his voice, in that simple but earnest "Please" did indeed give her pause long enough for him to plead his case.

"You should not leave. I should. But not before I have apologized profusely. Groveled for a bit, perhaps."

Was he attempting to make a joke? At a time like this? The utter nerve of this man. She could not stand it. She pulled her arm from his grip.

He did not even seem to realize what he had done. And he continued speaking, completely unchecked.

"Give me an opportunity to explain myself."

She hesitated, altogether unwilling to put herself in a position where she might be insulted again.

But her pride, her stubborn nature, would not allow her to back down. She would not let him have the satisfaction.

No, that would not do.

She straightened her spine and met his eyes, head held high to show Mr. Jameson the enemy he made today was not quite defeated yet.

"Say what you have to say."

He opened his mouth and then closed it again. It seemed, now that he was free to speak his mind, he seemed unable to do so. He proffered what might constitute the start of an apology several times, only to trail off again after a few words.

Her patience was now paper thin.

"Mr. Jameson, if this is your idea of an explanation…"

He cut her off. His hands hanging down by his sides now balled into fists.

Was he angry at her? He was the one keeping her waiting.

"Dammit, I am no good at this, admitting when I am wrong. Miss Marin—"

"I know I have been unfair to you. There is no excuse for my behavior, except to say that for whatever reason, you get under my skin like no one else has, like someone I knew long ago."

Her breath caught.

He continued. "And I do not expect you to forgive me. But I…" He broke off once more, perhaps trying to find his words. He almost looked like a caged animal. Eyes a little wild and desperate in a bid to make her understand his reasoning. "I am out of my depth. I feel like I am trying to lead my sister through enemy territory, blindfolded and unarmed and with no knowledge of the lay of the land myself. I do not understand how your world works, and I have unfairly blamed you for it. It was easier than facing my own shortcomings."

She should have walked away as soon as he finished speaking. She should have walked away and never spoken to him again. It was what he deserved. But there was something in his voice, a vulnerability that demanded to be acknowledged. And it needled at her heart.

So, she remained silent, waiting for him to continue his strange, inappropriate, and seductively candid explanation. He had her firmly ensnared here and he likely had no idea.

Damn him.

"When my mother passed away, I did everything I could to make sure Vivian would be provided for no matter what that meant for me. I made sure she was taught to read and write, so she could support herself if necessary. Finding her a husband never occurred to me because it was more important that she was well prepared should anything happen to me. My plans for her never included dancing or painting or playing the pianoforte, and that was how it should be. What would a girl like her, of her social standing, need to play the pianoforte for? But now, every measure I put into place for her future has been made worthless. Suddenly, the things she needs to learn are altogether different, and some days I cannot help but wonder, what if this does not last? What if it all turns out to be a mistake, and we wake up poor once more, having wasted all this time on useless accomplishments?"

He had started pacing up and down on the landing. His arm brushing against hers with every pass. But he stopped in front of her now, though his gaze remained fixed to the floor. "I have always been the one to take care of my sister, to guide her through life. And for the very first time, I cannot do that, and it terrifies me."

She waited, wanting to see his face before she passed any judgment on his words. She had only known him a few weeks, in this new chapter of his life, but she had come to realize that his eyes always told the truth of what he was feeling.

He looked up, and it nearly stole her breath. He looked so vulnerable, open, and earnest in his admission. His eyes implored her to understand. To forgive him. To help him.

And she, despite her earlier anger, despite knowing better, was willing to give it.

But she still needed to say her piece. As much for herself as for him.

"I understand your struggles better than you think. I was not born to this world. My parents earned their way. And as a family of color, we have had to work twice as hard to earn and keep our place here. I am glad to know your personal struggles, to understand you a bit better. But none of those struggles are my fault. It is not my fault the life I have grown up living works by different parameters than the one you planned for your sister. It is not my fault that the things I have been taught to consider vital, the things I am now teaching Vivian, are not at all helpful in procuring an independent income."

She was simply tired—tired of being insulted and pretending not to be hurt by his increasingly well-placed barbs; of constantly being judged by him and gradually starting to agree with his harsh verdict. She needed it all to stop.

"It is not my fault that I am doomed to be vain and useless, as you so eloquently put it."

He opened his mouth as if to protest, but she would not hear it. He meant what he said, and they both knew it. Why pretend otherwise? So she lifted a hand to bid him stay silent, and miraculously, he obeyed. "And yet some days, I despise myself for it."

There, the secret was out, one of many she held in her heart. And Mr. Jameson was staring at her in astonishment. It made her skin itch with the overwhelming urge to run and hide. The admission hanging out between them like a lingering foul smell. But she pressed on.

"I may be living a charmed and sheltered life, but I am aware that most people are not. I was not always in this privileged position as I said before. I know that there are people out there who would do anything to have my money and opportunities, and that, to them, it might seem like I am squandering them all on frivolities like balls and parties. But within my circles, from my perspective, most days it feels like I have no opportunities at all, and certainly no power. Yes, I have leisure enough to be reading the most instructional books, and yet I am not expected to read much at all, and certainly nothing of scientific or political insight. And why would I need to know politics? I am not meant to partake in shaping the country's fate, I am merely destined to warm the hearth of some man who does, to raise his children and entertain his guests. So, for you to come here and call me useless… believe me, Mr. Jameson, a large part of me knows that I am."

By now, the expression on his face had changed from shocked and empathetic to angry. It was only that hint of sympathy and concern she had glimpsed weeks ago that told her he was not angry at, but for her—a thought as strangely comforting as the softness in his voice when he said, "I… I truly am sorry that you feel that way."

And she believed him. With all her heart. Something she would never have suspected could happen even an hour earlier.

The question was, what would she do with it? Would she reject his apology, as she had every right to? Would she accept it, and everything else he seemed to be offering with that look and those words, that righteous anger on her behalf? The answer, as is the case so often in life, was a lukewarm compromise. She would accept his apology, but nothing else.

"Then if you wish for me to continue mentoring your sister, let us agree never to speak of this again."

He looked as if he wanted to protest, but she had enough. The day's events now beginning to weigh heavily on her mind and body.

"I would like to go home now. Please, excuse me."

She moved around him to continue walking down the stairs. This time, he did not try to stop her, and for that, she was grateful.

"Let me get you a carriage, then."

Normally, she would have pointed out it was less than appropriate for a young lady to take a carriage on her own, not that it had ever stopped her before. But in this moment, she wanted nothing more than to get away from him, or, more accurately, from the version of herself she unleashed around him.

So, without protest, she allowed Mr. Jameson to hail a carriage and put her inside, and only when the door closed, and the driver took off did she let the rigidity drain from her posture as she leaned back into the cushioned seat.

Since only a few streets divided the Marin residence from the Jameson's, she was home in a matter of minutes and looking forward to fleeing to her room and taking to bed.

And that was exactly what she did. She had a ball to attend at the end of the week and a debutante to prepare until then, and she would do so with the same diligence that she brought to every project. But tonight, she would make use of the supposed frailty of the fairer sex to retreat to her room and read and brood to her heart's content.

Chapter 10

Elijah arrived at his sister's first ball, his first ball, in ill-fitting shoes that pinched his toes, and a very bad temper. Both of which were connected, and neither of which were very beneficial to his enjoyment of the event.

If he could, he would turn around and go back home immediately. He had no patience for all this frivolity. Because along with shoes that did not fit, his conversation only days earlier with a certain young lady weighed heavily on his mind.

She was wary of him and had been withdrawn and quiet whenever he was around. Not at all like the person he had begrudgingly gotten to know over the last few weeks. And he did not blame her, not after the way he behaved.

Her change in attitude toward him meant that their interactions were very much limited to the exact kind of meaningless exchange of words that he absolutely hated.

And if he were to be completely honest with himself, he had to admit that he missed the way things used to be. He had succeeded in silencing the one person that may have been one of the only people worth getting to know in this world of fake smiles and forced politeness.

But it was not only the loss of a potential friend and ally that weighed on him when he looked at her, it was the way she seemed to be holding herself back from him now. And the fact that, as painful as it must have been for her, their conversation on the staircase the other day had given him a deeper look at the person she was.

The whole picture, whereas before he had only gotten glimpses of a few pieces.

He knew the confident and feisty version. But he had no idea behind the measured smiles, tailored gowns, witty retorts, and impeccably enunciated words, Miss Isabella Marin was just as lost and angry as he.

And that knowledge made it impossible to enjoy the silence she now bestowed upon him, no matter how much he had wished for it before. So, he made a decision, that he would work hard to regain the lady's trust, no matter what it took.

And oddly enough, it was things he had learned from her that might aid him in doing so. Contrition, flattery, charm—all were useful tools. He never thought he'd have to use them with her.

He searched the large room, full of more opulence than he had ever seen before, looking for her, all while Vivian clung to his arm, bouncing up and down excitedly.

"Oh, Elijah. Is it not wonderful? Nothing like those simple dances we attended in the past. We should take a turn about the room. Isa will have already arrived, and I would very much like to see her."

He would like to see her, too, but he could hardly admit that to his little sister. She was not known for keeping secrets.

"Let us find her, then," he said quietly.

He lost track of how many eager young men and anxious mothers introduced themselves as they wandered the periphery of the room. Was he expected to remember every single one of their names? Not to mention the daughters he had yet to meet?

Vivian looked to be in heaven, reveling in all the attention.

And so it begins, he thought wryly. His little sister was firmly out in society. Everything would be so much different from now on.

The idea made his heart ache with sadness. And standing in a sea of silk gowns and starched suits, beautiful music swelling around him, he felt very alone.

"Isa," Vivian exclaimed, dropping his arm and pulling him from the downward spiral of his current thoughts.

He looked up, searching for the young lady.

And there she was, in a vibrant olive-green gown that set her beautiful brown skin aglow. It reminded him of warmth and heat, a fire smoldering. Her hair was pulled halfway back with clips while the other half cascaded over her bare shoulders, a beautiful waterfall of soft silk. His fingers itched to know if it felt the way it looked. A small tiara glistened atop her head.

She stole his breath away. For Miss Isabella Marin outshone anyone else here. Even the extravagant splendor of the Whitney's ballroom looked dull in comparison.

Her eyes met his. And in this light, they looked warm and welcoming. Two deep pools impossible to look away from.

He stepped forward, giving her a bow. She curtsied in turn and then seemed determined to dismiss him. Before she could, he clasped her gloved hand and pulled it to his mouth to kiss it softly.

He did not miss her quiet gasp, or the way she stiffened immediately after.

"Miss Marin," he said, a small smile forming on his lips. "You look absolutely lovely."

She pulled her hand away and stepped back. His words were met with only icy silence and slight nod of her head.

He almost laughed at the predictability of it, but she would not appreciate that, he knew. Isabella Marin was as stubborn as they came. And he could not fault her for it. He welcomed it, deserved it. But he would keep trying, keep working to show her his apology was sincere.

And suddenly, Mr. Marin was there, his wife on his arm. He had not had the pleasure of meeting Mrs. Marin yet.

"My dear, may I introduce you to Mr. Elijah Jameson. Mr. Jameson, my wife, Mrs. Selena Marin."

She extended her hand to him. "A pleasure, Mr. Jameson," she said as she looked him up and down.

Isabella has her eyes, he noted. But where Isabella's were warm and bright, Mrs. Marin's seemed shrewd and cold. He felt judged, and he had only just met the woman. Was this how Isabella was always made to feel?

The lady excused herself almost immediately, no doubt finding him lacking.

"Do not mind her, lad," Mr. Marin said with a laugh. "She means no harm."

He doubted that very much. He had to conclude that she must be in the camp of those who found him and his sister to be "less than" as in less than themselves. He had hoped Mrs. Marin would be more like her daughter in that regard.

Mr. Marin proceeded to prattle on about club business and to inquire about the state of Jameson Steele. All while Elijah nodded along and answered as best he could while keeping an eye on his sister who was now being led out onto the dance floor.

He noted that Miss Marin seemed to be watching as well, and this eased his worry greatly, which only served to remind him of how much he had come to rely on her without realizing it, and how shamefully he had treated her in return.

Would she ever forgive him for his mistakes? Or would this stand between them forever? He wanted more than anything to speak with her, to apologize again.

It was only a short while later when he received unexpected help from his sister.

After dancing the first three sets without so much as a break for refreshments, his little sister floated by, a gaggle of admirers in tow, saw him, and then Miss Marin only a few feet away and exclaimed, "Elijah! What are you thinking? Here Isa stands without a dance partner, and you have not offered? Mrs. Fisher would be horrified. You are lucky she has not noticed yet. And if you do not ask Isa to dance immediately, I will track her down and inform her."

He did not doubt her, and he dared not contradict her. Certainly not when his sister had created an opportunity for him to have Miss Marin's undivided attention.

And before either of them could protest, Vivian had grabbed Miss Marin by the hand, pulled her over to him, and shoved them toward the dancers currently getting in formation in the middle of the room.

Aware of the curious looks of the surrounding couples and remembering well the effort it had taken Miss Marin to prevent him from making a fool of himself in just such a situation, he quickly turned to face her and bowed just as Mr. Dugray had taught him.

"May I have this dance?" he asked, not bothering to hide the pleading in his tone.

Would she reject him?

But the lady, either too stunned or too polite to decline, gave him her hand and let him guide her into position. He felt the tension leech from his body, only to return again moments later when he realized what he was about to do.

He actually had to dance now, in front of all these people. A feat he hoped to manage reasonably well by copying the dancers around him.

One last look at his partner to assure himself she would not flee, and then the first strains of the music reached his ears, and they were off.

***

Isabella was more nervous than she cared to admit as she placed her hand on Mr. Jameson's shoulder. His firm, very broad shoulder. She suppressed a shiver when his hand snaked around her waist, coming to settle on her back.

It seemed this man's mission was to confuse and confound her. His touch, his warm body, his close proximity had her blood singing, her pulse racing.

In the most delicious way.

And yet his words, his judgment, his hurtful accusations enraged her and made her feel so very exposed.

In short, she was confused.

It certainly did not help matters that the very dance they had chosen—or rather, which Vivian had chosen for them—was a Waltz, so intimate.

Mr. Dugray had the presence of mind to include it in his lessons, but they had practiced it much less than the other dances. Mainly because Mr. Jameson insisted he did not need to know it because it was unlikely he would be dancing at all.

She would laugh at the irony of it all if she were not so very nervous, and still very cross with the gentleman. Otherwise, she might have delighted in rubbing his nose in his mistake.

She took a breath to steady herself and sent up a silent prayer. Because there was a very distinct possibility that this undertaking would end in disaster.

She was stiff and unyielding as they began the dance. Try as she might, she could not relax. The conflicting feelings fighting a war in her heart and mind made it difficult to focus on being a good partner.

And to think she had wanted to poke fun at his skills. Now she was the one fumbling her way through, resisting Mr. Jameson's attempts to lead and leaning so far away from him she had to dig her fingertips into his shoulder just to avoid being flung off as they turned the corners of the dance floor.

And it seemed her partner's patience was wearing thin.

Tightening his grip on her back, he pulled her closer, angled his head down, and murmured in her ear, "I believe that for this dance to proceed the way it was intended, you will have to trust me."

She scoffed. Even though she knew he meant she should trust him to lead her in the dance, the words felt pointed. She glared at him and his eyes widened for a moment before softening, the apology in them was clear.

So, when he began whispering instructions, she let them wash over her and willed her body to follow. "Let some of that tension out of your shoulders, let me guide you, and trust that I will not let you fall. I have you, I promise."

Those words, so similar to what she had said to him in her family's drawing room. That she would defend him, should he need it.

Did he remember it? Replay their intimate moment over and over in his head as she did?

Unlikely.

He drew back and smiled, warm and reassuring, and she decided, perhaps foolishly, to take him at his word.

Lowering her shoulders, she tried to let some of the rigidity seep out of her posture while she loosened the too-tight grip of her fingertips on his shoulder. And felt him strengthen his grip on her instead, just enough so he could comfortably hold and guide her.

It took only a handful of turns until she finally relaxed, letting her body mold to his ever so slightly. The beautiful music and the beautiful room and this beautiful night finally worked its magic upon her.

Now firmly anchored in place by her partner's hand, and by the unexpectedly firm trust it inspired in her, she let herself ease into the sway of the music. With their bodies so close together, she could register his movements immediately, thus allowing her to adjust as needed so he could navigate them around the room. And soon it became so effortless and so seamless, she felt as if she was flying. As if they were flying. Together.

And since it was not every day that one got to experience such an exquisite feeling, she decided to allow herself, for once, to just enjoy it. To enjoy him.

To banish all thoughts of Mr. Jameson's inappropriate remarks and her own inappropriate responses, all thoughts of appropriateness in general, and just... fly.

Her partner, it seemed, was having much the same experience, for when she finally dared to look at him again, with a smile she found impossible to suppress, she discovered her exuberance mirrored on his face.

His annoyingly handsome face was completely transformed by a wide, joyous smile that threatened to take her breath away.

Instead of the usual glares and disapproving grimaces. Tonight, she was presented with deep dimples and a plethora of laugh lines surrounding his light brown eyes, and she knew, instantly and without a doubt, that she was seeing something precious. Something rare and wonderful. Something she had hoped to see again since the moment he walked into Mrs. Fisher's drawing room. His smile that evoked so many memories in her.

She held his gaze, hoping with everything in her that he would do the same. She desperately wanted to look into his eyes, unbidden and uninterrupted. To see the man he really was. That up until tonight, and that night on the staircase, she had barely seen a glimpse of.

Because despite her misgivings about him, what was happening between them now eclipsed all of it.

He held her gaze, head tilted down toward her, eyes now dark and smoldering, and for the span of what may have been a thousand years or just a few heartbeats, there was no one in the crowded ballroom but the two of them. And God help her, but she wanted to stay in this beautiful place for as long as she could.

The magical feeling held until the very last notes of the waltz, and only when they were forced to do so did they slowly, reluctantly let go of each other and step apart.

She tried very hard not to notice the absence of him.

It was the arrival of Mrs. Fisher, who evidently had been watching the entire exchange, that pulled her from her daze. And she just managed to curtsy and move out of the way of the couples setting up for the next dance.

Mr. Jameson seemed to have no such problem, as he cheerfully addressed their friend.

"Let me hear your verdict, Madame—did I avoid making a fool of myself and thus my sister by association?"

"You did indeed, young man. I was quite impressed by your skill. You are much improved after only such a short time. And the two of you made a very pretty picture together. It is rare to see two people so beautifully in tune during a dance, so perfectly harmonized. You should be very proud."

Isabella felt the blood rush to her already heated cheeks at the remark. Unable to meet her dancing partner's eyes, she simply nodded and muttered a meaningless reply, forcing herself to remain composed instead of fleeing the room.

Luckily, a footman arrived with a tray of refreshments just then, and when she had gulped down half a flute of champagne and finally dared to look at Mr. Jameson again out of the corner of her eye, there was nothing to indicate he felt as embarrassed as she.

She barely suppressed an eye roll; of course he would be unaffected. Or was he only pretending?

She would not let herself entertain the thought.

Mr. Jameson turned to face her. "And you, Miss Marin? Did my skills meet your high standards?"

His tone was light, teasing. Was he flirting with her? Or at the very least, trying to joke?

She could play along.

"Seeing as my toes were the ground you chose to test your skills on, I dare say you could do with a little more practice," she said, her lips lifting into a smile. They both knew full well that he never once stepped on her toes.

He flinched, exaggerating for comic effect, then pressed a hand to his chest.

"You wound me, Miss Marin. In fact, I feel I am being judged much too harshly after I worked so hard during our lessons. We cannot all be as practiced as you. I should like to see you keep your balance while on a ship ravaged by the waves as I have had to do. Then I could do some critiquing of my own."

She laughed. A full-on laugh that shook her whole body.

And he stared at her for a moment with—was that fondness in his eyes?

She blinked before answering him. "Perhaps I would surprise you."

Now would be the moment to tell him. Do you not remember Elijah? Do you not remember me?

His incredulous chuckle both told her how likely he thought that was to happen and goaded her into wanting to prove him wrong.

"I have in fact been aboard a ship during rough weather even, years ago. I was just a little girl while my father worked aboard those ships. If I was unable to accompany my mother to work, I would join my father. We were aboard a ship he was looking to purchase for his company. I am sure you know that along with banking he also deals in import and export. Anyhow, as my father and Mr. Fisher were discussing the most dreadfully boring things, I would always want to sail on a ship. And a friend dared me."

It was you Elijah, you dared me. But he still had not connected the dots it seemed.

She smiled mischievously at Mr. Jameson's baffled expression before continuing, "So, I hid. And when they took the ship out for a test, I went with them. By the time anyone noticed I was gone, they were away offshore. The weather turned, and well—I am sure you can figure out the end of the story."

"I have a hard time believing that."

"Oh, you may believe it. I would tell you to ask my father for confirmation, but I am afraid the memory alone will send him into conniptions. I was banned from going out for a month after that, and Mr. Fisher took away the lovely tea set he had given me for my birthday as punishment."

She regretted her last sentence immediately. To Mr. Jameson, her punishment must sound ludicrously pampered, and she expected him to say something scathing along those lines any second now.

But instead of pointing out once more what a charmed life she led in his eyes, Mr. Jameson simply studied her for a moment, his gaze assessing but not hostile.

"So what happened to that little girl who just had to be aboard a ship?"

Her circumstances changed and she never looked back. Until now.

"She grew up and was told she was a lady and should never behave in such a manner again. A ship is no place for a lady, after all."

That was a direct quote from her mother, but she would never tell him that.

"That is a shame. Seems like the perfect place for you. Out on the sea, in the wide-open space. Carefree."

The way they used to be, together.

She cocked her head to the side, trying to find the hidden barb behind the observation. But his expression was open, friendly, and the words harmless enough. It seemed he really had meant to compliment her.

Add that to the list of tonight's oddities.

Perhaps, she thought as the evening went on, that his harsh words the other day and her humiliating response had led to something good after all. Perhaps now there would be peace between them. Perhaps with those most basic misunderstandings cleared up, they could finally become friends.

She found she did not hate the idea.

In fact, she desperately hoped it to be true. And over the course of the evening, as Elijah talked and laughed with her, brought her refreshments, and asked her to dance a second and third set—the latter of which she reluctantly declined as etiquette dictated she must, that little spark of hope grew and grew.

By the time she descended from the Jameson's carriage at dawn, Elijah having insisted upon making sure she arrived home safely, she could concede that he was someone she wanted to continue getting to know, this older, wiser, new version of him. Not the boy from her past, but the man she hoped would always be in her future.

The ride home had been comfortably quiet. The silence only broken when Mr. Jameson helped her down from the carriage, and whispered a soft, "I am truly sorry for the things I said." And then kissed her gloved hand.

She squeezed his hand in hers for only a moment, hoping he understood.

She forgave him.

And when she slept that night, she dreamt of him, too.

Chapter 11

With Vivian's debut being such a success, the Jameson's were soon inundated with invitations to all kinds of social events.

To Isabella it was exciting, and it made her incredibly proud. But poor Mr. Jameson was struggling, probably not wanting to think of all the young men who were now interested in his little sister.

And he seemed overwhelmed by all of it.

So Mrs. Fisher and herself volunteered to help him screen the invitations, weeding out the most obvious of fortune hunters and those who likely only regarded the Jameson's as shiny new toys.

She had even noticed, among the piles, a few invitations from the mothers of eligible young ladies addressed specifically to Mr. Jameson.

She had seen some of those young ladies at the Whitney's ball. Those invitations went straight into the decline pile. Fortune hunting vipers most of them. She may not know exactly where she stood with Mr. Jameson, but she would not let him be turned into an object of curiosity or ridicule.

And she would not let him be taken advantage of.

To her continued surprise, the gentleman kept up his pleasant and polite behavior toward her. A week later and he was still going strong.

In short, their peace was holding, and she allowed herself to settle deeper into this budding friendship.

As they attended dinner parties, balls, and gatherings, took walks and carriage rides in and around the park, and attended the theater, she always looked forward to spending time with him.

And now that she and Mr. Jameson were on better terms, they could focus their joint attention on Vivian. She was now out and had the attention of several young men. They needed to discuss the rules of courting should any of the men catch her eye.

But though Vivian had danced and talked with many of the young men who now came calling almost daily at the Jameson residence, it seemed none of them ever left a particularly lasting impression.

It was surprising, but also something Isabella was perfectly fine with. Vivian should take her time and choose someone for love rather than money, someone she considered her best friend.

Nonetheless, their schedules were always full, especially since Vivian insisted they keep up their dancing lessons, and Mr. Jameson made the same demand with regard to Vivian's educational reading. After only a few weeks of this, Isabella was beginning to feel exhausted.

And that was why the idea her father just proposed to her made her almost want to sob from relief.

She had just returned from a theatrical matinée with Mrs. Fisher and the Jamesons when her father greeted her by the door, waving a letter excitedly.

"How would you like a trip to the seaside, my dear?"

"In the middle of the season?" she asked, surprised but only just so.

It was an odd suggestion, but she was rather used to odd suggestions from her father and had learned to only try and defer him from his plans when they threatened to give her a headache or threaten a scandal, like the time he wanted to inform his business partners that his daughter helped balance the books. He was so proud of her accomplishments he sometimes got too enthusiastic. But a trip to the seaside, while a little unusual at this time of year with event upon event to attend, was not anything to write the papers about.

"I have only just received a note from Mr. Fisher. He's returned from a business trip and wants to have a day of rest and relaxation. Mrs. Fisher will likely pack a lunch. So, what do you say?"

She felt her features relax into a fond smile at her father's unabashed excitement. He and Mr. Fisher had met upon her parents' move to the city over twenty years ago. They built up their business and investments together and had been close friends ever since, and Isabella adored him, although she did not get to see him nearly as often as she saw his wife.

So where was the harm in taking a little break from the hectic season to meet a beloved family friend and get some fresh air? It may even be a good idea to spend some time apart from a certain pair of siblings.

They'd been spending so much time together lately. And she was beginning to wonder if it was too much time. Because she found that a certain gentleman was on her mind far too often.

It was... distracting.

Earlier, for example, she had barely paid attention to the comedy play at the theater. Instead, she spent almost the entire time watching Mr. Jameson, whose enjoyment of the event seemed derived not so much from the theatrical spectacle but from watching his sister's delight in it.

Yes, it was absolutely distracting.

Perhaps it was indeed time for a respite.

But no sooner had she had the thought when her father dashed her hopes.

"And what do you say to inviting our new friends? I am sure Mr. Jameson would enjoy an opportunity to be out on the water again. And Frederick will be happy to observe his protégé faring so well."

She opened her mouth to protest, but one look at her father's excited face had her closing it again. There were times when she could persuade him to abandon his often-eccentric plans, and other times when no power in the universe could do so. Clearly, today was one of those times.

"That sounds lovely, Father. A wonderful idea."

Her father immediately sent word to the Jameson's about the spontaneous excursion.

And it was only after the two siblings accepted did her father bother to mention that this trip would be several days in length.

Meaning she would have to endure Mr. Jameson's presence for an extended period of time. No breaks.

Was her father trying to torture her? It certainly seemed that way.

The plan was for everyone to stay at the Fisher's cottage.

So, after a day of preparations, she and her father left their townhouse in a flurry to collect the Jamesons.

"Isa, Mr. Marin, it is so good to see you both," Vivian said as she greeted them with a curtsy after descending the steps of her home. "Thank you so much for inviting us."

Her father smiled down at the excited young lady. "My pleasure, my dear. I know how fond of you my Isa is. And I know she will enjoy your company over the next few days."

Isabella rolled her eyes. Bless her father's heart. He was only trying to make her happy.

"Yes, thank you, sir," a deeper voice said from behind Vivian.

Mr. Jameson was now descending the steps, carrying one luggage trunk while a footman followed behind him with another.

"Entirely my pleasure, lad. Shall we go?"

They all nodded and began to pile into the Marin's carriage.

She could not decide what would be worse, having to sit next to him or across from him.

Sitting next to him would mean being pressed against him. But sitting across from him would mean having to constantly avoid his gaze.

The decision was made for her when Vivian moved in front of her to sit next to her brother.

"Let's go, Isa," she whined, bouncing up and down in her seat.

She breathed a sigh of relief while also tamping down her disappointment. There was no way to win, she thought wryly as she climbed into the carriage, and they set off down the road.

***

Her father, and Mr. Jameson in particular, were in high spirits. They talked excitedly of the ships they might see and what the weather might be like, and what Mr. Fisher might have encountered on his business travels.

Vivian just stared out the window completely enraptured. She pointed out aspects of the scenery, which she had never really encountered before: animals roaming, beautiful fields of flowers, and groves of bright green trees. To her, everything must have seemed so perfect and romantic, not unlike the things she read about in novels.

Isabella envied that quality in her friend, to look at the world with such innocence.

She no longer had that luxury. The secret she had long kept buried made sure of that.

But as the city faded away, and she breathed in the fresh summer air, she let her mind wander to the days ahead.

All things considered, her life was perfect at this moment, secret or no secret. And she was happy, she thought, as she looked around the carriage.

So much so that when she looked up to find Mr. Jameson watching her, she found it easy to smile at him reassuringly and welcome his bright smile in return.

Several hours passed in both comfortable silence and excited chatter before the sea came into view.

Vivian's squeal of joy was catching, and Isabella found herself feeling the joy. Even Mr. Jameson leaned forward to take in the sight, his eyes alight with wonder.

She leaned forward slightly to ask, "Are you happy to be back here, then?"

With me, like when we were young. Would being here again finally spark a memory? She wanted so much for him to remember.

He looked over at her, the ghost of a smile on his lips. "I am. I did not do ship work often. But I have missed it, the openness, the salt air, the freedom, and some good friends." The glint in his eyes made her wonder. But then, his smile turned to a frown.

"What is it?" she asked quietly, gently.

"It was hard work, scrubbing the decks and pulling in the lines. Back-breaking work and not at all glamorous."

Not like you, he seemed to say as he avoided her gaze. But he knew her better now, knew her history. So maybe it was less about her position and more about his own now.

She wanted to reach out to him, to comfort him. But circumstances prevented it, so she simply caught his eye and said, "I am glad to be here with you."

And despite her misgivings the day before, it was not a lie.

His answering smile was dazzling, yet soft. She tried to ignore the pounding of her traitorous heart.

The carriage came to a stop near a dock on which stood Mr. Fisher and a few young sailors. They all descended, and the driver went on to deliver their trunks to a waiting Mrs. Fisher. Their friend was not fond of the sea or sailing.

Greetings and introductions were made all around before Mr. Jameson was inundated with questions from a few familiar faces.

Perhaps that was his worry, what his friends might think of him. Showing up here in his fancy new clothes, completely ensconced in his brand-new life.

While she and Vivian went ahead to the large ship moored to the dock, Mr. Fisher and her father followed close behind.

The Abigail, named for his loving wife, was Mr. Fisher's pride and joy.

She snuck glances at Mr. Jameson as they went. Marveling at his loud boisterous laugh and generally carefree manner, not at all like the man she had first encountered only a month ago, who looked so uncomfortable in his own skin.

With every second that passed, he seemed to shed more of the high-class, wealthy young gentleman he now was and take on more of the man he used to be.

By the time they ascended the gangway and reached the ship's main deck, Mr. Jameson was a man entirely set free, looking far more at home here than she had ever seen him anywhere else.

And that was a sight to behold indeed. His coat was unbuttoned, his collar loose.

The bright blue sky above them, dotted with soft white clouds, the expanse of royal blue water that stretched on for miles around them was nothing compared to the sight of him.

And she could not stop staring

His stance was relaxed, but sure as he leaned against the railing, even as the ship swayed gently from the waves below. A gust of wind tugged at his dark locks, effortlessly teasing them into the kind of fashionable disarray certain men probably spent hours trying to achieve each morning.

He was, anyone could see, completely in his element walking the length of the ships' deck—and for a brief moment, she wondered what it would feel like to stand by his side, atop the ship's bow as it rolled out to distant shores.

Just the two of them, and the sea, and the sky. And the blissful quiet.

Turning away from him to face the railing, she blinked away the romantic notion.

And yet, the sound of his voice, coming from just behind her, that deep rasp, set her heart beating wildly in her chest.

"I am surprised you are out here on the deck instead of hiding."

She smiled; he was teasing her.

She heard him step closer, but still where she could not quite see him.

She turned her head to look over her shoulder, glancing at him. He was smirking, and his good mood was inspiring her own. She smiled back.

"Hmmmm. Yes, well, this time I have permission to come aboard. No need to hide."

He moved even closer now.

What was he doing? She swore she could feel the heat of him at her back. The ghost of his breath was a whispered caress at the nape of her neck.

"That is true. But it does sound fun."

Hiding together he seemed to say. Just the two of them, alone.

She whirled around to face him, less because she actually felt ready to face him and more to suppress the sudden desire to lean into him. It would be so easy. And she did not want to think too much about it. If she did, she might let her feelings for him outweigh her quest for full independence.

She looked up into his eyes, eyes that made her want to melt. When had this happened? When had he cast such a spell on her?

She should scold him for standing too close. For teasing her. For offering to hide away with her. It was not proper.

But, glancing around, she saw that no one in their party stood near enough to have heard the exchange. And no one was looking at them.

Mr. Fisher was currently showing her father some new and marvelous navigation apparatus, and Vivian was basking in the undivided attention of every sailor within sight.

It was just the two of them. And there had been no malice behind his words, no intention to humiliate her—just gentle, good-natured teasing between friends.

Just friends.

"Are you sure you want to run away with me, Mr. Jameson?"

"If you have need of me, I am," he said, his words a rumbling dark whisper.

She gasped. They were teetering on the edge of something, she was sure. And it set butterflies alight inside her.

But she had no opportunity to respond, not even sure how to do so, when Vivian suddenly appeared by her brother's side to demand a tour of the ship. Mr. Jameson obliged—but not before sending her one last conspiratorial look that made her feel like she was part of some secret plot.

And this was the best kind of secret.

She let out a laugh before moving off to find Mr. Fisher and her father. She would like a tour herself.

***

Sometime later, after they had all been sufficiently impressed by the beauty of The Abigail, her father suggested they abandon ship for a late luncheon.

A few of Mr. Jameson's friends joined them, and they were a jolly group indeed. *Probably a bit too jolly*, Isabella thought, as her father suggested the young people go for a walk along the harbor wall.

"You will enjoy that more than listening to two old men prattle away," he said with a gentle push to her shoulders to get her moving.

Subtle, her father was not. He wanted some peace and quiet.

It was not entirely appropriate to have this many young men and only two young ladies, as there was no real chaperone for Vivian. But her older brother was among the group, so perhaps that could be overlooked. And Mr. Jameson looked so happy to be among his friends, Vivian so excited by the attention, Isabella could not bring herself to voice her thoughts.

So, she silently followed the group down the gangway and to the low stone wall that separated the sea from the road. Birds screeched overhead as the wind blew around them. That salty sea air, sharp and bright, tickled her nose. It was a perfect day.

One of Elijah's friends, a charming man named Mr. Rodriguez, offered her his arm. She hesitated. Would Elijah mind? She glanced around, searching for his face to gauge his reaction. He was close by, frozen, watching. Her heart soared, but she had no real reason to decline his friend. So she graciously accepted Mr. Rodriguez and off they went, Elijah pointing out things of interest and his friends supplying the names of the biggest and most important ships moored within their sight.

All in all, it was a cheerful, informative afternoon.

Informative in ways she had not anticipated, as she stole another glance at Elijah.

But when her eyes landed on his face, she found his attention was elsewhere and she quickly averted her gaze.

She had not realized that his gaze was firmly locked on her hand, resting quite comfortably on the arm of his friend.

Chapter 12

Elijah smiled to the sound of laughter, as he had for the past week. His sister had done so much of it on this trip; he would need to thank Mr. Marin again for the invitation.

The birds overhead called out to one another as the waves crashed nearby. The open air a welcome change from often stifling and crowded streets of the city. He was going to miss the noise, of waking up to a house full of people each morning. Not that Vivian did not provide plenty of noise every single morning back in the city, but this was different. More people, more voices, more life breathed into the air.

It reminded him of his life before. The constant, steady stream of people in the streets, horses pulling carriages, stray dogs looking for scraps, and his friends calling from below for him to join them for some fun.

But, if he was being completely honest, what he was really going to miss most was hearing Miss Marin's voice from somewhere nearby, always. Her laughter, her quick comebacks, the way she always seemed to be singing a tune, and spending every moment of every single day with her. Not that he would ever admit that out loud.

A shriek pulled him from his thoughts as he sat in the warm sand on this small stretch of the beach, they walked here most afternoons. He shielded his eyes from the sun to look up and out at the water.

Another shriek and then, "No, Vivian," just as his little sister sent another splash of water into Miss Marin's face from where she stood at the water's edge. She laughed and splashed back but moved no further in.

"Please, come in, Isa," Vivian whined.

She shook her head. "It's too cold."

That got his attention. He had never known Miss Marin to shy away from anything. He would have expected her to charge headfirst into that water and drag him with her just because she could.

He stood up, dusting the sand from his pants as he went. Vivian waded in a little deeper as he came to stand next to Miss Marin. Her posture was rigid.

"Are you alright?"

"I am fine," she snapped.

He kept his eyes on her face as he said, "You do not seem fine."

In fact, she seemed scared, eyes watching the waves like they might snatch her up at any moment.

Was she afraid?

Vivian waded into the water, her bright yellow dress visible below the surface. She loved to swim, though she never had much opportunity to do so. The public bath houses were sometimes an option on particularly hot days. But this was her first visit to the beach. He smiled as she splashed around and waved at him, laughing.

He turned back to Isabella. "Do you not like the water, Miss Marin?"

She shook her head slowly. "It is beautiful. I have just always been frightened of it, open water. That is why I never learned to swim."

"But then why stow away on Mr. Fisher's ship when you were younger? Did you not worry you would fall overboard?"

She laughed as she turned fully to face him. Her eyes were wide and bright. "You would immediately think of that. I do not know why, but the thought never occurred to me. Probably because I had a friend there with me egging me on. He was a real scoundrel."

There was a glint in her eye as she said this and a hint of pleading. Was she trying to tell him something?

She continued then; the glint gone. "I just wanted to be out on the water in a way that felt safe, I suppose. It was not until my father scolded me, face pale and frantic, that I realized how much danger I put myself in. Both my parents tried to insist on swimming lessons afterward, but I have never been able to handle it."

He could understand that. Some things are just too much.

"I am terrified of spiders. Ask Vivian, anytime I see one I have to ask her to remove it."

She laughed, the sound like the sweetest music playing only for him. "Thank you for telling me."

He nodded before inquiring softly, "Do you never go in the water, then?"

"Only when my father is here to escort me."

Ah, that would explain it, then. It was only himself and the young ladies that walked down to the water today, their last little adventure before departing for home this afternoon. The three elder adults having chosen to stay behind and have some time to themselves.

An idea occurred to him. But would she put her trust in him?

"I could go in with you if you like?" He waited, hope blooming quietly in his chest.

She looked into his eyes, searching, before she looked down at her dress. A soft blue color that reminded him of the sky above. "My mother would be furious if I ruined this dress."

The hope began to ebb away when she said with a sparkle in her eye, "And if that is not a good reason, then what is?"

She clasped his hand in hers and pulled him into the water, stopping when it reached just below her hips. And when they turned to face a coming wave, he tightened his grip and found himself hoping she would never let go, hoping she would always choose him to lean on.

Their little group spent one lazy, bright, and carefree week by the water during which he learned far more about Miss Isabella Marin than he ever expected to. And by the time they returned to the city, it seemed safe to truly consider her a friend. She almost always met him with a smile instead of a scowl, her teasing was more funny than harsh, and they could talk at length without it devolving into some kind of disagreement.

And after all the anger and annoyance and constant back and forth of their previous relationship, it was a great relief.

It was so easy now to talk and joke with her, to ask her advice when Vivian proved to be a mystery to him, and to have someone at his back who would defend him when needed. An occurrence that seemed all too frequent in the days that followed their little getaway.

He had become very close with the Marin family in a very short amount of time, that was true. And there were people who seemed to think it was something he had planned. People who only saw where he had come from and what he lacked. People who assumed he was after a secure position, who somehow could not grasp the concept of friendship between two young people of the opposite sex.

Elijah, it seemed, had gotten incredibly lucky in securing friendships with the Marin's. In only a few short weeks he found that he would be willing to defend Miss Marin, reputation be damned.

And he had no idea the opportunity to do so would come sooner than he expected.

***

"Elijah, are you ready?" Vivian asked, standing next to him on the grass outside the conservatory.

He nodded. "Yes, it is just..."

"Just what? Do not be nervous. You have done this before, you know," she said, teasing him as she loved to do.

"That is just it, Vivian. I am not nervous at all. And that is what concerns me."

Vivian laughed, shaking her head. "Oh, big brother, only you would say something like that. Never satisfied."

And then she moved through the open doors, leaving him to brood in the warm summer night air.

The second ball he, Vivian, and Miss Marin attended at the Whitney's was a ball very similar to their first one.

A sentiment which, as soon as it passed through his mind, reminded him just how far he had come in this new life. Only a few months ago he could hardly have imagined attending a ball in the first place. Now the experience barely caused more than a twinge of annoyance at donning uncomfortably formal clothes and spending a night squeezed into an overheated ballroom with too many perfumed strangers.

And that was what gave him pause as he entered the building. How normal this all was now.

Of course not everything about balls, dances, and the like was terrible. Apart from a few strange fads – he would never understand the allure of jellied meat molded into foreign shapes—the food was excellent. The champagne always provided a pleasant buzz. And he even found a select few young men whose company he did not mind.

Dancing, too, was something he found he took to quite easily, especially once Mr. Marin had taken him to see a cobbler for a pair of shoes that was vastly superior to the pair he had worn to his first ball. Add to that the persistent teaching of both Mr. Dugray and Miss Marin, who continued to volunteer as his lesson partner, and he found that he actually enjoyed dancing.

But, though, he had, by now, found the courage to ask several young ladies to dance. And had, encouragingly enough, never been turned down, he still preferred to dance with Isabella Marin.

A secret which he would surely take to his grave.

For as accomplished as many of the other ladies were, none of them seemed to mold themselves to his body so easily, to follow his lead as if they were reading his mind, to subtly take over leading when he momentarily forgot about a succession of steps and found himself at a loss as she did. None of them smiled the way she did when a waltz was announced. They did not laugh as he bowed and extended his hand, memories flashing through his mind of their first official dance. No one else shared their secrets.

None seemed brimming with life the way that she was when they came to a stop after whirling around the room, as if the pulse of every living creature was pumping through her veins in that moment. In such a way that made him want to stop time and stay that way forever.

None, in short, were quite like her.

But it would not serve him to favor her. Because a man in his position was expected to take a wife, and he and Miss Marin were just friends. He needed to focus his attention elsewhere.

That did not make the task any easier.

Even with the persistent, yet well-meaning Mrs. Fisher encouraging him to indulge the many young ladies who often vied for his attention. She encouraged him every chance she got to find anyone who might be able to elicit the necessary tender feelings within him that would lead to a marriage proposal.

He did not have the heart to tell her that even with his newfound fortune, marriage was a goal he had no intention of striving for anytime soon. It was still an abstract concept to him, as foreign and useless as the attentions bestowed upon him by young ladies who knew no more than his title and fortune.

But as he watched Miss Marin flit about the room, having taken a break from dancing to fetch Mrs. Fisher a drink, for the first time he found himself wondering if there could be something more behind the idea of marriage than the joining of two titled families. If, perhaps, there could be friendship, too, and trust and admiration...

With the right person, could there be more?

It did not escape his notice, the way his mind always strayed back to her in these moments. Since their visit to the sea, he missed her constant presence. He missed seeing her sleep softened face across the breakfast table. He missed walking in the gardens only to look up and see her sitting in a window of the library, reading. And he missed her face being the last one he saw at night before he laid down to sleep. It unnerved him and excited him, the idea that maybe she could be the right person for him.

His thoughts were interrupted by a sudden, eerily well-timed utterance of Miss Marin's name from somewhere off to the right. He turned, scanning the groups of people nearby until he landed on four young men huddled near the wall. They were tracking Miss Marin through the room.

His cravat suddenly felt too tight. All the noise faded away until all he could hear was their conversation.

"The Marin girl is not unsightly."

"Isabella Marin? No, not in the least. A very pretty face and figure to be sure. But could you imagine marrying her? Bedding her?"

Upon hearing the words, he promptly choked on his champagne. He was not included in the conversation, thus the question was not directed at him, but his mind was quick to answer. Yes, he could imagine it, all too easily.

How she would throw all propriety to the wind and pull him toward her with that blaze in her eyes that always spelled trouble. How that flush of her skin would make an appearance again, as it did whenever she was feeling a particularly strong emotion. But not the polite pinking of her cheeks that she showed to the world, but the deep, rosy pink he liked to evoke in her when he made her laugh. How her voice would turn husky like it did when she teased him about something, until she would cease forming words altogether and resort to sighs and moans alone...

"Like bedding a doll. Cold and unfeeling."

Elijah froze as the words hit his ears and he turned to find the owner. A pompous looking young man with a pinched face and too much grease in his hair.

The man's conversation partner chuckled and gave some kind of response, but he could not hear it under the angry roar in his ears. He had heard his fair share of bawdy remarks, and made a few himself, but never in his life had he said anything so insulting about a lady, be she an heiress or a maid.

Was this how they saw her? Cold and unfeeling. They did not know her at all. And they never would if he had anything to say about it.

He was about to turn around and give the cad a piece of his mind, hands clenched into fists, when a commotion nearby drew his attention—a commotion in the exact place where he had just seen Miss Marin, Mrs. Fisher, and Vivian.

Setting down his champagne flute on an empty tray passing by, he hurriedly pushed through the gathering crowd, frantically searching for her.

Finally, he lay eyes on Miss Marin, her face alarmingly pale and ashen, staring at something in horror. He followed her line of sight to a man standing with another woman, the look on his face like a young boy caught with his hand in the cookie jar.

He turned back to Miss Marin and reached her with only seconds to spare before she crumpled and fell into his open arms.

Chapter 13

Isabella was not at all prone to fainting fits or hysteria. A young lady only emotes in private, her mother would always say. The only exception being when one was being courted by a man.

And while Isabella did not fully prescribe to that idea, she prided herself on having nerves of steel. She was no stranger to her feelings, but she was no delicate flower. In fact, she had never fainted once in her life. So, returning to consciousness after having apparently done so was a dizzying, disorienting, and unfamiliar experience.

There was nausea first, then the feel of smooth fabric under her fingers. A couch maybe? The smell of burning wood hit her, a fire. She was no longer in the ballroom then. The room was much too quiet, and she did not feel the buzz of dozens of bodies around her.

Blood pounded in her ears; her skin felt cold and clammy. Her heart raced. Sheer panic.

Until she realized she was not alone, she was safe. Elijah was bent over her, holding a vial of smelling salts to her nose. She jerked her head to the side to escape the sudden stench of ammonia and was rewarded with a low chuckle. The sound a balm to her frayed nerves.

"I had been given the impression that you were not the fainting type, Miss Marin."

His flippant words would have irritated her were it not for the slight strain in them, the hint of worry in his eyes when she turned her head to look at him again.

His freckles and warm brown eyes were a great comfort. He smelled of ink and cinnamon as he always did. His curls fell just above his eyes as they always did. The familiarity of him serving to steady her heart and even out her breathing.

"What happened?" she asked when she finally felt ready to speak.

"You had a bit of a fainting spell, proving once and for all that you really are a very genteel young lady. Congratulations."

She would have snapped at her friend in a decidedly not genteel manner if she had not been so busy trying to remember what exactly caused her to faint of all things. The heat had probably been a factor, but there was something else...

And then the memory returned to her, and she bolted upright, ignoring the flash of vertigo at her sudden movement.

"Slowly now."

He sounded uncharacteristically tender; the worry still evident in his voice. Normally she would be interested in that worry, flattered even. But she had no time for that, not with the memory of him that assaulted her again.

She brushed off the glass of water he pushed in her direction with an impatient wave of her hand, her vision filled with black spots as her head spun.

"Are you going to faint again?" he asked.

Was she?

She took a deep, slow breath.

No. But she was far from alright.

It had not been just the heat, the stifling heat of dozens of bodies in fancy clothes. It had been being pulled into a group of laughing party goers by Vivian only to be faced, unexpectedly, with a certain man and his beautiful wife.

She would never forget the look of pure horror on his face when he saw her—an expression that likely mirrored her own. So very different from the looks they had traded only three years ago. When the world seemed so bright and full of hope. When everything still made sense, and her heart was full.

But looking into his eyes in that moment just drove home how very naïve she had been about the whole affair. A very apt term if ever there was one for what they had done.

In the span of seconds, she recalled the way he looked at her back then, the promises he made, the pretty things he had whispered to her. A finer actor there never was. And she, a true fool. A fool who fancied herself in love.

Now there was only pain and humiliation to accompany those memories.

And he was just standing there, staring. And the room was so hot. And the music so loud. And everyone would know her shame. And there was no way out of it—so she fainted.

Her body taking the only means of escape it had.

"What happened between you and that man?"

She flinched. She had not thought anyone noticed the extent of her emotional turmoil, let alone that her fainting spell was caused by the mere sight of a man who should not be more than a passing acquaintance. But of course Mr. Jameson was far more observant than she liked to give him credit for.

She knew what she should do – deny even knowing the man, chide her friend for so much as insinuating anything might have happened between them, and then distract him before he could ask even more probing questions.

She needed to get out of here, fast, before anyone noticed that she was alone in a secluded room with a young gentleman of no relation. As it was, the gossip was surely spreading like wildfire as the minutes ticked by.

But she did the opposite. Because the look in his eyes made her feel like maybe he would understand. That he would not judge her.

And she was tired of being afraid. She wanted him to know her, even the parts she did not like.

She sat up fully on the chaise lounge, Mr. Jameson scooting over to give her the room. She looked down at her hands, the color having returned. But her stomach was now in knots, unsure of exactly where to start. How much should she disclose? She was confident he would never expose her secrets, but this was something she had been trying to avoid for so long.

"What do you think happened?"

"Something that hurt you."

He was so willing to give her the benefit of the doubt. She was not sure she deserved it. But it was nice to know that someone was on her side.

"He…" She averted her eyes. Telling him this, speaking of such things was completely inappropriate. But she could do this. She wanted to do this.

She raised her eyes to meet his gaze head-on. "He seduced me. Three summers ago. Mr. Hayden is his name. Dean Hayden. It was my first season and he, charming and handsome and supposedly eligible, showered me with attention. He was not the only one. But he was the only one to seem interested in something other than my money. And in a world where I often felt out of place because of the color of my skin, he made me feel like that did not matter. That should have been my first warning sign. Because while my Mexican heritage is not all I am, it is a part of me, and it matters.

But there is no mistaking me for a passive victim here—I was all too willing to be seduced. Part of it may have been rebellion, the thrill of doing something reckless and romantic. He spoke of love and fate and a trip to the country to elope, things any young lady in my position would be happy to hear. I had always planned to marry for love. So when we managed to find ourselves alone for an extended period of time, it seemed silly and wasteful to postpone the inevitable. What could be so wrong about exploring our desires? By that point he had mentioned marriage, and it all seemed like an absolute certainty to me. And so, we did." She averted her eyes again.

What must he think of her?

She swallowed hard, tears began to fall, and she forced herself to continue. "Except, after that night, nothing else ever came to pass. He did not marry me, obviously. He never met me the following day as we had planned. And neither did he send any word of explanation. In fact, he disappeared from the city all together. Tonight was the first time I have seen him since."

She shuddered at the memory of her own naiveté, her face flushing with shame even as she held Elijah's stormy gaze. "By mere coincidence, I later learned that he had been secretly engaged and married her mere days after our secret meeting. He never had any intention of following through on his promises to me. I was merely a dalliance. Something fun to pass the time, apparently." She laughed, the noise sounding hollow even to her own ears.

Elijah was still looking at her quietly, hands balled into tight fists at his sides, and she could only imagine how angry he was right now. Likely fuming at having his sister publicly associated with someone like her.

"The affair was hushed up before it could turn into a scandal. My mother helped with that, of course. My father has no idea. I could not bear the thought of him knowing. So please do not say anything. Vivian's reputation should not suffer through her association with me. But I fully understand if you wish to cut ties with me now. I know I am tarnished."

Now he looked confused as well as angry, and she found herself wishing this whole night were over. That she was at home in her bed, hidden away from the world, never to be seen again. This was why she had tried to avoid each season since that first, knowing that she might either run into Mr. Hayden and his lovely wife, or have people learn of her horrendous mistake and use it against her.

People only knew that there had been possible marriage intentions between her and the gentleman. But that was enough to make them whisper and stare. She had wanted to flee to their home upstate and become a recluse. Rational? No. Dramatic? Yes.

But her mother insisted she be present. That she find a husband as soon as possible so that they could "Put this whole ugly mess behind them."

So she showed up for yet another season, put on a smile, and did her duty, fully expecting to hate every moment. And to fight with her mother every single day.

But meeting Vivian and helping her to prepare for her debut had been such a delight. Such a welcome distraction. A chance to make sure another young lady did not make the same mistakes she had.

She was so lost in her own tumultuous thoughts that it did not register with her that he had moved. But suddenly he was kneeling on the floor right in front of her reaching a handout to cup her face. His other hand rested on her knee, and she could feel the heat of it through the fabric of her dress. The hand that rested on her cheek was gentle, tender.

So he leaned into the touch, savored it.

It was only when he started softly brushing his hand along her knee and she felt a shiver run down her spine that she pulled away. And now she did brush him off, ripping away his hand and jumping to her feet, feeling betrayed by the feelings it evoked in her. Now was not the time.

And despite what she tried to tell herself, his actions made her nervous. Bringing up memories of him that had long been dormant. She knew better, she knew him. But before she could stop herself, harsh words burst forth.

"You mistake my honesty for permissiveness, Mr. Jameson."

His eyes widened. Confusion evident. "Excuse me?"

But she could not stop herself. "Despite what you might assume after hearing my story, I am not a loose woman."

Her words made his expression clear up in understanding, only to immediately darken with anger again.

"Are you accusing me of trying to take advantage of you, when all I meant to do was offer comfort?"

"I do not know what you meant to do, but your behavior is far from appropriate."

He still looked angry, and the doubt crept in, crashing through her mind like a hurricane. Maybe he really had just wanted to offer comfort, and had simply gone about it very clumsily? In which case he was probably very offended just now. She looked at his face, preparing herself for the inevitable eruption, for a lecture about not judging people based on their social standing, for anger and derision she would welcome at this moment. It would echo her own feelings toward herself.

Instead, he took hold of her gloved hand, gently so as to allow her to pull it out of his grasp.

Her heart ached. He was too good. Too good for her.

"Not all men are like him."

She stared at their linked hands for a moment, the warmth of his skin tangible through her silk gloves. Then she looked up to find his expression just as gentle as his voice and his touch were.

"I know that. But it appears I forgot, at some point. I wish I could believe it once again."

In the silence that fell between them now, her voice seemed to echo, small and defeated and not at all the way that she used to be, before everything. Before him.

"One day, you will."

He sounded so sincere that she wondered if it was somehow possible for his conviction to seep into her through their joined hands. And though she doubted it was, she still felt a little stronger as the seconds passed in silence, their hands and gazes linked until he gave himself a little shake, released her hand, and stood up.

"I told Vivian to find Mrs. Fisher and have the carriage brought around. I am sure by now it is waiting for us outside."

Nodding, she gathered her shawl from the chaise and started walking toward the door, but she had not even made it halfway there before her courage abandoned her once more and she slowed down.

So many people witnessed what had just happened... and like Mr. Jameson, some may have guessed why.

Her feet felt like lead, getting heavier with each breath she took, until she came to a stop a few feet from the door. There was a mirror hung up on one of the two tall double doors, gold-framed and polished to dazzling clarity, but what she saw in it was anything but dazzling.

Her reflection showed a sallow young woman, hair and dress in complete disarray, her usually lively brown eyes were dull and flat, her posture limp and defeated, and for a moment, she had trouble recognizing herself.

How different she had looked when she first made her entry into high society, with graceful, impeccable posture and perfect manners thanks to her overbearing mother. She commanded every room upon entering it, even at her young age, because her mother expected nothing less. She knew how to steer a conversation in the direction she wanted it to go and to make the right partners appear before her for exactly the right dance.

Her mother pounded it into her over and over. "We earned this, Isabella. You deserve to be here just as much as anyone else."

She possessed the unchallenged confidence of a young woman of fortune, beauty, and position who knew well her place at the top of the ladder, and never even dreamed of getting pushed off—only to fling herself off for a silly affair.

Not for the first time, she was bitterly aware that she had given Dean Hayden more than just her virtue on that fateful summer night. She had given him power over her, and maybe a bit more tonight.

During months and then years of silence from him, she reassured herself that she had, by some stroke of luck, managed to evade the punishment that usually befell young ladies who misstepped as she had. She thought if she retreated from everything, there was no way this could follow her around.

Mr. Jameson was right behind her; she could feel him at her back. And now with dread and panic rising within her at the thought of what lay outside those doors, she turned toward him, desperately searching for an anchor in the stormy sea she was trying and failing to cross.

"How can I go back out there when everyone knows?"

"Nobody knows. Vivian told the old gossips that you passed up dinner in your excitement for tonight's ball. Which, in addition to the heat, must have caused your fainting spell. That should be enough to satisfy them. No one will be able to connect your distress to Mr. Hayden's presence."

"You did. And his wife will. She knows, I can tell. She knows what happened, and she probably hates me for it. She may have spread the word already that I am a liar and a temptress and a worthless, wretched creature. She will want to get her revenge, even though her husband has already taken everything from me."

She expected him to try and comfort her, to say something reassuring and gentle and futile. What she did not expect was the flash of fury in his dark eyes, the hard, unsympathetic edge in his voice when he replied.

"He has not taken everything from you; not even close. You still have your wit, and your grace, and your strength, and as far as I have seen, no one and nothing can take those from you. You are not defined by one youthful mistake, unless you let yourself be. Your value lies not in how full your dance card is or how impeccable your reputation, but in the fact that you extended a hand to an obscure young heir and his sister and helped them navigate this social quagmire. You helped me even when I did not deserve it. You are selfless and kind. You are a good person. That is what you are worth. Know your value, and never let anyone else define it for you."

His passionate words left her reeling with the possibility that he might be right. That everything he said could be true. But the veil of dejectedness that had covered her in the years and months prior to the Jameson's entry into her life had lowered over her again, dark and heavy and now weighted with burning, poisonous fear. She shook her head, unable to believe him.

"That is all good and well, but you are forgetting that I am a woman, a woman of color too. Nothing is easy for me. Not a complaint, just the truth. And in my circles, a woman, no matter how smart, strong, or accomplished, is nothing without the right man."

He looked at her for a long moment, and from the stubborn jut of his chin she could practically see him refusing to accept her words.

"In my opinion, you never could be nothing, Isabella."

Her eyes widened. Her breath trapped inside her chest. This was the first time he had ever uttered her name. And oh the way it made her heart flutter.

The timbre of his voice had shifted, had become so warm that she could practically feel it on her skin, feel his words taking hold inside of her, making her strong.

It was so intense, this feeling. So intense that she had to turn her head away for fear of being burned by it.

Just then, the door was pushed open, allowing in a flushed Vivian and a positively frenzied Eric Whitney following behind her.

"Isabella! Are you unwell? I found Miss Vivian searching for a servants' entrance and saying that you needed a way to exit the premises unseen, and I have since been sick with worry over you."

She blushed, mortified to have her friend witness her humiliation. But too overcome to think of any reassuring excuse. Luckily, Mr. Jameson saved her from having to explain.

"There is no need to worry, Miss Marin is in excellent health. She merely suffered from being hungry. But a discreet exit is exactly what we need right now, my friend. Lead the way."

Mr. Jameson extended his hand, a look of irrepressible determination on his face, and said with a voice full of comfort and compassion, "Let's get you home."

And she took his hand, holding tightly to it, all the way out to the coach waiting to take them away.

And held it all the way home.

When she lay down to sleep that night, she swore she could still feel it. The weight of it, the heat of it. And it brought her great comfort.

Chapter 14

Three days after what Elijah now referred to as, "the incident," Isabella had yet to emerge from her bed.

At least according to Vivian who visited with her for a few hours each day. And though he wanted to as well, he had yet to do so. As much to give her space as to get some.

Because also since "the incident" he found that he had started to refer to her as Isabella. No longer Miss Marin, if only in the privacy of his own head, and the one time out loud. But it was a paramount shift. One that he was entirely unsure how to deal with.

Especially since every time Vivian mentioned her name, his face would turn bright red. Or he would immediately start coughing to cover up the sudden pounding of his heart. As if his sister would somehow be able to hear it.

His awkwardness was so apparent, Vivian had taken to constantly asking if he was alright. And he would have to fend her off by inquiring after Isabella.

Isabella. He cared for her, very much. And this nasty business with a certain man weighed heavily on his mind, on his heart.

That was how he found himself making a very unexpected and definitely ill-advised visit. But it was a visit he felt needed to be made, for moral reasons if nothing else. Or so he told himself again and again.

And so, he set out, for the first time in his life, to defend a lady's honor.

He had no idea when it happened, but he was now firmly implanted in Isabella's affairs. She deserved someone who was willing to defend her. Someone to care about her happiness, her struggles, her well-being.

Something that had been severely lacking, even from her parents, this past year.

He could lie and say that he was doing it for his sister. Because she was so concerned for her friend. But what would be the point of that? He would only be lying to himself since no one else knew what he was up to.

It was the memory of Isabella's face when she told him about her dalliance with Mr. Hayden.

Her eyes haunted and tired, her voice hoarse from all the tears. What must it have cost her to tell him everything? Only after seeing her home that night did he realize that he had never had a chance to reassure her that this secret was safe with him. He could kick himself for it. Was she fretting over it? Was that the reason she had not left her home?

By his estimation she had already suffered a great deal, and he wanted to end that suffering.

And so, he walked up to this door on Park Avenue and knocked. He tried not to look as angry as he felt. That could come just as soon as he was invited in.

He would do whatever it took to protect Isabella and her reputation.

And so it came about that he descended upon the Hayden residence unannounced, ready to impress upon him, just how abhorrent his behavior was—with his fists, if necessary.

What he had not expected was to be led into the drawing room to face the man's wife. Someone he had no particular quarrel with.

So overwhelmed was he by this unexpected turn of events that he barely remembered his manners—manners that Isabella made him learn by heart during their etiquette lessons—gracing the lady with an awkward bow before he all but blurted out, "Forgive my rudeness, but is your husband not at home?"

"He is not. He goes riding in the park every afternoon. But I would be happy to pass along a message, Mr..."

She was looking at him expectantly. Of course. The footman had announced him as a visitor, and he had yet to introduce himself to Mrs. Maria Hayden.

"Elijah Jameson, madame." He bowed again.

"Right. So, Mr. Jameson, is there anything in particular you needed to speak to my husband about? You seem in rather a rush," she said as she wandered over to the large window overlooking the street. Hoping to spot her husband perhaps?

He must have looked a fright now that he paused to consider. He practically sprinted away after breakfast this morning, barely stopping to run a comb through his hair. At least he remembered all of his clothes.

There certainly was something he needed to discuss with the man, but it would be the height of indelicacy to bring it up in this situation, so he fumbled for an excuse.

"Nothing urgent, no. Just a few questions pertaining to matters of business."

She turned to regard him, the lady's face showed how little she was convinced by his excuse. Her eyes were hyper-focused on his, narrowed in suspicion. "I was not aware you and my husband had any business together. Your name does not sound familiar to me. In fact, I do not remember him ever mentioning you. And yet you felt free enough to call on him at home." She took a few steps closer to him while still keeping a safe distance.

"We have only been acquainted for a short time, and very superficially." He was lying through his teeth by now and cursing the moment he decided upon this course of action. His mother always used to say he loved to act before he thought things through. Old habits and all that.

Instead of helping Isabella, he was likely making things much worse. How had he ever thought this to be a good idea?

He needed to get out of there. He cast his gaze about the room, desperate for an escape. The door to the room was behind him, but he could not just run. That would only make him look worse.

He was a fool. A lovesick fool.

He paused, his breathing was now sharp and shallow.

Love. He loved her. He loved Isabella Marin.

Because only love would drive him to such a recklessly stupid idea.

When had it happened?

Was it her wit? Her constant teasing? Her laughter? How beautiful she looked when she danced? It was all of that and more. So many small moments weaved together to create the tapestry of his feelings.

It was everything. Isabella was everything.

Someone clearing their throat got his attention. He looked up. Right, Mrs. Hayden, still watching him.

He needed to get away from this woman's inquiring gaze and sharp questions. "I only heard from a mutual acquaintance that he made some profitable investments as of late and wanted to ask for his expertise for my own dealings."

There, that was a plausible excuse. Now to make a quick, clean exit.

"But I can easily come back some other time or convey my questions in a letter. I do not mean to impose upon your time, madame."

He bowed stiffly and made his way to the door, trying not to appear too hasty. But before he had taken not two steps, the lady's voice stopped him in his tracks.

"Did you come here to speak to my husband about Miss Isabella Marin?"

He froze, wondering if he could still flee or if such an action would only confirm her suspicions.

"Please tell me the truth, Mr. Jameson. Please."

This time, her voice was enough to make him turn back around – there was such pain in it, he could not ignore her. He might be angry, but not with her. And for him, kindness would always win out. Even with a stranger.

Never mind that after only a few short moments with Mrs. Hayden, he could see that she was not a woman to whom pleading came easily. And she was shrewd to have figured him out so easily. Because of that, he sensed that lying would do him no good here.

"I did."

Her face hardened at the words, and she clutched at the chair next to her, squeezing until her knuckles turned white, but she remained silent, waiting for him to continue. And he felt he owed it to her courage to tell her the truth.

"The night of the Whitney's second ball, three nights ago, she told me how your husband had mistreated her three years ago. I felt it my duty to see her honor protected."

Now that he had detailed his intentions out loud, he realized how ridiculous he sounded—and how angry Isabella would be if she ever found out what he was doing. Vivian too. He could only imagine the lecture and smack about the head he would receive from his little sister.

Protect her honor? He had a feeling that was the last thing she would want. And he knew she certainly did not need him to fight her battles. But he, in his helpless desire to do something, anything since she told him about Mr. Hayden, had come here and made a fool of them both.

She would likely never forgive him this folly, should she ever discover that it occurred. But it was too late now to think of all that.

Mrs. Hayden narrowed her eyes at him again, her quiet desperation now gone. And with a sinking feeling in his stomach, he knew what she would ask, what she probably already assumed. Because why else would he be here, defending Isabella's honor?

"Are you engaged to the lady, then, or otherwise connected?"

He was an idiot. An absolute idiot.

"No. We are not connected by anything other than friendship."

Oh, how he wished he could say otherwise. How in the world had it come to this?

He was a fool. A fool in love.

"But Miss Isabella is very dear to me and to my sister. And since no one else felt it their responsibility to do anything about the situation, I decided to take it upon myself."

"So, you mean to challenge my husband to a duel?" the lady asked, eyebrows raised in question, her hands knotted in front of her.

He almost laughed at the absurdity of the suggestion. Was that something people still did? Perhaps the very wealthy or the very foolish. Of which he was both, he had to reluctantly admit.

He shook his head and took a step closer to her and away from the door. His fists were clenched in frustration. "No. I mean to talk to him, impress upon him the error of his ways, and make sure he will never under any circumstances disclose to the world what happened between him and Miss Isabella."

"Why? Should not other hapless men be made aware that there is a temptress in their midst, preying upon innocent men?"

He smiled sardonically—his anger beginning to simmer again. Of course, the lady would think that. She had to think the best of her husband. He did feel for her. But he would not let Isabella's name be slandered so. "I do believe an honorable man, married or not, would not let himself be preyed upon, no matter how tempting the lady in question. Unless he wanted to be caught.

Isabella is not without some fault. But I believe your husband knew exactly what he was doing."

Something flickered across the lady's face for a moment, a sign perhaps of an unwelcome realization? And as much as he hated causing anyone any pain, he knew this was his moment to drive his point home.

"I know this must be difficult to hear, but... your husband was not a helpless victim of seduction. Nor, I hope, is he a villainous cad by nature. He may simply be a man who made a terrible decision, and now others are suffering for it, yourself included. But the fact remains that, no matter who is most to blame, Miss Isabella bears the full brunt of its consequences. And she will more so if the full extent of it becomes widely known. While your husband simply went back to his comfortable home and married his beautiful fiancée, Isabella stood and still stands to lose everything if word of this gets out. The burden to decide if the punishment for her youthful indiscretion should be this harsh lies entirely with you now. I am sorry that your husband put you in this position. That he would entertain another woman while engaged to you. But Isabella is not solely to blame here. I do not know you, Mrs. Hayden, but I hope you are merciful enough to make the right decision."

"Does she still love him?"

"I cannot speak for her or to her feelings. But I can assure you that, whatever they are, she does not intend to pursue your husband. She merely wants to get on with her life without having the threat of ruin hanging over her head every waking moment. You can give her that reassurance by promising to keep your knowledge of the affair to yourself. And persuading your husband to do so as well. He owes her that much. And if he is any kind of a decent man, he will do it."

There was a long, heavy silence as she pondered her decision. All while he tried to calm his nerves and keep his mouth shut. This moment would decide if he had made a very grave mistake in coming here; if instead of helping his friend, he had only exacerbated her situation.

"Very well, then. I will keep quiet if she promises to stay away from my husband."

"I am sure that is a promise she will be more than happy to make." If he ever dared approach her with it, of course. For his part, Elijah would much prefer it if Isabella never found out about this visit.

His words once again triggered a change in Mrs. Hayden's demeanor, a softening of her features, and when she spoke again, she sounded melancholy, almost defeated.

"Whatever else you may be to Miss Marin, you are a good friend. I hope she values you accordingly."

He did not know how to respond to that, to something that spoke directly to his heart. So instead, he focused on Mrs. Hayden. On how grateful he was for her easy acceptance.

"She owes more gratitude to you, madame, for being gracious and forgiving."

And with a bow and a kiss of her hand, he took his leave.

Only time would tell if he had done the right thing.

***

Four days. Four days of sitting by her bedside, holding her hand and trying to make her smile. And apparently Vivian had enough.

At least, that was the impression Isabella got as her friend barreled into her room with a barely there knock and a mouth full of sass.

"I must say, I am very disappointed in you," Vivian said to her in lieu of a greeting.

She opened her mouth to defend herself but was denied the opportunity, as Vivian bowled over her half-hearted response.

"I expected better of you than to hide yourself away in here."

"I am not hiding. I was merely overcome with a summer cold. You know that, you were here only yesterday."

"Yes, you look quite at death's door. The same as yesterday. And the day before that. And the day before that," Vivian said with a roll of her eyes. "Meanwhile I have been fielding invitations, fending off gossiping old biddies, and Elijah is running about town defending you left and right."

Isabella stopped cold, taking a moment to breathe before setting aside her book as she tried to process those words. How exactly was Mr. Jameson trying to help her? And why would he do such a thing?

And defending her to whom exactly?

That thought alone was unnerving enough to propel her to her feet, feeling the need to be ready for whatever calamity Mr. Jameson, she still could not think of him as Elijah, was about to bring to her door. She quickly grabbed some clothes and ducked behind her screen to get dressed.

"What did he do?" she asked, trying not to sound as panicked as she felt.

"Who?"

"Your brother."

"I merely meant to impress upon you how your friends worry when...'

"Vivian," she snapped. Her patience was gone, and she needed the truth, or she may well combust.

"He went to confront Mr. Hayden," she said quietly, the worry plan in her voice.

Still in her chemise, Isabella stepped out from behind the screen again to stare at her friend, feeling the blood drain from her face and freeze in her veins.

Vivian hastened on, clearly hoping to reassure her. "He did not tell me until after the fact. I do not think he was planning to tell me at all. But I could tell something was up and I got it out of him. Do not worry, though, no harm was done. He did not even meet the cad at home."

"There was no duel or other such nonsense?"

"He had no intention of challenging the man. Elijah detests violence. And he said you would probably be very angry if he killed him. Though I am sure that was a joke," she said with a laugh, though she did not look entirely convinced now.

What a mess.

"In this moment I think I might not be too unhappy if Mr. Hayden killed him. How dare he take such action on my behalf."

Despite her righteous anger, she regretted her words the moment she said them. The thought of losing Mr. Jameson filled her with cold dread. And what a tasteless thing to say to Vivian.

"I am sorry, Vivian. I did not mean..."

"Oh, there is no need to apologize. Elijah can be a bit rash and stubborn. And thick headed. Our mother always used to say he was inclined to act before he thought. It is quite understandable to be upset. He really had no right to interfere. Even if it is because he cares for you so."

She blinked, both from the shock of Vivian labeling someone else as rash. But also...

Mr. Jameson cared for her?

She knew. Yes, realistically she knew this. He had shown her that night, treating her with kindness and respect. But it was another thing entirely to have his sister confirm it, and with such nonchalance.

Vivian continued on none the wiser. So she put those thoughts away for now.

"But you must believe me, no harm whatsoever will come from his visit. Your secret is still safe."

"How can I be sure of that?"

"Because Elijah made sure of it." Stepping closer, Vivian took Isabella's hands in hers. "You have helped us so much these past months. Now you need to trust that we can help you. Can you not find it in yourself to do so?"

Could she?

On the one hand, the thought of Mr. Jameson acting so impertinently on her behalf was infuriating, and the possibility that he might have only exacerbated the situation filled her with dread. On the other hand, she was incredibly moved by the idea that he had taken it upon himself to help her, to defend her, to believe her and her story without question. It was more than anyone had ever dared to do for her, and she wondered how on earth she deserved such devotion.

If Elijah had failed in keeping the man silent, she was as good as ruined. But if he had succeeded, then she may yet have hope for her future.

With a shaky smile, she grabbed her friend's hand, squeezed it tight, and said, "I can certainly try."

Vivian squeezed her hand in turn and then squealed with excitement. "Wonderful. Now we shall enjoy the delights of the season together once more. It is flying by. I can hardly believe we are already into July. You have been sorely missed these past few days, let me tell you. Elijah makes everything boring and educational. You provide the fun."

She laughed. It was nice to be seen that way., as someone who provided joy. No one had ever told her that before.

While she continued to dress, Vivian rattled off a list of places she had been forced to visit, much to her chagrin. It seemed that, in her absence, Mr. Jameson had dragged Vivian to lectures and museum tours. Things that left the girl itching to get back out amongst her peers.

Isabella had barely finished tying the back of her dress when Vivian was dragging her out the door, still complaining of the injustices she had suffered through.

"And then we hardly got to speak for being positively beleaguered by ladies. It is no exaggeration to say that they fell upon us in droves; it was the most ridiculous thing."

That particular piece of information lodged itself in her mind, and suddenly putting on her glove seemed an impossibility, her movements turning fitful and imprecise.

Vivian did not seem to notice.

"And Elijah seemed to enjoy every moment as I stood there waiting, can you imagine?" Vivian prattled on as they descended the stairs. "Oh, but here he is now."

She looked up, breath catching as her foot hit the floor. Her face suddenly felt hot. For there was Mr. Jameson, standing in the hall with her father, presumably having returned from lunch at the club. They went several times a week together as she understood it. She still had not decided if she liked that particular development or not, Mr. Jameson and her father being friends.

Not when her own feelings for the gentleman were so hopelessly tangled up with their shared past and his apparent oblivion to it.

Vivian skipped down the last few steps, completely at ease. Not a care in the world for all that had occurred over the last few days.

And Mr. Jameson? He was looking at her. His coffee-brown eyes full of warmth and tenderness. Her pulse pounded and her skin felt tight. When he looked at her that way, it was hard to think straight.

She had to pour all her energy and focus into the simple task of walking, of moving closer to him. And by the time she reached him, all she could think to do was smile. No curtsy, no polite greeting, nothing. She could only smile because she was so very happy to see him there. She had not realized just how much she missed him until she was in his presence again.

He seemed nervous, likely thinking she was about to scold him for his actions. But she had already decided to forgive him, and so she did the only thing she could think of and winked at him.

He laughed. Light and airy and carefree, his shoulders relaxing and the tension visibly draining from his body. And then he graced her with that smile she loved so much. Soft and sweet and a little shy.

"Well, Mr. Jameson, your sister has lured me out of my room. Have you come to whisk me away from my home?"

"You have wholly uncovered our nefarious plan. I was ordered to suggest taking a walk in the park, to tempt you with the promise of fresh air."

So off they went, her hand securely tucked into the crook of Mr. Jameson's arm, and Vivian and her father following close behind.

The sun was shining and there were birds singing and the grass was a beautiful bright green.

And when Mr. Jameson stopped to pick a wildflower and presented it to her, her stomach swooped, and her smile widened. And for that moment, everything felt right.

Chapter 15

After her brush with scandal, Isabella was admittedly reluctant to be fully out again. Try as she might, the specter of trouble followed her wherever she went. So nervous was she that she often imagined Mr. Hayden was lurking around every corner just waiting to spill her secrets.

But she found distraction with Mr. Jameson and for that she was endlessly grateful. Over the past week he had allowed her to teach him all manner of innocuous tasks. He pretended to be interested in learning to sew, asking question after question about different patterns, and he indulged her daily stroll through her garden as she picked bouquets to give when she paid calls. He followed her around with a basket, the smile never leaving his face.

But for her next endeavor, she resolved to teach him how to steer a horse-drawn carriage. Something he would actually enjoy. And if anyone asked, she would swear up and down that it was not her idea.

The gentleman had, rather unwisely, mentioned his inheritance of a rarely used but well-cared-for Phaeton during a visit to his club. At which point several of the gentlemen present had invited him to join them for trips to the countryside. The only problem was, Mr. Jameson did not know how to drive.

Even more surprising was that he was the only one who did not see a problem with this. That she knew how to drive, and he did not would be another fact to file away in the category of things she would enjoy teasing him about.

"I never needed to know how," he said, trying to defend himself when she had questioned his lack of skill.

"Then I shall be the one to teach you," she had happily declared the previous day during their usual walk. "We cannot very well have you making a fool of yourself, can we?"

"No, we cannot have that," he said, looking at her with a wistful expression she was not able to decipher.

Being a somewhat proficient driver was one accomplishment she usually kept hidden. "It is so unlady like, Isabella," her mother always complained.

But being fiercely fond of her independence, she had long ago pestered her father into showing her how to drive their trusty old cart. Over the years, she progressed to practicing with her father's Phaeton in an attempt to cheer herself up during a particularly boring summer when she was fifteen. In short, she had been spoiled into possessing the very skill Mr. Jameson now needed, and there was no question of not passing it on.

As always, she dutifully voiced her doubts about the appropriateness of the scheme, though she hardly meant it. And as always, she had been summarily ignored.

It was a dance that she and Mr. Jameson were experts at by now. She would come up with a fun and absolutely inappropriate idea and pretend that it was his. She would swear up and down it could never be done, and he would ignore her until she relented. Both of them laughing and smiling the entire time.

It always made her think of their activities as children. Running wild and causing mischief, but always managing to avoid being caught. She no longer waited with bated breath to see if anything triggered his memory. But there was always a single ember of hope in her heart.

"You are truly a menace, Miss Marin," he would say. That twinkle in his eye that hinted of mischief making her heart flutter.

At the very least, she managed to convince her father to have his groom drive the carriage out of town so they could begin practicing out in the country, far away from prying eyes.

Or so she thought.

She, her father, Mr. Jameson, and Vivian found a secluded little park with a pond, agreeing that it would be the perfect place to have lunch the driving lesson was over. It was a perfect summer day, as it had been almost the entire season thus far. The air was warm, but not humid. The skies were clear and the greenery was bright and lush. She could not remember a more perfect summer. And as she watched her companion steer the carriage effortlessly, she wondered if he was not the reason it felt that way.

His presence in her life like a light chasing away all the darkness.

After taking a few laps around a small copse of trees, the party descended to partake of the picnic they brought along. While Vivian spread out their blanket and rustic feast, Isabella was busy demonstrating to Elijah the proper care of the horses when a lone carriage approached.

She intended to pay it no mind, only glancing up out of sheer curiosity—and promptly froze mid-movement. For the man approaching them, on a curricle so high-seated it bordered on the ridiculous, was none other than Mr. Hayden.

She had expected to run into him again, had told herself to be strong if she did, to not let her fear overtake her. But she was not ready for him to suddenly burst into this most innocent moment.

Not wanting to let him see her discomposed yet again, Isabella stepped out from behind the carriage to greet him with a perfectly executed curtsy. She would take a cue from Vivian, no thoughts, only actions.

Mr. Hayden's cart came to a stop aside theirs, and he let his eyes rove over the small party. Her father was heavily engaged in his book, and for that she was grateful. It would spare her having to lie to her father.

The man's eyes came to linger on her for a long moment, his face softening into a wistful smile that she was almost tempted to return. Fool that she was.

He was still a snake. And a terrific actor. And nothing about him was genuine.

His smile disappeared as suddenly as it had come when Mr. Jameson stepped up beside her. She glanced at him and them at Vivian who was lurking quietly in the background. She had likely guessed who the man was if she did not recognize him from the night at the ball.

While her father, thankfully, still did not seem at all interested in the situation. Bless his heart.

Mr. Jameson shifted closer to her, their shoulders and arms now touching. His body was tight with tension.

Mr. Hayden said with a nasty smirk, "I do believe we have recently become acquainted, is not that right, Mr. Jameson?"

She glanced at him, shock likely evident on her face. Why had he not told her they had met? Last she heard, they had not crossed paths. His eyes widened slightly before softening, and his hand brushed up against hers. An apology.

They could discuss it later.

Mr. Jameson nodded curtly in reply. "Yes, at the club."

He supplied no further information,

Mr. Hayden nodded at the Phaeton behind them. "I see you are practicing with a fine vehicle. Care to take it for a race?"

Isabella groaned inwardly. What trouble would this lead to? He had probably heard about Mr. Jameson's lack of skill and intended to show him up.

His suggestion was met with silence. Thank goodness.

She watched Mr. Hayden closely because he likely was not finished. Had he always been this obnoxious, and she had been too taken with his pretty face and charm to notice?

"Every peer worth his salt ought to be able to boast of having won at least one race. What do you say, Mr. Jameson, would you like to try your hand at it right now? At the very least, it will impress the ladies."

He glanced at her as he said this. He was goading, making her friend out to be less than because he did not possess a certain skill. The nerve of this cad.

Her friend had remained uncharacteristically calm. Noticing his unusual restraint, she felt a surge of pride. He had apparently taken her counsel to heart and decided not to make a scene in public, and for that she was both grateful and flattered.

And so very proud. He had come such a long way.

But of herself, she was ashamed. Here was a man who had wronged both her and another innocent woman, who now taunted her very dear friend. And she was resolved to say nothing for the sake of propriety?

That would not do.

Before she could think better of it and before anyone else could get a word in, she grabbed Mr. Jameson's hand and pulled him around the carriage away from prying eyes.

"You will race him," she whispered.

He laughed, actually laughed at her. "Isa—Miss Marin, you cannot be serious?"

And now she laughed. "Have you ever known me to back down from a challenge?" she asked, eyebrows raised in question.

"But he did not challenge you, he challenged me."

"And you would do nothing? It is only a race, you can do this," she said as she touched his arm in reassurance.

He watched her for a moment, maybe steadying himself, and then he nodded and climbed onto the seat.

She climbed atop the seat next to him, pushed the reins into his hands, and said in her most haughty voice, "Mr. Jameson will be happy to accept your challenge."

A flash off to her left caught her eye. Vivian was practically jumping up and down, excitement clear on her face. At least they were all getting some entertainment from this unprecedented situation.

Mr. Jameson gave her a short, determined nod as he gripped the reins tightly. He was ready to begin. It sent a secret thrill through her that they knew each other so well now that they could communicate such things with just a look.

Mr. Jameson maneuvered the Phaeton into position next to Mr. Hayden's and then motioned for Vivian to come forward and give them a starting signal. She did so eagerly, waving her handkerchief with an expert flourish.

Only moments ago, she had been smiling and happy. But the look she gave their opponent was so full of disgust and hatred, Isabella wondered how Mr. Hayden did not drop dead immediately.

She was immensely proud of both of her friends today.

Her father, she noted, was still blissfully unaware, now having fallen asleep on the picnic blanket. It would be quite funny if they were not in this current situation. They could all have a good laugh about it later.

She watched as the wisp of linen fluttered down to the dirt path at Vivian's feet, and off they went. She felt the wind whip against her face, the hair at the back of her neck loosening slightly from its knot. She breathed in deeply, wanting to remember this particular feeling of freedom for as long as possible.

For a short while, they were matched evenly, their horse's head-to-head as they raced along the broad country road. But soon, Mr. Hayden pulled ahead.

Perhaps it was the fact that his vehicle was lighter than theirs, perhaps his horses were fresh out of the stable, or perhaps he simply managed to urge them faster, but he kept pulling further and further ahead.

Suddenly, Mr. Jameson was nudging her arm and looking down quickly at his own hands before glancing at her. Was he having some kind of trouble? With a growl, she yanked the reins out of her companion's hands and found that they were entirely too tight. She loosened them a little, and the horses promptly sped up. She turned to shoot Mr. Jameson a questioning look, only to find him already watching her, smiling at her, head cocked toward the road ahead of him.

Her brow furrowed in confusion, she glanced at him quickly. He was still smiling, with a smugness that was not there before. She turned her eyes back to the road; they were almost head-to-head again. Had he tightened the reins on purpose to get her to step in?

His next words confirmed her suspicions.

"Go get him, Isa. You can do this."

Isa, he had called her Isa. And oh, the way it filled her with joy, like air filling her lungs. Mr. Jameson. Elijah. Her Elijah. He knew her, and she adored him for it.

Go get him, he said. You can do this. And so, she did, giving the horses the full reins. Within minutes she caught up before completely overtaking him. And then she was racing ahead at full speed, triumph surging wildly through her.

Her hair had finally come loose from the wind, strands of it whipping about her face, and her arms were soon straining with the effort of holding on to the side of the box so as not to go flying off.

But she need not have worried. When a bump in the road threatened to topple her over the side, Elijah's hand closed around her arm and held fast. And she could devote all her attention to winning this race, with her partner by her side.

Soon Vivian came into view, indicating the completion of their lap, and she urged the horses on one more time. They were almost two full lengths ahead when they passed their starting point and officially cinched the win.

She pulled the horses to a stop and turned to face Elijah. For now that she had a moment to think, he was Elijah to her, her very dear friend. She whooped with delight and then threw her arms around his neck, squeezing as tight as she could.

He hesitated for only a moment before wrapping his arms around her waist and squeezing far more gently.

"You were amazing," he whispered, his breath tickling her ear.

She breathed him in, reveling in this quiet closeness, this moment just for the two of them. Before she could speak, the moment was broken as their opponent pulled up beside them.

She pulled away reluctantly to meet Mr. Hayden's eyes, and she found him levelling her with a disdainful look.

Instead of congratulating them on a well-earned win, he remarked,

"I fear the company you keep is not doing you any favors, Miss Marin. I would sooner expect such a reckless display at a corner pub than around persons of our rank."

How had she ever liked this man? He was the most ridiculous and petulant child.

Instead of defending herself, she simply burst into laughter—clear, loud peals of it that echoed across the fields. The fact that it was not proper to do so was not lost on her, and she was sure Vivian would call her out on it later, if only to tease her.

But she could not help it. To be laughing in the face of the man who had risked her ruin, was the most delightful thing she could have ever imagined.

With one last disgusted look in her direction, Mr. Hayden cracked his whip and sped off.

Gradually her laughter died down, and she was able to regain her breath and her composure. She had never behaved so shamelessly in her entire life—or felt such triumph.

And she had but one person to thank for it.

Turning to Elijah, she laid her hand gently on his arm and said, "Thank you. Thank you so much."

"I did nothing you could not have done by yourself."

She blushed. The confidence he always seemed to have in her was nothing short of breathtaking.

"Perhaps not. But you gave me an excuse to do it, and for that I thank you. You are a true friend."

He smiled bashfully, looking this way and that as his hand came up to rub the back of his neck, knocking his cravat askew in the process.

"I assumed it was the best way of giving you a chance at vengeance short of handing you my pistol and calling for a duel."

She laughed. "You do not have a pistol. And a duel? Perhaps if this were seventy or eighty years prior."

"Lucky for Mr. Hayden, then."

"True. Because I just might have taken you up on the offer."

"I do not doubt it."

The smile accompanying his words was warm, affectionate, and perhaps held a hint of pride—just enough to make warmth blossom in her chest.

She wanted to touch him again. To tell him all the things he made her feel. But she could not bring herself to do it. Instead, she quickly clambered off the seat and took up a spot on the blanket with her father and Vivian.

And proceeded to ignore Vivian's broad grin.

Elijah joined them moments later, seated so close to her that their arms repeatedly brushed against each other.

And thus passed the shadow of her first season, chased off by sunshine and laughter and the unexpected, unmitigated triumph of winning her first race.

Chapter 16

With Isabella persuaded to return to society as his sister's companion, Elijah was not ashamed to admit the relief he felt. It was good to be back to business as usual as the season continued to move on. Those few days without her felt like an eternity.

Yes, because he missed her. And he loved her. A fact he was still having trouble processing. But also because having to keep his sister entertained was an incredibly difficult task.

Thankfully the two ladies returned to their regular activities with relative ease. Paying calls and volunteering their time at charities and attending a few gatherings. All the while he, Mrs. Fisher, or Mr. Marin were asked to chaperone whenever necessary.

Mrs. Marin was never included. Something he learned to appreciate. On the rare occasion he came in contact with Isabella's mother, he got the distinct feeling that she did not really care for him. As evidenced by the fact that she never said more than two words to him if she could help it.

But his sister was in good hands, his relationship with Isabella strong. And for the first time since he began his new life, he could say that he was happy. He could now focus the majority of his attention on his own affairs, namely the running of his business. He settled into a routine of being in the office from 8 a.m. to 3 p.m., five days a week. His evenings were spent either at his home, or the Marin's, and on occasion, the club. And the weekends were filled with all manner of high society activities with Isabella and Vivian by his side.

He had come to enjoy his work: learning to understand where materials came from, how they were made, and where they went. And he was surprised to learn that some of the buildings he passed by each day were ones built by his company. It was living history, and he was happy to be a part of it.

He had responsibilities, people to look after, and he'd be damned if things went sideways under his care. With Mr. Marin as his new teacher, he learned new things every day, greedily soaking up whatever knowledge his friend passed along. Though the man was honest enough to admit his own shortcomings.

"You ought to be schooled by my wife in these matters—in her hands rests the true bulk of our affairs. That is why she so often travels back to our home in the country while I remain here with Isabella."

That must be why Mrs. Marin was rarely seen. He assumed it was her obvious dislike for him. But perhaps he was regarding himself too highly to think that the lady would be absent solely because of him. Isabella would say that was his big ego getting ahead of itself again.

He laughed quietly to himself, and Mr. Marin continued on with a smile and a soft chuckle.

"You see, my wife is the pragmatic one. Me, I am too prone to get lost tinkering and experimenting and would soon let our house burn down above our heads if left to my own devices. But this puts me in mind of a most promising scheme," Mr. Marin exclaimed. "As soon as the season is ended, you and your sister will simply have to accompany Isabella and I to Marin House and stay for a while. You will learn as much from my wife in a single day as I would teach you in a week. And the hunting is fantastic in our little corner of the world. And that I can most certainly teach you well."

The idea greatly appealed to him. He sometimes heard Isabella speak of her home to Vivian, in such reverent tones that he had become quite curious. The place must be a veritable Garden of Eden to make the pragmatic Isabella turn so lyrical. He was eager to see the place for himself, and curious to see the lady in her natural habitat, among the wildflowers and long grass. Where he imagined each day would see her looking as radiant and happy as she sometimes did here, as she had when they danced, when she joked around with Vivian, and, most freshly impressed upon his mind, when she beat Mr. Hayden at their race.

He would give almost anything to see her so happy all of the time.

The lady had bewitched him, and she did not even know it.

Would he ever have the courage to tell her?

***

But life intervened, as it was wont to do, when Vivian received her first offer of marriage some days later.

And then promptly turned it down. It should have been an omen of things to come.

His little sister being proposed to was incredibly polarizing for him. On the one hand, finding a husband was one of their tasks this season. And among the young bachelors he had met so far, Mr. Whitney was as well-meaning, polite, and well-situated as he could possibly wish a young man to be.

And Isabella vouched for him, which was another mark in his favor.

On the other hand, his sister was still so young, and he was loath to part with her.

But no sooner had he begun to accept the idea of her marrying did Vivian announce her decision to reject him.

And Elijah was left reeling.

All of his questions as to why yielded no results. Vivian simply and emphatically stated that while she liked and respected Mr. Whitney greatly, she could not find it in her heart to marry him.

And Elijah in turn could not find it in his heart to try and persuade her to change her mind. After all, his sister's happiness was not to be subordinate to any other matter, marriage included. And had he not money enough now to allow Vivian to make her own choices no matter the result?

So, the matter was settled with relative ease. But there seemed to be something in the air where marriage was concerned. Because only days after Vivian turned down her proposal did she offer him another interesting piece of information.

"Isabella has a suitor," she shouted at him upon bursting into his study with no preamble. He had been attempting to balance the books. He had an accountant for this, but he was trying to learn things himself. And he was failing miserably, which of course made him think of Isabella. She was good at this sort of thing.

He sat back in his chair and looked up at Vivian, confused and hoping desperately he had heard wrong.

"She what?"

Vivian rolled her eyes, seemingly annoyed at his confusion. "Isabella. Our Isa has a suitor," she said, placing her hands on her hips.

He knew exactly why he was not happy about this news, but why not his little sister

"What happy news for her," he ground out, wishing suddenly that Isabella's suitor was such a terrible and unpleasant person as to make it impossible for her to accept his attentions.

It was incredibly petty of him, but he could not find it in his heart to care right now.

"I would not be so sure of that. The man puts me in a bad humor, always going on about his many accomplishments and his social connections. And Isabella clearly cannot stand him, yet she encourages his attentions."

That gave him pause. He looked up at Vivian, eyebrows raised in question. Isabella was hardly the type to hide her feelings. He knew that from experience. So why would she pretend with this man?

Or was she not pretending at all, and Vivian was merely projecting her own feelings onto the situation?

It was not an impossibility. In fact, it was more likely than Isabella pretending to like someone.

Hope was gone again.

"Perhaps she really does like him, and you are only seeing what you wish to see?" The words hurt him as they left his mouth, but they had to be said. He only wanted Isabella's happiness. And if she had any romantic feelings for him, he would know by now. He continued on, "Plenty of people start out at odds and still find themselves falling in love."

Wishful thinking on his part, but Vivian did not need to know that.

She gave him a strange look. "I know that. But I am quite sure this is not the case here." She fell silent momentarily, pondering something. "We shall have to keep a close eye on him, find out what kind of man we are dealing with."

"I do not believe Isabella would appreciate such meddling."

"Psh, meddling! We are merely looking out for her. Isabella is our friend, after all—we cannot let her marry just anyone." With that bold last statement, she was off again, banging through the door and stomping down the hall.

The noise put a smile on his face. Vivian never did anything subtly or quietly, and he hoped that would never change.

He sat back in his chair; eyes fixed forward on nothing in particular. The clock in the room struck two as he recalled Vivian's words. "We cannot let her marry just anyone."

On that fact, at least they were agreed. But while Vivian's intentions were honorable, the way he felt for Isabella made his decidedly less so.

Would she ever forgive him if he meddled in more of her affairs?

He honestly was not sure. And he was not willing to risk her presence in his life to find out. His aching heart be damned.

But as it turned out, Vivian was about to make more trouble than Elijah ever bargained for, and it all started with that turned down marriage proposal.

***

He was used to letters changing his world in the span of a few seconds.

But he never expected this letter.

He had just returned from yet another ball, this one particularly exhausting. A ball during which he spent the entire night watching Isabella fawn over a certain suitor. A Mr. Carlisle, who in Elijah's opinion, looked every bit the smug cad. And he wanted so badly to express those feelings to his friend, especially when he could see how vexing she found the man.

But he could not find the courage to do it. So, he left as soon as was acceptable and expected to return home to his sister who was laid up in bed with a cold.

Only he found an empty house and a letter addressed to him sitting atop the mantle in the sitting room.

The letter in question turned out to be the only trace of his supposedly sick sister in an otherwise empty house, and no sooner had he read it that he turned white as a sheet and sank down on the nearest chair, completely stupefied.

He did not know how long he sat there when suddenly there was a great commotion outside the door and Isabella burst in, holding a letter also bearing Vivian's handwriting.

His stomach dropped. This was no joke. He had hoped in his desperation that maybe Vivian was having a good laugh somewhere over this cruel trick. He was angry, of course, but he would forgive her after giving her a stern lecture.

But Isabella standing there in front of him tore that hope to shreds. When had his hands started shaking?

"Elijah," she yelled. "Vivian—she—! Oh, good lord, did you get a letter, too?"

And even in this moment of uncertainty, hearing his name on her lips for the very first time made something tighten in his chest.

She was still out of breath, and judging by her slightly damp hair had run here through the soft drizzle showering the trees outside.

Water dripped on the floor in a steady cadence, and her hair was plastered to her face.

His fingers twitched, the urge to tuck a wet strand behind her ear so strong, he clenched his hands tight.

Dammit. He needed to focus.

He nodded dumbly in answer to her question and held out the letter for her to read.

She did so while anxiously pacing the length of the room.

His eyes followed her every step.

"I cannot believe her. Eloping? What is she thinking? What is he thinking?"

The "he" in question was Mr. Dugray, Isabella's friend and his and Vivian's patient and faithful dancing instructor—or so he had thought.

How could this have happened right under his nose? Under both their noses, he thought as he watched Isabella.

"But there has to be some sort of explanation. It cannot be as she writes. I cannot believe Mr. Dugray would ever do such a thing... he is an honorable man," she lamented, sounding very close to tears.

She was likely taking this very personally, and he did not blame her. It was the same for him. He had failed as an older brother.

"Even honorable men do dishonorable things if they fancy themselves enough in love," he said through clenched teeth.

The remark likely came out sounding like a very mean-spirited comment on her own history, and he regretted it immediately, but thankfully she ignored his interjection.

"Of course, we must go after them immediately. How fast can your groom have your carriage ready? Although perhaps we should rent one instead. It would not do to be recognized once we begin our search. And we shall need money too."

He was now staring at the letter still clutched in her hands, thoroughly overwhelmed by the night's events and only roused from his stupor when Isabella stood before him, hands on her hips, to look at him expectantly, her eyes were full of fire.

"What are you waiting for? Will you not go after her? Oh, but we must!"

"We?" he asked with a furrowed brow. The word croaked out through a painfully dry throat. He pulled at the collar of his shirt which suddenly felt too tight.

"Of course, I am coming with you," she said, her voice hard and determined.

"Absolutely not. Vivian is my sister. My responsibility."

"And mine as well. I was the one who promised to guide and chaperone her, to keep her safe from fortune hunters and rash decisions. I was the one who introduced her to Mr. Dugray. This is my fault, and I will not be kept from trying to prevent an even more dire outcome. So either you take me with you, or I will be forced to sneak into my father's coach house and take our coach myself."

"You would not do such a thing."

He almost laughed. She absolutely would and he knew that. But he had to try and put her off. This was his burden to bear. And he did not want her to have to shoulder it too.

"Come now, Elijah," she said with a smirk. "You know me better than that by now."

Her eyes were all fire and smoke. Just the way he liked them most.

Did she have any idea how much he loved her?

He studied her quietly for a moment. Everything from her defiant glare to her stance—solid as if she was readying herself for withstanding an attack—told him that to try and dissuade her from accompanying him would be a waste of precious time.

But a little while later, as he took her silk-gloved hand to help her into a hackney carriage, he thought perhaps it was better this way.

To not be alone in this.

To be with Isabella, who was equal parts strong and savvy, and determined to brave the coming storm with him.

What more could he possibly need as long as he had her?

Chapter 17

Only an hour later they were on their way through the city in a rented coach just as Isabella had suggested.

Under normal circumstances she would have poked fun at Elijah. She would have teased him about how he was wrong, and she was right, that he could not have stopped her from accompanying him and they both knew it. The whole thing would have been such fun.

But she had not the heart to make him feel any worse than he likely already did.

In truth, seeing him this way, so dejected and miserable put her on edge. His hands were clenched tight, his shoulders hunched, his foot tapping endlessly against the floor of the carriage. She was so used to hearing him laugh and seeing him smile that the absence of those things was like a darkness seeping into her veins.

So cold and hollow.

And she wished nothing more than to offer comfort, but could not see a way to do so without showing her heart completely.

Instead she focused on problem solving as her companion was in no fit state.

It had taken some time and a fair amount of money to convince the postmaster to rouse a driver and ready a set of horses at this late hour, but it was worth every penny if they were able to prevent trouble.

The letter indicated Vivian and Mr. Dugray ran off to a small town upstate. Apparently, a man there was known for marrying couples in secret.

How in hell would people even discover such a thing?

She would certainly have a few choice words for Mr. Dugray when they came upon him.

By the time they finally left the city, sun soon started to rise in the east.

She spent the majority of the time coming up with ways to minimize the scandal. All while Elijah stewed and simmered over his apparent failure.

"We could bring her to Marin House. Hide her away for a few weeks. I could stay there with her while you return to the city. Should anyone ask, I was called home when my mother suddenly fell ill, and Vivian accompanied me to be by my side in this difficult time. My mother lives reclusively enough that no one should have visited her while we were on the road. None will be the wiser."

She looked at him, eyes beseeching, hoping to pull him from his misery.

But poor Elijah could scarcely muster the enthusiasm to respond with more than a meaningless murmur and instead turned his head away to stare out the window.

She could not fault him. Worry and tiredness were so clearly etched upon his face that she was sure the image would forever be burned into her memory.

She wished nothing more than to be able to smooth those worries away. To trace the lines and contours of his beautiful face and feel the softness there. To feel the lips that made her laugh and the mouth that riled her up. The sun-kissed skin that reminded her of sand, warm beneath her fingertips.

She fell silent then.

There was no point to her forced cheer and false reassurances. She knew he would not hear a word of it until his sister was safe again.

The next few hours passed in anxious silence, revealing a bleak, overcast day that did nothing to lift her spirits.

The slow, torturous passage of time allowed her to agonize over when and how this event could have occurred at all.

She had let Vivian down. She had let herself down. And she had let Elijah down so shamefully.

After all, had it not been her responsibility to not only introduce Vivian to society but to keep her far away from its many pitfalls and temptations?

Should she not have guarded the girl against this? Especially after her own failed attempt at an elopement. Did she not know better?

Perhaps if she had not been so focused on her own mistakes. If she had not been so focused this past week on entertaining the suitor her mother had insisted upon, the suitor she was trying to rid herself of as soon as possible, perhaps she could have prevented this.

If only she had been honest with Vivian about her past.

Elijah likely blamed her as well as himself. How could he not?

She should have seen the signs, should have recognized what she had once experienced, an independent and headstrong girl falling for a handsome man.

Elijah could never have. No matter how hard he tried. He could not possibly be expected to spot the first signs of a tender attachment formed by a young female heart.

But looking back, she could see it, what was happening right under their noses.

The way Vivian always managed to bring up Mr. Dugray in conversation, the subtle changes in how she interacted with other young men, the over enthusiasm for every dance lesson.

Too little, too late.

When Elijah at last spoke, she half-expected him to rebuke her himself. Instead, his voice was tense but gentle, yet so sudden it made her jump.

"We should stop soon. Get some rooms for the night. You must be exhausted."

She shook her head emphatically. "We would lose too much time. Better just to change horses and push on. I am fine."

"I cannot force you to spend another night on the road."

"You are not forcing me if I am perfectly willing to do so."

He looked skeptical, his eyes shifting back and forth and his eyebrows raised in question, clearly about to protest another time. The man was entirely too stubborn for his own good.

And that was coming from her.

But she was determined not to let him. She had done enough damage; she would not let him waste precious time for her comfort, even if every bone in her body ached from being tossed about at this punishing pace and her arm was sore from trying to hold fast to the door.

"One night without a soft bed will not kill me, I assure you."

He only nodded in acknowledgement, what little energy he mustered to speak gone again.

And so, they continued as she suggested, only stopping to partake of a brief meal as their horses were changed and their driver took his leave in exchange for a better-rested substitute.

Although she meant what she said and her determination to find Vivian was quite unwavering, she found, as the day wore on, that she was exhausted. Her eyes drooping shut in regular intervals long before the sun had fully set.

Not that she could have slept. With every step the horses took on the rough road, the carriage shook and rattled, and she shook and rattled with it.

To make matters worse, she had not had time to change out of her silk evening gown and tightly-laced corset, making her both cold and uncomfortable.

So there was no risk of her falling asleep on poor Elijah, she thought as she watched him. He had not dozed off once. How exhausted he must be.

As if he had sensed her thoughts, Elijah chose this moment to turn his head and fix his eyes on her, studying her for a long moment while she tried to look brave and unaffected. But all her efforts were powerless against the cold, and try as she might, she could not stop from trembling with it.

He pulled back slightly to hold out his arm, his coat billowing out like a giant bat's wing. Were she less tired, the sight would have made her giggle. As it was, it only confused her.

"What are you doing?"

"Come here."

"Why?"

"So you can have some of my warmth and be at least moderately more comfortable. We have a long ride and a difficult mission ahead of us. Since you insisted on accompanying me, you should make sure to rest so you can be of some use when we reach our destination."

She rolled her eyes. This man. He always had to have the last word.

That, too, had not changed from childhood.

Oh, but that offer, it was tempting. Between the cold, her uncomfortable attire, and being tossed about in this rickety menace of a vehicle, it would be just what she needed.

But for all their recent intimacy and her feelings for him, being so close to him was beyond unthinkable—not just for propriety's sake but because her insides had developed a habit of tightening like a spring whenever he touched her.

So she silently rebuffed the offer, lulled by the landscape rushing past the window against a rapidly darkening sky.

Her resistance lasted until the next bump in the road sent her into the side of the carriage. It was only Elijah's outstretched hand on her arm that kept her from smacking her head on the window.

She was sure he only intended to steady her, instead she ended up draped across his chest, her face a mere hand's breadth away from his.

"Now will you stop being so stubborn?" he asked, his rasping whisper sending chills up her spine.

Heavens. He was so warm. Deliciously, enviably warm and, judging by the way he leaned back into the cushions, rather comfortable as well. He had no wretched pieces of clothing inhibiting his breathing.

In short, he was everything she was not right now, and everything she wanted to be. And being this close to him felt so very good.

Too good.

Too tempting to resist. So, she would not. But first, she had a problem that could only be solved with his assistance.

She should not even be considering asking this of him,

But she was so terribly uncomfortable.

She moved to sit gingerly on the edge of the seat with her back turned to him. Slipping her cloak off, she turned to look at him over her shoulder. With a racing heart and deceptively calm voice asked, "Would you be so kind as to play the lady's maid and untie the laces on my corset so I can loosen it?"

When her request was met with silence, his eyes wide and searching hers for the hint of a joke, she rushed to explain, "My maid laced me up so tight for the evening that I can scarcely move. I will not be able to do much leaning like this."

"I should not... That is, I could not possibly," he stammered, a blush now staining his cheeks.

She had never seen him so flustered.

It was adorable.

She rolled her eyes, attempting to keep her cool, even as she felt anything but. Of course he should not—he should be nowhere near her corset.

And she should not have considered this an option, letting him undress her, let alone suggest it out loud. But she wanted to be warm and comfortable, and she would not rest until she was, impropriety be damned.

"You were the one to offer to make me more comfortable. Are you rescinding that offer now?" He would not be able to resist a challenge, especially one coming from her.

Silence again, for so long she was starting to get impatient. No matter that his hesitance was entirely justified.

Then, suddenly, she felt his fingertips on the back of her neck, so very warm, but shaking ever so slightly.

He was nervous.

His hands were rough and clumsy as they felt around for a button to undo the top of her gown.

Taking pity on him, she reached back to unfasten it, trying to ignore the flash of heat that shot through her when their hands met, and he sucked in a sharp breath at the contact.

With the first barrier out of the way, she tried to focus on something, anything else while he pushed aside her gown and petticoat just far enough so he could fumble around for the laces.

His uneven breathing was harsh in her ear as he bent his head to get a better look at things.

Her mind refused to focus on anything besides his hands, and the heat of them through the thin material of her gown, and so very gentle on the exposed skin of her lower back.

A promise. A whisper of what could be, if only she would let it.

The carriage hit another bump, and he reached out to steady her, hands coming to rest on her waist.

He gave a gentle squeeze, and she only just managed to stifle a groan.

As his hands slid back up to her laces, she could feel the callouses on them, no doubt a remnant from his past life. The contrast of rough and smooth was heaven and sin made real.

The feeling served as a stark physical reminder of who she was with.

This was Elijah. Her friend. A man with no romantic designs toward her.

And yet, his touch evoked a scorching desire within her.

Already her cheeks were burning, her breath coming in short, shallow gasps, that she only prayed he took no notice of. She needed this delicious torture to end.

And yet, when the knot finally gave and he released his hold, allowing her a few moments to loosen her laces before buttoning up her dress and releasing her again, she found that she already missed the feeling of his skin on hers.

She shuddered and yanked on her cloak with such force she nearly tore the fastening.

She dared not look at him as she scooted back on the seat and folded herself into his side. She sat stiffly, and determinedly stared straight ahead.

For several moments, he simply left her like this, propped against him like a lifeless doll.

But the cold seeped in again and she shivered.

In a flash, his arm was around her shoulders and her form molded to his side, allowing him to wrap her into the fold of his overcoat. The delicious wave of warmth washed away the last of her decorum, and with a little sigh, she wrapped her arms around his waist, allowing her icy hands to be thawed by the heat radiating from his chest.

It was a situation unlike any she had ever found herself in before. She felt both incredibly comfortable and a little uneasy.

Was she forcing herself on him?

"What is the matter?" came his deep voice from somewhere above her.

"What do you mean?"

"I can practically hear you thinking."

She laughed. "I only just—That is, I only wondered if I was making you uncomfortable?"

His soft chuckle ruffled her hair. "You could never make me uncomfortable."

She smiled about to respond when she felt the ghost of a kiss pressed to her hair.

Or perhaps that was just her wishful thinking as she finally drifted off to sleep.

And in her dreams, she heard his voice.

"Sleep now, Bella. Sleep."

Bella. No one had ever called her that before. No one.

Chapter 18

The second day of their trip found Elijah in quite a state, his head spinning with worry.

He was worried about his sister, of course he was. Was she safe? Was she now Mrs. Dugray? Did she regret her course of action?

But there was nothing at all that could be done about it, not if they were already married. There was only gossip and judgment to face. Nothing new for him, really. He still hoped they could stop it. But the journey had given him time to accept what may happen. He would always be there for his sister no matter what.

Perhaps that was why, even though he was concerned for his sister, he also found himself reliving memories of last night, and then chastising himself for doing so.

It was not only the thought of what had happened that consumed him, but what he wished would have happened. When Isabella allowed him to open her dress to expose her neck, he had felt the overwhelming urge to press the softest of kisses to her beautiful, golden skin.

When her hair, tousled and half-undone as it had become from the rough trip, brushed the backs of his hands, he itched to touch it and run his fingers through the dark rivulets, like water on a hot summer's day.

When his hands moved beneath the fabric of her dress to peel it from her body, he had desperately wanted to keep going, to beg her to let his fingers travel down further until they met the bare skin of her lower back.

To travel around the soft curves of her waist, over and up her stomach, just to the bottom of her breasts. So hot and full. Not small like many of the other young women.

No, Isabella was perfect. Her body in all its fullness was perfect. And he longed to set his eyes upon it. His hands ached to travel down over her belly button, lower to the top of her mound. Lower and lower into the wet, warm heat of her, fingers dipping in and out. A perfect moment.

So many unexplored roads leading to the sweetest of treasures. Just the thought of it threatened to undo him.

He glanced over at Isabella. The hour was still very early, and she was sleeping peacefully curled against his side.

Waking next to her, safe and warm in his arms did something funny to his heart, and he was loath to let her go, but they still had a task to complete. So he focused his thoughts on the day that lay ahead of them.

One more change of horses and they would arrive at the village. The task then would be to find where Vivian was hiding. She would be angry, he knew. And so, the situation was to be managed delicately.

He would try so very hard to keep his anger in check. Perhaps Isabella would help him do that? She was always a good buffer between the two Jameson siblings.

Isabella would need to keep a very low profile. It was best that both of their presences in town be kept quiet.

Apart from her father, who she had managed to get a note out to yesterday morning, no one knew what they were up to. And he made no objection, likely because he believed Elijah's intentions toward his daughter were only that of a friend.

That was for the best. And he hoped for everyone's sake they could keep it that way. If not, they would soon be in a scandal of their own.

They would also need a place to stay for the night, so he and Isabella could have a proper rest. And a larger carriage for the return journey because they would be traveling home with Vivian

With all this to think of, he could not afford to idle in improper thoughts of his traveling companion. She risked much coming along on this journey and he was determined to show her the respect she deserved, even in the secrecy of his own mind.

She deserved that and so much more.

And in the cold gray light of morning, his fantasies were made to seem all the more unlikely. But perhaps that was for the best. Perhaps that notion would make it easier to accept that what occurred the night before would never happen again. That it likely meant nothing to her.

No matter how much he wished it did.

But in the darkest, coldest hours of the night, before he had allowed sleep to claim him, Elijah let those thoughts run wild.

Dreaming of days and nights spent with Lady Isabella Marin. Their bodies joined together in love. Their lives tangled together in every way that mattered most.

But it was not to be. And there were more important things to think of.

He was tired and weary, and fear for his sister's safety was never far from his thoughts. So, he had taken some comfort from the soft, supple body pressed up against his. He savored the scent of her skin, vanilla and jasmine, and her soft breathes against his neck. His own skin dotted with goose flesh at the feel of her mouth so close to him. With her safely in his arms he drifted into a deep sleep. Who could blame him for taking comfort from her just this once?

It was nothing more than that. And it never would be.

When the sun finally crested the horizon, he disentangled his body from hers and shifted down the seat. She woke slowly, confusion in her eyes as she watched him.

"Whatever is the matter, Elijah?" she asked, voice thick and rough from sleep.

If only she knew.

He shook his head, offering her a smile. "Nothing at all. It is only that we will be making our final stop in a few moments. I am going to step out and stretch my legs. You should go back to sleep."

He shrugged out of his coat as they came to a stop and covered her with it.

"Oh, no. You will be cold. You do not need to—"

He cut her off, giving her a sharp look. "I insist."

She smiled and then nestled comfortably into the folds of the coat, burrowing her face into its collar with a little sigh.

He exited the carriage, breathing in the dew-filled morning. His body was sore and achy. His throat was dry, and his skin felt itchy and tight. He needed a drink and a wash. But such luxuries would have to wait for a little while longer. He walked a few feet down the road and back, stretching his arms above his head as he went. His back cracked and popped in that satisfying way. He took a deep breath of cool fresh air, the invigorating feeling of sunshine warming his back.

He stopped to chat with the driver for a few moments to make sure he was fit to continue on. Once he was satisfied with the man's answers, he climbed back inside the cab. Only this time he took extra care to give Isabella ample space. He would not allow himself to be lulled by her again.

By the time their carriage approached the border of the little village, his head was filled to bursting with thoughts of his sister, his entire body coiled like a spring with nervous tension.

Isabella must have noted the change in him because she scooted down the seat to fit herself against him again before taking his hand in hers and squeezing it tight.

If her unexpected gesture had surprised him, it was nothing compared to the effect of her next words, and the confidence with which they were uttered.

"We will find Vivian. I am sure of it. Just as I am sure that she is safe and happy. No matter if her actions were wrong, your sister is quite smart. She can handle herself well, no doubt thanks to you. And whatever you might be feeling now, understandably so, Mr. Dugray is a good man, an honorable man."

"Honorable?" He could not help but sneer, wholly offended by the thought. "I see no honor in this situation. Quite the opposite I would say."

"Do you not trust my judgment? If you cannot have faith in them, have faith in me, Elijah."

His heart ached. He felt like such a failure, letting his sister run off like this. But he looked at Isabella, that lovely fire burning in her eyes and the fight went out of him. He wanted so much to be like her, so strong and confident. But he could not find either of those things in himself just now. "I cannot seem to find faith at all. Not even in you."

She pulled his hand up with hers to rest them intwined together against his face, cradling it.

"Then I shall have enough faith for the both of us."

As was so often the case, her words stunned him into silence—her earnest optimism and gentle sincerity only deepened the hold she unknowingly had on his heart.

It gave him just a little bit of hope.

It was this small sliver of hope that he clung to now, turning his hand under hers to cradle it in his palm. The contact calmed him enough to stop the nervous fidgeting of his legs.

And Isabella, no doubt reassured by the barrier of her silk gloves between them, let her hand remain in place.

***

Isabella began the second day of their wild journey confused and angry.

Her head was well and truly a mess.

For a few blissful, dazed hours between sleeping and waking last night, she felt warm and safe and cherished in a way she never had before.

But then she remembered where she was, in a carriage on the way to prevent her friend from falling into scandal. She remembered what she had done last night, what they had done, what she had asked Elijah to do, and the reality of it all came crashing into her.

She should be embarrassed, ashamed. But that was the problem; she felt neither of those things. And that harsh truth was enough to chase away the bliss and peace of those quiet hours.

Heaven help her, but she was in love with him. The past two days had made that perfectly clear.

She loved him. And so she was afraid. Because Elijah had overlooked her improper behavior before but how many more times could he see proof of her indecency before he decided that she was a bad influence on his sister? Or a stain upon his own character? This blissful state would not last, it could not last.

Not with the baggage she carried. Not with their shared past still unknown to him. How would it look in his eyes that she had never spoken up about it?

She could not bear the thought of it.

Which was why, as they entered the village and she noticed the worried tension in his body, tangible even through the layers of clothing between them, she could not leave him alone in such a state. She wanted to be there for him the way he always seemed to be there for her.

And he seemed to take strength from it.

"You are too good to me, Isabella," he whispered, his face now so close to hers.

"Not at all," she whispered back. "Quite the opposite, really."

His eyes. She could get lost in them. And those lips, so full, red like the brightest summer berries.

She shifted closer, drawn to him the way she always seemed to be.

To have this man rely on her for strength when her very life strove to convince her of the inferiority of her own sex was a completely surreal experience. It filled her with so much gratitude and love for him she could hardly stand it.

And it only made her all the more determined to see this current predicament they were in put to rights.

Vivian and Mr. Dugray had at least a six-hour head start by their calculations. Which meant that there was still hope that the two were not yet married.

They were able to procure a room at the small inn in town, the lobby was warm and inviting, with light oak furnishings and wall's the color of a robin's egg. This turned out to be a great first stop because the innkeeper was a terrible gossip, a short middle-aged woman with a mop of blond hair pinned to the top of her head, and she was all too happy to point them in the direction of Vivian and Mr. Dugray.

They found the aforementioned gentleman in the blacksmith shop of all places. He was sat near the door, in a pose that suggested he had been waiting there for quite some time. He was roused by the slam of the door as they entered and immediately stood up to greet them.

What must they look like? Hair wild and clothes wrinkled from travel and sleep. Not that such things really mattered in situations like this one. But she would have paid good money to see her reflection right now.

She opened her mouth to demand answers from the man as to Vivian's whereabouts, but she never got that far. Because the moment Elijah spotted his sister's presumed husband, he launched himself at Mr. Dugray with a sound she could only describe as a feral roar, stopping short a mere hair's breadth from his face to snarl, "Where is my sister, you scoundrel?"

The man did a remarkable job at keeping calm as Elijah gripped his jacket tightly, and he replied evenly, "She is at my aunt's home in the neighboring town while I have taken lodgings here. No one has seen us alone together or heard of her intentions to elope. Your sister's reputation is perfectly safe. But I still have every intention of marrying her."

"The hell you will," Elijah snapped as he raised his hand, drawing it back for what she could only guess would be a very sound punch.

She only just managed to catch his arm mid-air, hanging on to it with all her strength.

"Enough! This will not solve anything."

For several long moments, Elijah hesitated, remaining poised for a fight, but she would not relent.

"Elijah, please," she whispered.

He looked down at her, so much hatred in his eyes. But also, so much pain. "Please," she said again. "Violence will not solve this problem." She squeezed his arm, reminding him of the position he was still in.

After a few tense moments, she felt him relax slightly and lower his arm. Her own fell back to her side.

Elijah stepped back until the two of them were shoulder to shoulder. She was about to speak again when he uttered in a low, menacing tone, "Well then, let us solve this like gentlemen."

And to her horror, pulled a wad of bills from his inner jacket pocket.

"How much?"

"Excuse me?" Mr. Dugray asked, his eyes wide and full of confusion.

"How much will it cost me for you to disappear from my sister's life for good?"

Mr. Dugray drew back as if the very suggestion caused him physical pain.

Isabella scoffed. She loved Elijah, and she understood his anger, but in this moment, he reminded her far too much of the worst kind of man. The kind who believed they could buy their way out of anything. This was not her Elijah.

Mr. Dugray stalked forward and shoved his finger into Elijah's face. He cut an imposing figure in his well-made suit. "I will not be bought off. I love your sister, and the only reason I will ever turn my back on her is if she tells me to."

By now, every single person in the cramped blacksmith's shop was watching the exchange. And she began to worry the longer they drew attention to themselves, the more likely that someone would recognize them.

And then the secret would be out and Vivian, along with herself and Elijah, would be well and truly ruined.

She spoke up before either man could say another word. "Perhaps we should discuss this with all concerned parties present. And in a much more private setting."

Elijah's eyes met hers for a brief moment before settling on Mr. Dugray again. From the rage still flickering in his dark eyes, she worried he may still try to hit the man. But it seemed the desire to see his sister won out, because he nodded once and turned to Mr. Dugray again.

"Very well then. Bring me to my sister, now."

He stormed off, presumably to procure a vehicle, and she and Mr. Dugray followed quietly behind him.

The pair stood near the entrance to the inn while secured their carriage. Mr. Dugray turned to her then, a sad expression on his face.

"I hate to see you tangled up in this affair, Miss Marin. I am sorry for it."

He sounded genuinely upset, and odd as it may be, that filled her with hope and relief.

He continued on. "I never wanted it to happen this way. Vivian and I talked of marriage, yes, but I had intended to formally ask for her hand, to do things the proper way. But a recent proposal spooked her, and then she was at my door two nights ago asking me to elope. She would not be put off."

Isabella laughed in spite of herself. That sounded so like Vivian. "No, I expect she would not. But if she was so set on an elopement, how did you convince her to go to your aunt's house instead?"

"I told her we could marry immediately, that I knew of a man who would marry us in a town upstate. The second part was true,

I do know such a man. But I made the driver change course later on."

"Could you not have dissuaded her before ever leaving town together?"

There she had him. She could see from his embarrassed expression.

"Perhaps, I could have. Or perhaps she would have made a scene in the street. I love Vivian deeply, but she is too impulsive for her own good."

She looked at him, waiting for further explanation. She would not stop until she had the whole truth.

He straightened up and looked her right in the eye as he said, "But more importantly, I did not want to dissuade her. And that is the whole truth of it, God help me. Vivian was afraid her brother would forbid the union, and I could not accept that. I am a selfish man where she is concerned, I freely admit that. But I know in my heart that we are right for each other, even if the union would not be considered a conventional one."

"And yet you did not get married."

"Because I could tell Vivian was unhappy about going behind her brother's back. She was quite distraught by the prospect of getting married without his approval. That is why she left him that letter."

"And yet you would now force his hand in the matter?"

He had the good grace to look ashamed, but there was also a hint of mischief in his eyes when he said, "We live in a world of classes, Miss Marin. A world divided by rules and money. But love does not know it. And I could never turn my back on a love like this."

He continued on, his tone a bit more serious now. "And as much as

I regret seeing you dragged here, I wonder if perhaps your presence may not turn out to be a blessing. You seem to have Mr. Jameson's ear. Could you not plead our case with him?"

She could not blame him for asking such a thing, now that she knew the depth of his feelings for Vivian.

But she was still so very angry with both of them for acting with so little regard for anyone else's feelings. She had seen firsthand the pain it caused Elijah. The worry and, she suspected, a feeling of betrayal at his sister's refusal to confide in him.

But she also saw the earnest guilt in her friend's eyes, heard the way his voice softened when he said Vivian's name. And he was right, society's rules were not in their favor, not in Vivian's and especially not in his.

Despite being more kind and accomplished than any well-born gentleman she knew, Mr. Dugray spent his life being overlooked or outright snubbed by most in high society. Only called upon to teach them his expertise, but never seen as an equal. The same way it would have been for her if her father had not made his fortune.

If anyone deserved happiness, it was him.

"I will not attempt to persuade Mr. Jameson against his own conscience. But I will tell him what you told me and let him make his own judgment with all of the relevant information."

He inclined his head in gratitude. "Fair enough. Thank you, with all my heart. You are a true friend, and I hope your involvement will not be to your detriment."

She could only hope. But that hardly mattered now. She was here for Vivian and Elijah. There would be time to worry about her own reputation later.

"He may not be as contrary to your cause as you fear. Mr. Jameson may be strict where his sister is concerned, but he is not without feeling."

He seemed surprised at her words, or perhaps at the softness and confidence with which they had been spoken, she realized too late.

But he was kind enough not to voice his thoughts, falling quiet instead as they spotted Elijah marching toward them.

His eyes were still all fire, his voice all thunder, when he ushered them into the vehicle, and his countenance during the trip was so hostile she did not even attempt to make conversation.

And she was admittedly angry at him for trying to bribe Mr. Dugray. She resolved to speak to him about it when they were back home. That kind of behavior was not something she could allow to pass unchecked.

She could only hope finding his sister safe and sound would make him more inclined to listen to the lovers plead their case. If not, she feared brother and sister might never recover.

Chapter 19

On the journey, Elijah had ample time to plan what he was going to say to his sister when he faced her.

But as they neared their destination, his anger settled and turned mostly into a heavy sadness. He was still angry, but he was also just incredibly worried for her safety. Having a little time to process his feelings made it clear, he was angry because he was afraid. And now that he found her, he could freely admit that.

They were ushered into the home by Mr. Dugray's aunt who immediately sent Isabella and Mr. Dugray out into the garden so the siblings could have a moment alone in the sitting room. A courtesy that Elijah would forever be grateful for.

The moment he laid eyes on her, he felt nothing but intense relief. All he wanted was to hold her in his arms.

Vivian must not have sensed this, because by the time the door clicked shut behind him, she was already standing to face him, looking as if she were ready to fight for her very life.

And he was not the least bit surprised.

"Just so you know, you have nothing to accuse Mr. Dugray of. He was a perfect gentleman the entire way here."

She sounded rather disappointed about that. He resolved not to dwell on it, for the sake of his sanity.

"We were never alone for a moment, except in the carriage, and one can hardly be compromised in a carriage."

And suddenly he was overcome with a cough, choking on his gasp of surprise. He knew full well just how compromising two people could be in the confines of a carriage.

He forced himself to take deep breaths. This was not about him, and if Vivian somehow managed to guess the direction his thoughts had taken, he would never hear the end of it.

But his own circumstance did give him pause. Was Mr. Dugray just like him? A man completely and utterly lost to the woman he loved. Could he really punish the man or his sister for being brave enough to act on their feelings? Especially when he was not? After all his talk to Isabella about women being more than their virtue, he supposed it would be rather hypocritical of him to apply different standards to his sister. And of course he knew that Vivian was smart and empathetic and beautiful no matter what she got up to when unsupervised.

But he was still afraid for her. She had a thick skin, that was true. He just did not want to see her hurt by unkind gossip.

And even if, by some stroke of luck or some of Isabella's magic, they managed to keep the whole affair a secret and get Vivian properly wed, the decision would have consequences.

With a heavy sigh, he sat down in the chair next to Vivian's an uncomfortable brown leather monstrosity that made him feel very small. His own home could use some redecorating, but at least his chairs were comfortable. And the walls weren't a garish red like almost every open surface in this room. He settled in and finally asked the question that had plagued him the entire way here.

"But how can it be that neither myself or Isabella had any inclination of what was going on with you and Mr. Dugray? I feel like quite the fool."

Vivian let out a laugh, the loud, sharp kind Isabella worked so hard to train out of her. "The two of you would not have noticed me entertaining every single young man who ever showed me interest because you were so distracted by each other."

A blush heated his cheeks instantly. How had she guessed his secret? He thought he had been so careful to hide his real feelings. And if Vivian knew, would she tell Isabella? The thought turned his legs to jelly, his palms were now slicked with sweat. He opened his mouth to offer some weak protest, but she cut him off with an impatient wave.

"Yes, yes, I know, you have never felt more than friendship and respect for Isabella, just like everyone else who knows her must respect her..." she rolled her eyes, then fixed them on him with a devious glint. "But if you give me leave to marry Mr. Dugray, I promise not to tell her of your true feelings."

"Blackmail, Vivian? I did not teach you that, and I doubt Isabella did either."

"Oh? So she is Isabella to you now? Not, Miss Marin?" she said with a smirk.

He fixed her with a glare, and she continued on.

"Perhaps I taught myself, since it seems to be the only way I can get anyone to respect my wishes around here. And just in case you had forgotten what they are, I shall remind you. I wish to marry

Mr. Dugray, and I wish for you to give us your blessing." Her voice softened and her eyes took on their characteristic warmth as she took his hand. "You are the only family I have, Elijah. I would hate to be married without you by my side."

As always, Vivian's honest affection threatened to sway him. He always found it hard not to give her everything she wanted.

He squeezed her hand before speaking. "I do not wish to miss such an important event in your life either. But you must understand even with the money I have set aside for you from the inheritance, Mr. Dugray will not be able to give you the kind of lifestyle you have become accustomed to. I daresay even someone as talented and respectable as him does not make buckets of money from giving dance lessons."

"And I will not mind. I have been used to a far different lifestyle for most of my life, as have you. We have lived on much less, and have we not been happy anyway? Money can only give happiness where there is nothing else to give it, to quote a famous author."

"And does Mr. Dugray agree with you on that point?"

Her face hardened.

"You mean does he only want to marry me for our new money? If he does, he is the best actor I have ever seen."

"But you admit that there is a chance? Your portion of the money is a large sum by any standard. Not to mention as your husband, he may have access to circles he is currently banned from."

"Or I may be banned from them as well. Come now, Elijah, you have lived among those people too. Does it not seem just as likely they will shun me as welcome him? This is the same stock of people who abandoned us when our mother fell pregnant with me. They turned their backs on us. As did our own family. I do not begrudge you accepting this new position; in fact I think we deserve it. But I would much rather be with the man I love and be shunned by society than the other way around."

He was stunned. Not by her determination, but by how well she had taken stock of her situation, and how calmly and maturely she had delivered the results of her examination. It was not an impudent child sitting before him, nor a flighty, overly romantic young girl. At some point, Vivian had grown into a woman who had chosen her path in life and would stick to it, come hell or high water.

He could not have been more proud, no matter his worries for her.

"You are quite decided, then?"

"You may know more of the world than I do, big brother. But I know my own mind. And I certainly know my own heart."

A sudden lump in his throat delayed his reply, but when he finally managed to choke out the words, Vivian's smile was everything he needed to know he had made the right decision.

"Very well then. It seems you may call yourself a bride soon."

Vivian's answering shriek was ear-piercing.

***

Before they were to return to the city, they had resolved to spend some time at Marin House. This was so they could claim that this was where their journey had taken them all along.

He was curious about Marin House and to see mother and daughter together in a more intimate setting. The way he imagined his mother would have been with Vivian were she still here.

The carriage jolted as it rolled over a pothole, and he was pulled back to the present. Vivian dozed on the seat next to him while Isabella watched him from across the small space.

"What was your mother like?" she quietly asked.

He stared at her for a moment. She always seemed to know what he was thinking. It reminded him of what his mother used to say, "Your face is an open book, my dear. So easy to read if one pays enough attention." The idea Isabella paid him enough attention to read his face filled his heart with joy.

He smiled. "In a word? She was strong. And fiery. Like Vivian." He chuckled. She was kind and always encouraging. We did not have a lot of money, but we had a lot of love. His cheeks reddened, and he ducked his head. "I am sure that sounds cliché."

Isabella leaned forward and grabbed his hand. "It does not. It sounds lovely. What was her name?"

"Abigail."

Isabella smiled. "I wish I could have met her."

"Me too." His chest constricted with the words. "I miss her so much. And yet I am so angry with her." The words were difficult to say. They felt harsh, but if there was anyone who would not judge him, it was Isabella. She squeezed his hand. Encouraged, he continued, "She used to tell us that she left her family for love. They did not approve of my father, so she ran. It turned out her family was right, but she would not go back. I do not know if it was her pride or if she was truly happier in her new life, but Vivian and I grew up not knowing anything of our family."

"Did you question her about it?"

He laughed. "All the time for a while. But eventually she put her foot down, and I did not push. I could tell it upset her. Looking back, I realize I was trying to protect her, to spare her feelings by avoiding the topic. But she was my mother," he snapped. "She was supposed to take care of me." He had never let his frustration about this show. It felt good to let it out, to raise his voice in frustration, to not hold in his feelings all the time. "I had to take care of Vivian after she was gone. We could have had family, safety, security, but she chose not to tell me anything. It is hard to reconcile the loving mother I knew with one who kept so many secrets. I do not know how to let my anger and love for her coexist."

Isabella cupped his face in her hand, and he leaned into her touch. "I cannot pretend to understand," she said. "But I do think it is alright for you to feel all those things. It is hard to realize our parents are only people. They're flawed and they make mistakes."

He loved how understanding she was. He smiled softly. "I know she would have loved you."

"Do you really think so?"

He nodded, "I do. You have been so good to us. A great friend to Vivian. You are invaluable to us."

She pulled away from him and gazed out the window next to her. His chest grew tight. "Have I upset you?"

She looked back at him, worry creasing her brow. "Sometimes I wonder if my mother truly loves me. I mean, logically I know she does. But I do not always feel it. Does that sound ridiculous?"

He shook his head. "Of course not. As you said, you are allowed to feel however you want. I do not know your mother well. But I would venture to guess she only wants the best for you, even if her methods and delivery do not make it seem that way."

She chuckled. "You are entirely too kind, Mr. Jameson." She relaxed into her seat once more. "Thank you," she said sweetly. "For being here with me."

"There is nowhere else I would rather be."

They settled into silence as the carriage rolled along. It was true, he would always prefer to be with Isabella than with anyone else, but he was nervous. He was well aware that Mrs. Marin did not much care for him, if her reception of him earlier in the season had been any indication. She must think him not good enough to be associated with her daughter. But his love for Isabella made him eager to leave her with a better impression.

And he wanted to know that his impression of her was not entirely accurate, that she was more like her daughter than she had previously let him see.

Only upon meeting her again did he see that she was not. She reminded him of Isabella on their very first meeting: Cool, correct, and very much displeased by his very presence in her home.

Chapter 20

In hindsight, Isabella ought not to have expected her mother to approve of her impulsive actions.

She was sure to hear about it later if the scathing glare her mother gave her before greeting their guests was anything to go by.

Her mother was the picture-perfect hostess, readying food and rooms and offering them free use of the gardens and library. The four of them proceeded outside to the gardens for a walk before dinner, and as soon as the siblings were out of earshot, her mother turned to her with a reproachful expression.

"Spending two, nearly three days alone on the road with an unmarried man? What were you thinking, Isabella?"

"I... there was hardly time to think. I only wanted to help my friends as they have helped me many times over these past few months."

Her mother's lips tightened into a thin line. "You know your father and I do not believe in this society's insistence on constricting and controlling a young lady's every move. We have certainly offered you a great many freedoms and have been disappointed before. I would hate to see the same thing happening again. Have you learned nothing at all from what occurred with Mr. Hayden? Repeating the same mistake twice becomes less a mistake and more of a pattern."

This was why she wanted so very little to do with her mother. Because of the way she felt when they parted. That she would never be good enough.

"Elijah needed me," she practically shouted. "I—I mean they needed me. He and Vivian both," she said quietly, glancing ahead to be sure her outburst was not overheard.

The two siblings were talking animatedly, none the wiser.

As she turned her gaze back, her mother's features softened, but the worry in them remained.

"You care for them both. That is admirable, to want to help them. To help him. But what about what you need, Isabella—a secure position, a smart match? Your situation is already precarious because you are not without a blemish on your reputation. Was helping them worth the risk? Because I should think not, and I expected better judgment from you."

Isabella fell silent, watching as the siblings emerged from between the rows of hedges, taking in the view of the sweeping natural gardens before them with exclamations of awe and delight. She knew what she should say, what she should feel—that nothing and no one was worth losing sight of her future.

But would it be much of a future without either of them in it? Without Vivian's infectious laugh or Elijah's beautiful smile. And the way he looked at her as if she was the very sun that lit up his days. No one made her feel the way he did. She was not willing to give all that up. But did she really have that luxury?

Elijah did, even with his new status. He was a wealthy, white man.

"But perhaps you have already started making plans toward that end?"

Her mother's tone of voice pulled her from her fantasies, and she followed her gaze, which was now fixed on Elijah. She sighed, rubbing her forehead where a headache was starting to bloom. Did her mother miss nothing? She could not have this. Not when there was no hope in it.

She shook her head vigorously. "No. Nothing of the sort has been said by either him or me. He cares for me as a friend only."

He knew her dirty secret. And while she knew he did not think less of her for it, there was no way he would take her. Not when another man already had. Besides that, he had never made any suggestion that he saw her as anything more than a dear friend.

"And what of the things that have not been said?"

"No such things have ever taken place."

It was not an outright lie. But it was also not the whole truth either. Elijah's behavior in the carriage had been nothing less than honorable, which Isabella could easily explain as a sign of indifference toward her. But there were other moments to disprove that theory: small touches that lingered where they should not have, glances that felt like they bore straight through her skin and to her very core, and feather light kisses to her hair as she drifted off to sleep.

Were these actions only that of a friend? She hoped not, but she dared not dream.

And even if those things meant what her mother was implying, such intentions need not necessarily end in marriage, as she well knew from experience.

"Mind, I am not saying you should marry him. Rich or not, he was not raised to live the way he does now, and no doubt knows little of our values. His allowing you to come along on this wild excursion certainly proves that."

Isabella rolled her eyes; her mother knew so little of her. "He did not allow me anything, Mother. I hardly gave him a choice but to let me come."

"Perhaps. But I am certain he put you in a position where you felt the need to accompany him in the first place."

"I felt the need to accompany him because I felt responsible for Vivian's well-being. She was placed under my tutelage, and I failed to support her when she needed it the most. The only way Mr. Jameson could have prevented that would have been by forbidding my presence in his sister's life altogether."

Which he might have tried to do very early on in their relationship, but she was not about to tell her mother that.

"And considering the situation you are in, would that not have been for the best?"

Her steps faltered on the path, so overwhelmed with anger at her mother's harsh judgments. Could she not see how much the siblings meant to her daughter? Did she care so little for her happiness? How could she not see that they were not so different from the Jamesons? Isabella was not born into this life.

In fact, she and Elijah had started in exactly the same place. But there was no way she was going to bring that up. It would only make things worse.

Her stomach soured at the thought of never knowing Elijah and Vivian as she did now. What would these last few months have been like without them?

Much lonelier, she was sure of that. She likely would have tried to hide away here, avoiding her mother at every turn until she was forced to interact with the first eligible young man who showed interest.

There would have been endless shouting matches between mother and daughter and many fake smiles.

Instead, this season was filled with laughter and happiness, despite her precarious circumstances. And that was all down to Vivian and Elijah.

If only her mother could understand that.

"It does not matter now. They are in my life, and there they will stay no matter what you think of them."

With those final words, she rushed ahead to join her friends, linking her arm with Elijah's as they stopped to admire a bed of roses.

***

They stayed at Marin House for two more days, and Isabella did everything she could to avoid being alone with her mother. Meals were filled with awkward silence and stilted conversations. There was no way the siblings did not notice the frostiness between mother and daughter but neither commented on it.

The day of their departure Isabella was packing up her things when her mother finally broke the silence, walking into her bedroom and taking a seat next to her on the bed.

"Isabella," her mother said quietly. "I do not want to leave things like this."

Isabella shook her head. "Things are always like this between us, Mother. You tell me all the things I am doing wrong and then you go off to do your own thing. Why are you free to do as you please but I am not? I only want the independence you have. You run this house when father is away on business. You manage the finances. Why can you not see that I want what you have?"

Her mother looked momentarily stunned, eyes going wide before regaining her composure. "I am married, Isabella. That is where my freedom comes from. I would not be able to live this way if not for him. I love him dearly; I am lucky in that. Many women are not so fortunate. That is why I want a good match for you. So you can have security and freedom."

Isabella took a deep steadying breath and spoke, "And Elijah would not give me those things? You would rather I marry a stranger?"

"His position is precarious. There is no guarantee he will succeed at keeping his grandfather's business afloat."

Isabella scoffed. "There is no guarantee the man I marry will be as kind and loving toward me as Father is to you. You would risk my unhappiness for the promise of money?"

"It is not so simple," her mother snapped.

"It is," Isabella snapped back. "But clearly you do not care. Now, please leave. I have to finish packing." She turned her back, effectively dismissing her mother. She had never spoken to her that way. Her heart pounded and her hands shook, but she breathed a sigh of relief that the words were out there. All she could do now was carry on and hope that maybe they had an impact.

She did not know what her future looked like, or whether or not Elijah would be a part of it as more than a friend. But maybe speaking the truth to her mother could be the first step in letting Elijah know exactly how she felt about him.

Chapter 21

The ride back into the city was long. Isabella entered her home in a dress that was rumpled beyond help, hair that was no doubt a tangled mess, and a weariness that demanded she sleep for a very long time. The promise of the comfort of her own bed called to her like a siren song.

Instead, she was ushered into the drawing room and greeted there by her father and Mrs. Fisher. She fought hard against the urge to roll her eyes. Now she had to sit and make small talk in her dirty clothes and itchy skin, covered in days of travel.

Mrs. Fisher stood up and moved swiftly to her side, grabbing both of her hands and squeezing tightly.

"Isabella! Oh, you poor dear! I came as soon as I heard. Of course everyone is talking about it!"

She glanced at her father, brows furrowed in confusion. Had something happened while they were away?

He cleared his throat before speaking. "I had trouble believing it myself, and yet everyone was so convinced…"

There was real pain in her father's voice, real concern on Mrs. Fisher's face, and dread slowly filled her as her mind raced through all of the terrible things that could have happened. Had someone died?

"Father? I am confused. Whatever is Mrs. Fisher doing here so late? Did something happen while I was away? Are you both alright?"

She knew, of course, what must be wrong. But she would not panic, could not panic, until she knew the full extent of the damage. And there must be damage, surely? Or else her father would not look worried. He was the most calm and agreeable person she knew.

His worry scared her more than anything else ever could.

Mrs. Fisher pulled her over to the couch. "Oh, you poor thing. Do you know nothing? You'd best sit down then; it is positively shocking." The lady waited for Isabella to get comfortable and then continued. "The whole city is talking about it. That you spent days alone with a young man in a carriage, and that you ran away to elope. Now, surely there is a very good explanation for such a rumor? An innocent mistake that led to its being spread falsely? Sadly, your father seems to have not been informed about the matter at all."

She looked over at her father, levelling him with a stern glare. He knew exactly what occurred, that there was nothing untoward. Why had he not relayed this to Mrs. Fisher? Did he not believe her intentions? The thought of it was enough to steal her breath. She could not bring herself to even look him in the eye now, could not bear to see him so angry and disappointed.

"There is a good explanation, but the bare facts are correct. I did take a trip upstate, but it was not I who eloped. I went to help a friend with the most honorable companion imaginable."

Mrs. Fisher sat down next to Isabella with a deep sigh. "I was hoping you would deny the whole thing. But I am glad to know the truth. Though I assume there is more to the story?"

Isabella nodded slowly, unsure of how much she should reveal. Obviously, her father had not informed their friend of the true reason for her absence, either because he did not believe it to be true or because he was trying to protect Vivian. She wanted to ask him, to plead her case, to defend her actions. She had expected this reaction from her mother, not from her father.

She was pulled from her musings when Mrs. Fisher said, "Vivian finally ran off with her dancing teacher, then."

Isabella turned to face her friend, her jaw hanging open in shock, but Mrs. Fisher only shrugged.

"I may be old, but my eyes are still as sharp as ever. It was difficult not to notice how much Vivian enjoyed her lessons."

"And you said nothing? Did nothing to prevent it?" Isabella could not hide her astonishment. And if Elijah ever found out about this, there would be no quelling his anger.

"Why would I? Mr. Dugray is a man of integrity, and young Vivian, a lady of means. There is nothing to be said against their union. Were she poor, or he a cad, I would have intervened a long time ago."

Isabella could not believe what she was hearing. "There is nothing to be said against the union itself. But they will no doubt be an object of ridicule well before the season is over and long after it has passed. And they kept it secret from everyone, including her own brother, and had him chase after them in frantic fear."

Mrs. Fisher only laughed and then patted her hand in the most patronizing way. "I see I need not ask you why you took a trip upstate with our Mr. Jameson. And I would be willing to bet that he gave his little sister his blessing in the end. Or else you would not have returned in such relative calm."

Isabella fell silent. Just the mention of Elijah and her heart began to race, thoughts of their trip filling her mind. Her cheeks were likely bright red, but Mrs. Fisher must have mistaken her feelings for embarrassment.

Placing a hand over one of Isabella's, Mrs. Fisher smiled at her again, this time with compassion.

"You were a great friend to them both, risking so much to help them. And I can only hope it is being repaid in kind. But, there is still the issue of the rumors. Something must be done. I am sorry to say that you and Mr. Jameson now have a reputation behind you."

Mrs. Fisher looked at her expectantly, eyes wide. And her father mumbled from behind them, "I agree."

What exactly were they getting at? Surely they could not be suggesting... It was only a trip to save his sister. Nothing more.

Isabella never got the chance to question them as chaos erupted from somewhere in the house, the sound of the front door banging open, and then someone bellowed, "Isabella!"

A moment later Elijah burst into the drawing room, his travelling clothes in the same sorry state as hers and his hair in wild disarray. He skidded to a halt in front of her, out of breath, his cheeks ruddy.

"Mrs. Fisher, Mr. Marin, Isabella…" He faltered for a moment, seemingly unsure whom to address first. His eyes wandered from her father's stony face to Mrs. Fisher's encouraging smile and to her own face. A face that probably looked something like a fish out of water, mouth flapping open and shut.

What in the hell was going on tonight?

Then, he abruptly turned toward her father and said, "Mr. Marin, may I have a word with your daughter? Alone?"

If her father looked shocked, he did not show it.

"You may."

What was it about Elijah that always made her father so willing to bend the rules of propriety?

Her father looked at her searchingly, as if waiting for some sign of protest. But she gave none.

Getting up from her place on the sofa, Mrs. Fisher made for the door, only stopping once near Elijah to pat his arm in a comforting manner before she said, "You are perfectly right, my boy. Even if it must be a terribly hushed and hurried affair, a young lady still deserves a proper proposal."

Isabella heard the words perfectly well, saw Mrs. Fisher's smirk thrown in her direction, and yet she failed to string them together in any kind of coherent manner. Only when the door closed, and Elijah addressed her did the fog in her head finally start to clear.

"I cannot begin to express how terribly sorry I am for all of this." Elijah studied her intently, but with a certain distracted air. "How are you taking the news?"

"I only just found out. Is it really as bad as Mrs. Fisher says?"

"Apparently it is. I was approached about it on the street before even setting foot inside my house."

"And are people really saying...?"

"People are apparently saying a great many things."

His fists clenched around the back of a nearby chair, leading her to guess the unflattering nature of what people were saying. The simple movement seemed to serve the dual purpose of expressing his anger and curbing it at the same time, and when he spoke again, there was nothing but bold resolve in his voice.

"How do we fix this? We must fix this for you."

"We cannot."

"Of course we can. We have safely returned my sister to town; we shall put an end to these rumors too."

"No, we cannot. There is no force as unstoppable as gossip; we can only wait until it has run its course. Luckily, this means you will come out of this affair unscathed. It is not so scandalous for a man to have a dalliance or two, though it is usually done more discreetly. But as soon as they have found some other scandal to delve into, you will be forgiven—men always are."

She could practically taste the bitter truth of her words on her tongue.

"And what about you?"

She wanted to kiss him just for asking the question. He cared more about her than he cared about himself. She knew that. And she loved him for it. So very much.

"I have played with fire again and been burned. A mistake repeated more than once is a pattern. And I am now receiving the punishment that should have befallen me years ago."

He looked outraged. Again, her heart flipped for him. "You did nothing wrong in that situation. That man tricked you into falling for him and then abandoned you."

"Even so, I was lucky to escape unscathed through that debacle. But now it seems that it is finally catching up with me."

"But what if... what if we could find a way to completely dispel the rumors?"

"As I said, that is not possible."

"I believe it is. You are not thinking big enough, Bella." He was looking at her with a gleam in his eyes, with a heat that she dared not hope to mean what she thought it might.

"Elijah. You cannot be suggesting what I think you are suggesting."

He nodded, looking completely serious. "I am. You could be a married woman. We could marry immediately. Go back to that little village and get married. And the next time you appeared in society it would be as my wife. And then you would be safe."

It was, of course, what everyone would expect of him now. To own up to his part in this mess and make an honest woman of her. He would do it for her, but she could not rob him of the choice to pick someone he really loved.

"I cannot ask that of you."

"You do not need to ask. I am offering."

"Then you are offering too much. There is no need for both of us to be punished for my stubbornness."

"There is no need for you to suffer for helping out in matters that should by rights be no concern of yours. I will not let your help in finding my sister be the cause of your unhappiness."

"And I will not let your desire to repay my help lead to yours."

He took a deep breath, then let it out in a frustrated huff, his hands coming up to ruffle already messy hair with unrestrained impatience.

"You are as stubborn as ever. Please, Bella. Will you not at least consider the possibility that this story need not end in disgrace and tragedy?"

She wanted to scream at him, to take him by the shoulders and shake some sense into him. When had such stories ever not ended in disgrace and tragedy, or at the very least in mismatched, regretful marriages?

But she said nothing because he chose this moment to bring his hand up to cup her face. The words got stuck in her throat when he traced her cheekbone with one rough thumb. She leaned in; she could not help it. She always ached for his touch.

"However much you may believe it, making one mistake does not have to keep you from being happy ever again."

The words laced the heat of his touch with a sharp hint of painful longing. And oh, how she wanted to believe them, and everything they could mean.

She brought her hand up to his, fully intending to pull it away. But when her fingertips met his warm skin, she found herself unable to do so. Instead, her hand came to rest upon his wrist.

He searched her eyes for what she did not know and then quietly he asked, "Do you not trust me at all by now? Can you not imagine that I mean to do well by you?"

She could imagine it; in fact, she could imagine so many things about him in that moment that words failed her amidst the roaring thoughts in her head. She nodded.

He stepped closer, so much closer, to rest his forehead against hers.

The heat of him was intoxicating. The way he smelled, of mint and wildflowers. Sharp and soft at the same time. Like the wild open air they inhabited during their walks on the journey home. Like so much goodness and hope.

"I would march up to your father this instant and ask him for your hand if I did not think you'd take offense at not being consulted first. I am serious, Bella. Marry me. Please."

"Elijah," she started out. She knew what she should say. And she knew what she wanted to say, but she could not bring herself to do it.

"Please," he whispered.

And then he pressed his lips against hers in the gentlest of kisses. Oh, the feel of his lips on hers, so soft and sweet the way she had always imagined they would be.

She knew it was wrong. But it did not feel so as she opened up to him, tilting her head to allow him more access.

She would allow herself this. This one small piece of him for only this moment in time. And then she would let him go. She had to.

He had worked too hard to gain some standing within polite society to throw it all away for her. He could do so much better; could find a wife who was soft-spoken and docile and unmarred by scandal.

Just one more moment, she thought, as his lips slid over hers. And then he gently increased the pressure so as to create a friction that she could feel in every nerve ending in her body.

Just this once, she promised herself as his hand locked around her waist and pulled her flush against him.

Just to say goodbye, she swore as his tongue stroked against her own, deepening the kiss, ravaging her. Ruining her. And she wanted it, welcomed it, sighing against his mouth when his other hand swept from her cheek to her neck to tangle in her loose hair. And her own hand found its resting-place over his heart.

She could feel herself starting to tip from "just this once" into "perhaps forever" when he drew back to ask breathlessly, "Is this not worth it? We would be so very good, Bella. We are so very good."

Reality slammed back into her, and she choked down the sob that rose in her throat at the reverence in his rough voice, the hopeful look on his face.

She had to set him free, but she was too much of a coward to look at him when she did. To see his flushed face, his smoldering eyes, and his lips, wet and plump from their kisses.

She committed them all to memory just then. That would keep her going when he was gone.

"You may speak to my father tomorrow."

But she would not be here.

By the time the sun began rising in the sky, Elijah was long gone, and she was on her way out of the city, fleeing to her mother like a scared child.

Elijah was simply going to have to understand. She had instructed her father to explain, and though he had vehemently protested, she had not let herself be swayed by him.

Elijah's story would not end well as long as she was in it. Without the burden of her stained reputation, he could go about his life as usual, and she would soon be forgotten.

These were the things she told herself on the cold, lonely ride to Marin House. But nothing could stop the tears that flowed freely, staining her cheeks.

She was sure this is what it felt like when a heart was truly breaking.

Chapter 22

Elijah Jmeson was now a jilted man. Which would be riotously funny if it were not so terribly sad.

Mr. Marin had been incredibly kind when he delivered Isabella's message. He expressed his sympathies and his hope that they could remain close. The trouble was, Elijah could barely look the man in the eye.

To say nothing of the fact that he could not even bear to set foot inside the Marin residence. His broken heart would not allow it. In the days that followed, he spent his time debating with himself.

Should he go to her? Demand an explanation? Did he hate her now? Should he?

He paced and obsessed. He replayed that night over and over in his head, dissecting every word and action. He lay awake night after night thinking of her face and the feel of her perfect lips against his.

But outwardly, he held it all together. He went to work, held meetings, received visitors, and helped his little sister plan for her upcoming wedding.

It was to take place next month in mid-September, and there was much to be done. Yet another thing that made him miss Isabella. She should be here for this. She would have answers to all the questions.

She had hurt him, deeply, and yet he wanted nothing more than to see her again, to hear her laugh, to see her smile.

And that was the root of all his troubles. He loved her so much that even her abandonment, her lie, could not turn his feelings.

He withstood Vivian's probing for several days more, not wishing to drive a wedge between her and her first and truest friend in this city. But Vivian was never one to be put off, and eventually, she persuaded him to give an account of what had occurred.

He was prepared for her anger. He was prepared to defend Isabella's decision, even if he did not understand it. He was not prepared for his little sister to smack him upside the head and declare him a "colossal idiot," though he probably should have been.

"Oh, I am the idiot?" he snapped.

"Yes," she snapped back. "You must not have been clear. Because Isa would never intentionally hurt you. She loves you too much."

Just those words and his heart ached. Did she love him?

Vivian continued on, "So she must have had a good reason for behaving as she did." She fixed him with a stern glare. "Did you sufficiently impress upon her the depth of your feelings? Tell her that you love her, and have for quite some time?"

He could feel the blood rushing to his cheeks at the mere thought of it. "I did not see the necessity of making a sentimental spectacle out of my suggestion. I merely offered to be a good husband, and to make sure she would come out of this entire affair with her reputation intact."

"You offered her a marriage of convenience?" Vivian's voice reached a pitch that stabbed at his eardrums. "Oh, Elijah. No wonder she declined."

"I hardly think me offering to help her was enough to rule me out as a husband. No, I am quite sure Isabella had good reason enough to reject me."

Vivian shook her head, half in anger, half in incredulity. "Your stubbornness first among them, I presume?"

He remained silent. He could think of a dozen more reasons why someone like Isabella Marin would not wish to marry him. But the thought that she of all people would give weight to any of those reasons hurt more than he cared to admit.

It did not seem like something she would do. Was it possible he had been wrong in his assumptions?

While his thoughts raced, Vivian spoke up again. "Did it ever occur to you that perhaps she would have been more than willing to marry you if she thought you were not asking for her hand only out of a sense of duty and guilt? But out of the deepest love and admiration for her?"

He shook his head, forcing the thought away for fear it would spark hope. He instead guided the conversation over to some business related to Vivian's fast-approaching wedding, and soon there was no more talk of Isabella, at least in their household.

But her name continued to haunt him all over town: in gossip relayed by the servants, acquaintances, and Mrs. Fisher, in the looks that seemed to follow him wherever he went—looks that seemed to waver between fascination and disdain–and in the passing comments from his peers, young men who congratulated him on successfully evading marriage.

No one had any idea that marriage had been his goal all along.

No matter how much he tried to convince people that nothing happened between the two of them, it was futile. No one cared, they only wanted something to talk about. But the very idea that he would treat Isabella with so little respect as to defile her in a carriage grated on his nerves.

He could only hope that Mr. Marin was not apprised of the talk about his daughter, and that he knew Elijah was doing everything he could to quell it.

Which was why, when he received an urgent invitation to visit Mr. Marin at his home, he assumed it could not be for anything good.

So it was with a great deal of trepidation that he arrived at the home and was led into Mr. Marin's study. To his great astonishment, instead of the shouting he had expected, he was handed a letter and instructed to read it almost as soon as he had crossed the threshold.

For one moment he thought the letter was from Isabella. Who else would deliver a message to him through her father?

He did not know if the thought delighted or alarmed him more. Would he finally hear what made him so unsuitable as a husband? Would he learn the hope that had lately burgeoned within him, that perhaps they might be suited to being more than just reluctant friends, was not a hope she could ever see herself sharing? Or would he instead finally receive an explanation as to her sudden departure. Or an apology? And would he even want any of it?

Before he had time to formulate an answer, Mr. Marin cleared his throat, and Elijah finally turned his attention to the letter in his hand. As soon as he unfolded the thick paper, he realized that he was not looking at Isabella's elegant hand, which he sometimes had opportunity to observe as she sat quietly writing letters while Vivian studied.

No, this hand, though somewhat similar, belonged to a different person, and curiosity bade him to start reading.

"My dearest husband," he only read the first line before he threw the letter back down on the table. "Sir, this is your private correspondence."

"Yes, yes. But it is from my wife, who is a very matter-of-fact woman, so you need not fear any intimate address. In fact, the letter is not concerned with either her or me, but with someone whose well-being I believe us both to have an interest in."

He hesitated, but eventually, curiosity won out. He picked the letter up again and continued to read:

My dearest husband,

I am afraid summer is holding a grudge this year, for there have been hardly more than a handful of sunny days lately; just constant drizzle. Luckily, the tenants have assured me that their crops have not taken any damage yet. But the weather does nothing to elevate the mood in this house, particularly in the case of those of us who are already dejected. I hate having to bring you such bad news, but none of my efforts so far have caused a change in Isabella's demeanor...

He paused—even reading the name caused him pain. And the idea that she was unhappy... it was unbearable. But he forced himself to continue reading Mrs. Marin's description of her daughter's despondency, torn between the urge to rush to her side and a brief satisfaction that at least she, too, was suffering.

She keeps herself busy, of course, but her heart is not in any of the activities she used to derive joy from. And she has started taking frequent and long walks which do nothing to alter her disposition. You know me to be a champion of healthy, vigorous walks myself, but in this weather, their constitutional effects are questionable at best. Alas, I am afraid our daughter is quite set on imitating the mournful heroines of just the kind of sentimental novels she used to sneer at, and drown herself on some muddy country lane. If you have any idea what to do, if you can think of anyone who might cheer her up, please let me know posthaste, or I will have to resort to locking her into her room just to keep her dry for once.

With sincere worry, your loving wife,
Selena.

Post Scriptum: Just as I am about to send this to you, my maid reports that the young man who has introduced himself as the heir presumptive to Marin House, the one who stands to inherit over Isabella, has been seen going down on one knee before her in the garden. I have not received report of her answer, nor have I been asked for my parental blessing, but her mood remains unchanged. If a proposal has been uttered, it did not add to her happiness—though perhaps it is her determination to make herself unhappy for the sake of someone else's happiness.

I know I am largely to blame for this. I pushed her to entertain the young man as a potential suitor, though I knew she has interest in another. I believe you know to whom I refer. Please, do what you must to get him here. I believe he is the only one who can reach her now.

Elijah lowered the letter with shaking hands and a dry throat to stare at a grim-faced Mr. Marin.

"I am afraid my wife's report is correct. I have had a letter from Mr. Carlisle. He is my heir, to inherit over Isabella. A slimier man there never was. He writes that he wishes to marry my daughter to 'keep the family together'. But I know he only seeks to have Isabella's money."

"But why must he inherit and not Isabella? This is America; women inherit here all the time," Elijah said, desperation in his voice.

Mr. Marin let out a shaky sigh. "It was my father. He invested money badly and nearly lost everything. Mr. Carlisle's father, a cousin, bailed him out. But only if his son was named my heir should I not have a son of my own."

"Which you obviously did not."

"No. It was not something my father ever considered. And I tried to fight it for Isabella, but there is nothing to be done."

Was this why Isabella refused him, so she could wed this Mr. Carlisle and save her family? He could believe it. She was selfless to the point of recklessness. And it was like she also felt she deserved no better because of her past indiscretions. But why would she not tell him? Did he mean so little to her? Or perhaps she really did want this mam?

Just before their wild journey, Vivian had mentioned that someone was courting Isabella. And that she seemed interested.

And then Elijah went and proposed marriage to her. He was such a fool.

"Now it is up to you to fix this, Elijah. That is why I invited you here," Mr. Marin said with a twinkle in his eye.

"I?" Elijah heard the bitterness in his own voice. "I doubt I have the power to have any effect on your daughter's wellbeing."

"Ah, but on that count, I believe you are wrong." Mr. Marin looked at him, blue eyes trapping him in place in an eerily familiar way. "I remember you; you know. I will admit it took me longer than I would like, but I remember you as a child getting into trouble with my daughter. I believe it was the summer right before we came into our money. She ten and you twelve?"

Elijah stood stunned, jaw nearly on the floor. How could he have forgotten? He cleared his throat. "Isabella bought me an ice cream. That is how we met. I—she was my very best friend for that single summer. She meant so much to me. But I never saw her after that. I never thought to try and find her. Life got in the way."

Mr. Marin smiled softly. "It seems you are getting a second chance. I do not know what exactly transpired between you and my daughter. But I do know that, whatever it was, it is making you both unhappy. I, therefore, suggest you leave for Marin House immediately and pay Isabella a visit. Perhaps you ought to tell her some of the things you told me the last time you visited this house."

Elijah clenched his teeth as he remembered the passionate speech he had made to Mr. Marin about his daughter the morning after his proposal—and the look on the older man's face when he had bade to him sit down and informed him of her departure.

"I do not believe she wants to hear them."

"On the contrary, my friend, I believe she needs to hear them."

"But I am not sure I can bring myself to say them again. Not when she made her feelings toward me perfectly clear."

Mr. Marin quirked a brow. "Are you absolutely sure? Enough to pass up this opportunity?"

He was not.

And it must have shown on his face because Mr. Marin said, "Something must be done. And you are the only one who can do it. I know you love my daughter. And I know you always will. As a father, that is all I have ever wanted. So go and get her, son. Please."

Maybe he was a fool. But he would try like hell.

Chapter 23

Two days. That was how long it took to get from his home in the city to Marin House. Not so long in the grand scheme of things, but alone and impatient, this journey felt endless. There was no little sister to nag him or a beautiful young lady to distract him. It was only him and his endless nerves.

It was almost comical that both times he had been to this house he was very nervous. Only this time he was welcomed much more warmly. It was almost like night and day.

Mrs. Marin smiled, if somewhat somberly, and said, "I see my husband understood my letter correctly. You will find what you are looking for in the garden."

Isabella had often mentioned that the gardens were the part of Marin House that she loved most, and Elijah found he agreed when he had occasion to walk there during their short stay on the way back from upstate.

Although he preferred the order and formality of the older part of the garden, with its accurately drawn lines, geometrical forms, and pleasing symmetries, he knew Isabella preferred the newer, more naturally styled area. It was full of brightly colored flowers and beautiful fountains, there were even lanterns that could be lit at night.

He could certainly understand why it spoke to her: the sloping lawns, winding lanes, overgrown little copses and thickets all fed her wild and free spirit.

It was in one of those copses that he found the woman he had been looking for, standing with her back to him under a tall willow tree.

When he laid eyes on her, he froze completely, remaining in place as he took her in for a few moments. A solitary and beautiful figure against a backdrop of green and blue, the sky having finally cleared as the sun chased off the last of the clouds.

She looked like a goddess of old.

But of course, the woman before him was no goddess. She was as human as he, and as vulnerable to rushed decisions and cowardly acts. And yet for all that she had hurt him, he was aware, now more than ever, of how irrevocably he was hers.

Having thus fortified himself, or rather, having realized that there was no way to avoid this confrontation without forsaking her forever, he marched on, calling out her name as he drew near.

Isabella turned, and for a moment, her face was awash with different emotions, changing and shifting as swiftly as light falling upon the shards of a chandelier. Then she exclaimed, "Mr. Jameson."

The use of his surname felt like a slap to the face; cold and meaningless now that he knew what his first name sounded like falling from her lips.

Was he no longer her Elijah? Except that he was, and had been since they first met so many years ago. Now that he knew she was the girl from his childhood, he could not fathom how he missed it. How many days and nights did he recall those memories of their time together? She was still the same in so many ways.

"To what do I owe the pleasure of your visit?"

Her face had settled now, every bit of honest emotion pressed back behind the polite mask he knew so well—though it had not been directed at him in quite some time. He wanted to wipe it off her face, or better yet, kiss it off.

"Your father sent me to inquire after your well-being."

Great start, Elijah. Really great start.

"He sent you on a fool's errand, then. As you can plainly see, I am as well as can be."

"Maybe. But your mother would disagree. Enough that she would send an urgent message to your father."

"My mother is a mother. If I am not coughing or sneezing, she will find some other imaginary ailment to worry about."

Her voice was as smooth as her features now, and so bright and chipper it hurt his ears. He remembered comparing her to a marble statue when they had first met, and that comparison seemed more than apt right now.

It hurt to see it, to see her reign herself in. This was not her.

And just the thought of seeing her condemned to a life of stone, of smooth smiles and even smoother excuses... It was wrong.

He was going to put a real smile on her face if it was the last thing he did. He needed to see it like he needed to breathe air. Her smiles were his sunshine.

"I would say she is right to worry. You left the city rather abruptly."

There. Now she would have to admit there was something amiss. She would have to explain.

But once again, he had underestimated his opponent.

"And I do apologize for that. But, I trust my father informed you of my departure?"

She would really lie to his face again? Did she care so little for his heart?

"He did," he snapped, some of his anger crashing back into him. He wanted to come clean, to tell her his true feelings and their shared past, but he could not overlook her lies again. He continued speaking, "He did not, however, explain why you lied to me so shamelessly." He clenched his fists, waiting.

There it was, the crack in her armor, finally. Her armor finally cracked, and she closed her eyes, her shoulders sagging just a bit. He pressed on.

"I had not pegged you for a cruel, deceiving person. At the very least, I had thought you had a good heart."

He knew she did. But that did not matter, not until she let go.

And finally, the stone cracked. She stood tall, cheeks flushed, eyes blazing, and she marched right up to him.

"And what do you know of my heart?"

More than you know, he thought. There was that fire he loved.

"Less than I thought I did, it seems," he said sharply.

"And more than you should," she snapped. "If you have enough information to speculate about its wishes. But it makes no difference what my heart wants."

The fact that she seemed to honestly believe that enraged him more than anything else.

"Does it want Mr. Carlisle?" he snapped.

The question came out harsher than intended, and her lip trembled for a moment.

But she did not yield yet, and he was glad to see it. This was the Isabella he knew. Stubborn and strong. And so wildly beautiful.

"Mr. Carlisle is willing to ignore the rumors about my supposed ruination, and for that I am grateful. Marrying him is my one chance at keeping Marin House and making sure my mother will be provided for after my father's death."

The words sounded hollow, as if she were reciting a script, and they only made him more determined.

"Then it should interest you to hear that Mr. Carlisle, along with Mr. Hayden, is the one who spread these rumors in the first place."

Her eyes widened in surprise, but a hint of mistrust remained. "How can you know that?"

"Eric Whitney told me just before I came here. He heard Mr. Carlisle telling Mr. Hayden that he saw us get into the carriage and leave town together. Apparently the two men are well acquainted, and they spent the following days spreading the most shameless tales about you."

"But why...?"

"Perhaps to make sure, should you return unmarried, you'd have no choice but to accept his offer. He had no way of knowing what we were really up to. But he knew he could twist it into something ugly."

He could see her taking in the words, could see anger creeping into her features, her eyes narrowed and flashed, her nostrils flared, her cheeks flushed.

How strange and refreshing it was to see her angry at someone other than himself.

But he would not let that distract him. This was the moment to make his point and drive it home.

"Knowing all of this, you cannot still intend to make yourself unhappy by marrying the man."

But her resistance, whatever was fueling it, was not worn down yet.

"And his plan worked, did it not? I have no other choice."

"Yes, you do." He took her hand and squeezed it, his voice now pleading. He would plead and beg until he was hoarse if that was what it took. "I cannot give you Marin House. But I can give you so much more. My love and devotion. My respect, my admiration. My money, my home. Anything. But above all else, my heart."

She shook her head, as if trying to will away the tears he could see glistening in her eyes. It was unbearable, to be so unhappy without her and see her just as unhappy, and not be allowed to ease her pain.

She choked back a sob before saying, "I cannot let you ruin your prospects by marrying me out of pity."

He froze for a moment, unable to comprehend her words. This was what had held her back? His prospects? He may not have done a very good job expressing the "depth of his feelings", as Vivian had put it, but...

"Pity?! You think I would marry you out of pity?"

"What else would it be? Anyone who knew of my situation would not so much as consider marrying me – unless they had your heart, and your determination to save everyone, even from themselves."

"If that is what you think of me, after all our time together, you know very little about me, or yourself. Otherwise you would know by now that pity has nothing to do with my suggestion of marriage, and you would be sure that no one who knows you could ever do anything for you solely out of pity. No, Isabella, where you are concerned, love and admiration must always come into it."

She was staring at him, wide-eyed and incredulous. But she did not protest, and she had not fled yet. That was something, enough at least to encourage him to continue.

For as scared as he had been of disclosing his true feelings, now that the word "love" had been uttered, it became much easier to step closer to her and continue speaking of it.

"I love you, and I will not accept any reason why I should not marry you except one, and that is if you do not think you could find it in your heart to love me back, in time."

There. He had poured his heart out. And now there was nothing to do but wait.

And Isabella, she... laughed.

She was laughing at him?

The sound was half-choked by a sob, but it was a laugh. And though it should probably irk him that his second proposal of marriage was met with outright amusement, he felt relieved at the reaction. At the very least, he had managed to cheer her up.

"In time? Oh Elijah, you really are a fool. I love you. I believe I have loved you since the day I first met you," she said as she caught her breath.

And then she leaned up and into him, pressing a kiss to his lips, lingering and deep and so very perfect.

Her lips were soft as silk. He reached to cup the side of her neck. Her skin was warm from the sun, and her hair smelled of the roses all around them.

Sunshine and roses. How perfect, his Isabella.

Nothing could be better than this, he thought as his lips moved against hers.

Until she pulled back just a whisper and said, "Since that summer we spent together on the docks, I have loved you. Do you remember?"

He nodded. How long had she known?

Her eyes closed for a moment, then settled on him. "Leaving you the way I did almost ruined me. I thought you only offered marriage to save me from ruin. And because I love you so, I could not allow that. It seems I, too, was a fool," she said with a smile.

He laughed. They were both fools. Fools for love.

Her betrayal still hurt; he would not pretend otherwise. How long had she known of their shared past? Why had she not told him?

He did not want to lose this moment, but he had to know. "Why did you never tell me that we were once well acquainted?"

She looked away and then back again, her eyes full of regret. "I assumed you would not remember. And that if you did, you would not like what you saw. I was ashamed of myself. I suppose seeing you again reminded me of how far I was from who I used to be. And then when you proposed marriage I could only see it as a sacrifice on your part. I did not think myself good enough."

His other hand came up to rest on her cheek. "I am not as selfless as you seem to think. Would I have kissed you as I did that night if I were only offering an escape instead of a love match?" he asked, mirth now lacing his voice.

"Well, I dare say you need no excuses now," her voice was firm, defiant almost, but the smile tugging at her lips was soft and lovely, "seeing as I am your fiancée."

He could not say who moved first, only that they were kissing again. Sighing and moaning quietly as their lips parted and their tongues tangled. He reached down to grip both her hips, pulling her flush against him, so hard for her already.

She broke away for a moment to catch her breath and he seized the opportunity, lips trailing along her jaw and down her neck, leaving wetness behind.

"Elijah," she moaned, and the sound travelled straight to his trousers. He was aching and trembling now as he pressed harder into her. She gasped.

"Wait," he said, pulling back, "perhaps we should stop." He did not want to push her into anything.

She looked up at him, eyes like liquid heat. "No. I need this. I need you. Please," she said as she pulled him with her until her back was pressed against the willow tree and he was against her again.

She stared at him as she placed his hand over her breast. "I want to wait until the wedding night, for... everything. But for now, I want us to explore each other. If you are agreeable?"

He nodded slowly. Surely he was dreaming.

"You must say it," she prodded gently.

"Yes," he whispered.

She pulled his lips to hers again, sucking and nipping, her tongue a fierce weapon. She tasted like sin and berries. Sweet and intoxicating.

He groaned, and finally, finally he was able to surrender. He kissed along her neck and down the column of her throat, licking the salt from her skin. His lips hovered over the tops of her breasts for a moment before she pushed his head down gently with her hand.

He chuckled. "Patience, my love."

"Please, Elijah."

He dropped to his knees and pressed his head into her stomach, breathing her in. She reached down and slowly trailed her fingers through his hair, scratching lightly. He moaned and she must have liked it because she pulled on his hair harder. He filed that information away for later.

His hand now rested on her ankle, and he trailed it up her leg, her knee, and then her thigh, squeezing the skin there. He watched her as he went, her eyes looking glazed from pleasure. Her silk stockings were cool to the touch, almost shocking compared to the heat emanating from the center of her, now only inches away from his fingers.

He moved up until his hands hooked into the band of her bloomers, pulling them down slightly. Isabella gasped.

"Are you alright, Bella?"

"Yes, oh yes. Please keep going, please."

He continued pulling until the bloomers were just below her bottom, and that was when he very carefully pushed one finger inside her as he stood up again.

He claimed her rosy, pink lips in a kiss, catching her soft, sweet moans as his finger moved in and out, deep, exploring her most secret place. And when she reached her climax, fingers digging into his shoulders, birds chirping overhead, the sound of her panting in his ear, he thought that this might be heaven.

Chapter 24

They started with her mother. Isabella was nervous, but Elijah insisted all would be well. And he was right.

"I am so happy for you, my darling daughter," her mother said as she pulled her in for a hug. "I know I have not been the most supportive. But I can see now that the two of you are so right for each other."

It was more than she ever dared hope for, and everything after that seemed easy by comparison.

Her father was ecstatic. Mrs. Fisher declared she had known this would happen all along. And Vivian immediately insisted they have a double wedding.

A suggestion instantly shut down with a "Not a chance in hell" from Elijah.

The transition from friends to more than was seamless. They attended dinners together, saw shows at the academy, and each night when they parted ways it was with a sweet, lingering kiss.

But in all that activity, they had yet to attend a large formal function, until the very last of the season.

"Are you sure you want to do this, Bella?" Elijah asked her for easily the tenth time that evening.

She laughed before turning to face him on their seat in the carriage. And as always, he took her breath away.

A few weeks on from that fateful day in the garden and sometimes she still felt it was all a beautiful dream. That this man, her Elijah, could not actually be hers.

But he was. And she was. And they were.

She reached out to straighten his bow tie before looking up at him with a soft smile. "I am sure, my love. I want everyone to know that we are together, so that we can put any lingering gossip to rest. I know this seems like such a big step, but to me it is no different than any other night we have spent together. So let people look and talk. All they will see is two people madly in love. I am not afraid. We have worked toward this very moment for weeks. I am ready."

He snatched her hand from where it now rested on his chest and brought it to his lips, nose skimming her wrist before he planted a soft kiss. His eyes flickered to hers, smoldering and dark, and she bit back a groan.

That day in the garden flashed in her mind. They way he had started slow, fingers exploring hidden skin. The torturous in and out until she was on the very edge of coming undone. Lips on the tops of her breasts again and again before he sunk to his knees a second time. Her breath caught in her throat as he ducked underneath her skirts and buried his face between her legs. His mouth so soft and his tongue so insistent.

"Ugh. Can the two of you not keep your hands off each other for one moment?" Vivian whined from her seat across from Elijah.

Her eyes opened wider, her face heating from embarrassment. It was too easy to become distracted where Elijah was concerned, and she really was trying to be better about it. She obviously needed more practice.

As the carriage came back into focus, Vivian spoke again, her voice like water thrown on flames. "Isa, please. I really do not wish to see you looking at my brother that way. Take pity on me."

And Elijah, the bastard. He only winked at her before settling back against the seat.

Isabella glared at Vivian. "You are one to talk, Mrs. Dugray. You and Wes are all over each other all the time."

"I can attest to that, unfortunately," Elijah mumbled.

And it was true. True enough that the two of them chose to move up their wedding to as soon as possible. They were married just last week, with Isabella and Elijah acting as best man and maid of honor.

Isabella sobbed the entire time, mostly because Elijah kept looking at her as if he could not wait for it to be their turn. And it would be soon. They would be taking the date previously set for Vivian and Wes, which was only a couple of weeks away now, in mid-September.

"Oh, shut up, Elijah," Vivian snapped.

Wes spoke up then, resting a comforting hand on Vivian's shoulder. "Hey, everyone calm down. I know we are all on edge, but everything is going to be fine. People will talk, but then they will move on. And by next season, there will be a new scandal for everyone to sink their teeth into. The four of us will be old news."

"He is right," Isabella said, looking pointedly at Elijah as the carriage came to a halt. "And it does not matter anyway, because we are here. No turning back now."

She looked through the window at the familiar townhouse. Lanterns lined the stairs to the front door, adding a pleasant glow to the already buzzing, warm summer night.

This was the final event of the season, and though she had never said it out loud, lest she worry Elijah, she was endlessly grateful that it would be hosted by a friend. No one would dare insult any of them with Mrs. Fisher as the host.

Since they returned to the city, newly engaged, she and Elijah had re-entered society slowly and cautiously. A lunch here, a dinner there, smaller affairs at first, where they would attract less attention, and then a few nights at the theater, always accompanied by Vivian and Wes to make it clear that Vivian was still very much a part of society and the family. And Mrs. Fisher took every opportunity to champion them, something for which Isabella could never thank her enough.

But this was the first time they would really be seeing people en masse. Isabella was both nervous and excited.

Elijah's hand on her back was reassuring as she stepped down onto the sidewalk and smoothed out her dress. It was one of her favorites, a light rose-pink color embellished with tiny flowers. The fabric was light, but full, with a skirt that swished when she walked.

It made her feel like a princess. And with Elijah by her side, she felt like she could conquer the world.

The room was resplendent. Dozens of candles cast a soft, warm glow. There were bouquets of roses and lilies and the occasional burst of bright yellow from a sunflower. Music played softly from the small band in the corner.

Looking around, she noted a few people openly staring at their group, some with wide curious eyes, some with judgmental glares. One woman sneered. Isabella stiffened for a moment, the urge to run strong. But she focused on Elijah's steady presence at her side and drew strength from it. They moved further into the room, spotting Mr. Whitney who gave her an encouraging grin.

She breathed a sigh of relief. They were not alone in this, and she had confidence that more people would come around. She now felt only excitement for the night to come, a stark contrast from the very first ball of the season. Tonight, she planned to dance and laugh and enjoy the company of her friends. The perfect end to this chapter of her life.

Mrs. Fisher joined them then, fawning over everyone as she always did.

"Mr. Jameson, Miss Marin. And the newlyweds. I gather you two are off on honeymoon in a few days?"

Vivian smiled, excitement clear on her face. "That is right. We will spend a week in Newport soaking up the very last of the summer sun. We are staying with a friend of Wes's aunt."

"And you two?" Mrs. Fisher said, turning to Isabella and Elijah. "How are the wedding plans coming?"

Isabella winked at her friend. "Just fine. I have handed the bulk of the work over to my mother. It was easier that way, and I really do not mind."

Elijah snorted, trying to cover it up with a cough

Mrs. Fisher only laughed before leading the foursome over to Isabella's parents. It was a rarity for her mother to attend any event, but she promised Isabella she would. It was still so new, having an open line of communication with her mother, but she liked it.

She felt Elijah tense at the sight of her mother, and she had to stifle a giggle.

While their relationship was far from perfect, they now had a mutual respect for each other. That did not mean Elijah was not still nervous around her.

Her reaction to their engagement really did turn things around for the Marin family as a whole, which was something Isabella was still learning to navigate. Little things like when she and her mother got a moment alone after the engagement announcement, she expressed how proud she was of Isabella for following her heart.

A far cry from the last conversation they had on the subject. It was the first time in so long Isabella felt her mother's love, and it gave her so much hope for the future.

It felt like more than a sign when the notes of a familiar tune invaded her thoughts and a wide smile broke across her face. Elijah's hand, resting on her waist, gave a light squeeze.

It was the perfect moment, made all the more perfect when he leaned into whisper in her ear, "What about it, Miss Marin? Would you care to dance?"

He remembered. But then, of course, he did, because her Elijah was perfect.

This was the song they danced to weeks ago. The night they danced as if no one else was watching. When they were still denying their feelings for each other, their hearts miles ahead of their heads.

"I would love to, Mr. Jameson. If you think you can keep up with me."

And when he pulled her into his arms moments later, it felt like coming home. As he leaned down to whisper in her ear, "I mean to try, Bella. I mean to try."